the AVENGERS®
and the
THUNDERBOLTS™

SPIDER-MAN: THE VENOM FACTOR by Diane Duane
THE ULTIMATE SPIDER-MAN, Stan Lee, Editor
IRON MAN: THE ARMOR TRAP by Greg Cox
SPIDER-MAN: CARNAGE IN NEW YORK
by David Michelinie & Dean Wesley Smith
THE INCREDIBLE HULK: WHAT SAVAGE BEAST by Peter David
SPIDER-MAN: THE LIZARD SANCTION by Diane Duane
THE ULTIMATE SILVER SURFER, Stan Lee, Editor
FANTASTIC FOUR: TO FREE ATLANTIS by Nancy A. Collins
DAREDEVIL: PREDATOR'S SMILE by Christopher Golden
X-MEN: MUTANT EMPIRE Book 1: SIEGE by Christopher Golden
THE ULTIMATE SUPER-VILLAINS, Stan Lee, Editor
SPIDER-MAN & THE INCREDIBLE HULK: RAMPAGE
by Danny Fingeroth & Eric Fein (Doom's Day Book 1)
SPIDER-MAN: GOBLIN'S REVENGE by Dean Wesley Smith
THE ULTIMATE X-MEN, Stan Lee, Editor
SPIDER-MAN: THE OCTOPUS AGENDA by Diane Duane
X-MEN: MUTANT EMPIRE Book 2: SANCTUARY by Christopher Golden
IRON MAN: OPERATION A.I.M. by Greg Cox
SPIDER-MAN & IRON MAN: SABOTAGE
by Pierce Askegren & Danny Fingeroth (Doom's Day Book 2)
X-MEN: MUTANT EMPIRE Book 3: SALVATION by Christopher Golden
GENERATION X by Scott Lobdell & Elliot S! Maggin
FANTASTIC FOUR: REDEMPTION OF THE SILVER SURFER
by Michael Jan Friedman
THE INCREDIBLE HULK: ABOMINATIONS by Jason Henderson
X-MEN: SMOKE AND MIRRORS by eluki bes shahar
X-MEN: EMPIRE'S END by Diane Duane
UNTOLD TALES OF SPIDER-MAN, Stan Lee & Kurt Busiek, Editors
SPIDER-MAN & FANTASTIC FOUR: WRECKAGE
by Eric Fein & Pierce Askegren (Doom's Day Book 3)
X-MEN: THE JEWELS OF CYTTORAK by Dean Wesley Smith
SPIDER-MAN: VALLEY OF THE LIZARD by John Vornholt
X-MEN: LAW OF THE JUNGLE by Dave Smeds
SPIDER-MAN: WANTED DEAD OR ALIVE by Craig Shaw Gardner
X-MEN: PRISONER X by Ann Nocenti
FANTASTIC FOUR: COUNTDOWN TO CHAOS by Pierce Askegren
X-MEN & SPIDER-MAN: TIME'S ARROW Book 1: THE PAST
by Tom DeFalco & Jason Henderson
X-MEN & SPIDER MAN: TIME'S ARROW Book 2: THE PRESENT
by Tom DeFalco & Adam-Troy Castro
X-MEN & SPIDER-MAN: TIME'S ARROW Book 3: THE FUTURE
by Tom DeFalco & eluki bes shahar
SPIDER-MAN: VENOM'S WRATH
by Keith R.A. DeCandido & José R. Nieto
THE ULTIMATE HULK, Stan Lee & Peter David, Editors
X-MEN: CODENAME WOLVERINE by Christopher Golden
GENERATION X: CROSSROADS by J. Steven York
CAPTAIN AMERICA: LIBERTY'S TORCH by Tony Isabella & Bob Ingersoll
THE AVENGERS & THE THUNDERBOLTS by Pierce Askegren

COMING SOON
X-MEN: SOUL KILLER by Richard Lee Byers
SPIDER-MAN: THE GATHERING OF THE SINISTER SIX by Adam-Troy Castro

Pierce Askegren

Illustrations by Mark Bagley & Jeff Albrecht

BYRON PREISS MULTIMEDIA COMPANY, INC.
NEW YORK

BERKLEY BOULEVARD BOOKS, NEW YORK

Special thanks to Ginjer Buchanan, Steven A. Roman, Michelle LaMarca, Howard Zimmerman, Emily Epstein, Michael Asprion, Ursula Ward, Mike Thomas, and Steve Behling.

THE AVENGERS & THE THUNDERBOLTS

A Berkley Boulevard Book
A Byron Preiss Multimedia Company, Inc. Book

PRINTING HISTORY
Berkley Boulevard paperback edition / January 1999

Edited by Keith R.A. DeCandido.
Cover art by Duane O. Myers.
Cover design by Claude Goodwin & Joe Kaufman.
Book design by Michael Mendelsohn.

For information address: Byron Preiss Multimedia Company, Inc.,
24 West 25th Street, New York, New York 10010.

The Penguin Putnam Inc. World Wide Web site address is
http://www.penguinputnam.com

Check out the Byron Preiss Multimedia Co., Inc. site on the
World Wide Web: http://www.byronpreiss.com

Check out the Ace Science Fiction/Fantasy newsletter, and
much more, at Club PPI!

ISBN: 0-425-16675-9

BERKLEY BOULEVARD
Berkley Boulevard Books are published by The Berkley Publishing Group,
a member of Penguin Putnam Inc.,
375 Hudson Street, New York, New York 10014.
BERKLEY BOULEVARD and its logo
are trademarks belonging to Berkley Publishing Corporation.

PRINTED IN THE UNITED STATES OF AMERICA

10 9 8 7 6 5 4 3 2 1

To the memory of Otto Binder, a man of many accomplishments, not the least of which was the first-ever Avengers novel.

ACKNOWLEDGMENTS

Special thanks to Kurt Busiek and Mark Bagley, who not only let me play with their toys, but got right there in the sandbox with me. Thanks also to Stan Lee and Jack Kirby, who created the Avengers; to Tom Brevoort, Steve Behling, and Mike Thomas at Marvel; and to this book's editor, Keith R.A. DeCandido, for ushering this work into existence, and for asking me to write the danged thing in the first place.

EDITOR'S NOTE

This novel takes place shortly after the Marvel comic *Avengers* (Vol. 3) #12.

Prologue

Alexandria, Virginia

Anyone who recognized the tall man was too wise to say so.

He came striding up King Street, as unmindful of the morning's bitter cold as of the human throngs who shared the cracked and weathered sidewalks with him. He was a big man, with a muscular build that was evident even beneath his black leather trench coat's billowing drape. He wore a peaked cap pulled low enough over his face that it obscured his features, and polished boots that went well with his military gait. He moved with the easy confidence of a man who was quite accustomed to having others get out of his way.

Certainly, no one blocked his path now. Instead, prompted by the same instincts that warn the mouse of the cat, or the fish of the shark, men and women scurried out of the tall man's way. Some stepped into the slush-filled gutters that flanked King Street while others sought the apparent shelter of shadowed doorways, but none remained on the walkway itself as he came near. Nor were any eager to return to the walkway after he had passed, at least not until his steady, almost marching pace had carried him well past them.

The effect was striking; he seemed to carry a zone of isolation with him as he made his way through the oldest part of the city, past the restaurants and antique stores and gift shops that waited so eagerly to separate tourists and locals alike from their money. After a dozen blocks or so, the granite spire of the Masonic Temple came into view and the storefronts the tall man passed became smaller and shabbier. Expensive restaurants gave way to working-class bars, antique galleries gave way to junk shops, and chichi gift emporia yielded ground to used bookstores, one of which caught his attention.

NEUTRAL TERRITORY BOOKS, the legend in its window said. Below that were the words, SPECIALISTS IN MILITARY HISTORY, NEW AND OLD, followed by, DAVID ERSKINE, PROPRIETOR. The window itself was dirty and flyspecked, and the shop's shadowed interior was barely visible through it. What could be seen, for the most part, were bow-shelved bookcases that had been crammed to overflowing, and a sales counter piled high with still more volumes. The tall man nodded, then opened the door and stepped inside.

Another man, stocky and bespectacled, with muttonchop whiskers framing a genial face, looked up from his work as the door's bell rang. "Howdy! I'm Dave," he said cheerfully. "Welcome to Neutral Territory."

The tall man removed his hat, eliminating the shadow its bill cast, to reveal distinctive features and a shaven pate.

Dave blinked in surprise and recognition.

"Hey," Dave said, a broad grin splitting his features, "I know who you are. I've seen you on TV!"

The tall man stepped closer. The monocle in his right eye glinted in the dim lighting.

"This is an honor," Dave continued enthusiastically. "I never thought I'd see *you* in here. Really, you might not believe it, but I've always been a big fan of *Hogan's He—*"

With speed and precision that bordered on the inhuman, the tall man's left hand reached out and his gloved fingers dug deep into the other man's throat.

Dave made a strangled noise and clawed with his own hands at the one that held him, trying desperately to weaken the tall man's iron grip.

Desperately, but futilely.

"I fear you have mistaken me for someone else," Baron Wolfgang Von Strucker purred, speaking English cleanly and precisely, albeit with the distinctive cadence and accent of a man whose first language is German. Without visible effort or strain, Strucker extended his arm fully and lifted his victim until Dave's sneaker-shod feet kicked at empty air, inches above his shop's floor.

Gloved fingers twisted, and there was a sound like pottery breaking. Dave writhed once as he convulsed in his death agonies, and then Strucker's hand opened. Immediately, the luckless bibliophile's body fell and lay motionless on the floor.

"An impressive display, if unnecessary," a third voice said, as another man stepped from a shadowed alcove. He was an average-looking fellow, with features that were remarkable only for their very nondescriptness. He had the look of a man who would melt without a trace into even the smallest crowd.

"But then," he continued, "I would expect no less from one of your accomplishments."

"A triviality," said Strucker, plainly unsurprised by the third man's presence. He spoke curtly, but not without good humor. "But hardly unnecessary. There were to be no witnesses to our meeting."

"Oh, the swine had to die, there is no doubt of that," came the response. "If nothing else, the exorbitant prices he charges for his dubious wares would merit his execution. I refer more to the method you used. Surely, the Death Spore virus would have done the job as efficiently."

"As efficiently, but not in so personally satisfying a manner. Besides, I saw no need to cause you discomfort or hazard," Strucker said, his thin, pale lips pulling back in a merciless grin. "At least, not now."

Visible through the pallid skin of Strucker's face, bruised-looking patches of purple tissue shifted and pulsed in time with his words. Strucker, feared throughout the world as a war criminal and terrorist mastermind, was much more than that. His entire body was, in effect, a walking biological warfare agent, the carrier for a deadly synthetic microbe. Once, the terrorist cabal he headed, Hydra, had employed the Death Spore in a global blackmail scheme. Now, Strucker used the living poisons embodied within him as a more personal weapon.

He could kill with a touch, and with less than a touch.

"You would not have done so," said the other man—somehow less nondescript now. The lines of his body and face rippled and flowed, changing like a film image that had lost its focus and was trying to find it again. When the blurring effect resolved itself, a very different figure stood where the portly, anonymous chap had been a moment before.

He looked like himself now. He looked like Helmut, the Thirteenth Baron Zemo.

He looked a bit like Strucker, too. Zemo was also tall, if not quite so tall as Strucker, and he bore himself with a similar carriage; both men were marked by the same odd combination of athletic grace and military bearing that hinted at a higher nobility. Like Strucker, Zemo wore a trench coat and boots, but while Strucker's face was exposed, Zemo's hid behind a tightly fitting hood of purple fabric that was held in place by a golden headband.

"Charming," Strucker said, "if not particularly impressive. A mask behind a mask. I presume the first effect was a hologram?"

"I have taken measures against your vaunted Death Spore," Zemo continued, as if the other man had not spoken. "I am immune to it, and beyond your ability to harm me."

His words sounded like a warning.

"I doubt that very much," Strucker said. "But the point is moot. We will not test the issue. We are here to do a bit of business, after all, and not to engage in inappropriate hostilities."

"So your summons said," Zemo said.

"Not a summons, but rather an invitation," Strucker said. "Issued only after many months of negotiation between our representatives, and couched in terms far more courteous than I would offer most." He smiled again. "I would suggest that you reciprocate that courtesy, Zemo, and cease your posturing. We are on neutral ground, after all, and, in effect, under a flag of truce. There will be many other days for battle. Let this one be for talk."

"What is it that you want, then?" Zemo asked. "I have other matters that demand my attention."

"More ploys? More games with the forces of order? Or do you still seek revenge against your precious Thunderbolts?"

In months gone by, Zemo, himself a criminal mastermind whose name appeared on many most-wanted lists, had executed a con game of breathtaking proportions. Fate had given him the opportunity in the form of a monster named Onslaught, whose attack had ended in the apparent death of nearly all the world's most prominent super heroes. During the period following that catastrophe, Zemo had assembled his own team of super-powered criminals and created new identities for them. Once, those same men and women had been known as the Masters of Evil, but for a time, a world nearly without heroes had embraced them as the Thunderbolts, the newest champions of law and order.

Apparent champions.

It had all been a ploy, of course, a stepping-stone on

Zemo's own projected path to conquest. Zemo's intent had been to gain the world's confidence, and then the world's control. He had succeeded in the former, but not in the latter.

The unexpected return of the world's true heroes—the Fantastic Four, the Avengers, and others—had put an end to that campaign, helped along a bit by the betrayal of Zemo by members of his own forces. Instead of winning a world to rule, Zemo had succeeded merely in adding new foes to a very long list of hated enemies.

High on that list of names were those of his betrayers, his erstwhile allies and teammates.

"The Thunderbolts," Zemo said, "and others who have been foolish enough to arouse my ire. Now, tell me what it is that you want, so that I can deny you, and then be quit of this tiresome place."

"*Ach*, the impatience of youth," Strucker said, "or, rather, of relative youth." Strucker spoke from the perspective of age; he was much older than he seemed. His birth had been in the century's earliest decades, and he had served Germany with distinction during World War II. Decades later, the same biological incident that had given him his death touch had imbued him with strength and vitality that belied his years, but his views had remained much the same. "You would do well to let the years teach you patience," he counseled Zemo soothingly. "It is a lesson beyond price."

Zemo's only response was a glare, evident even behind the concealing lenses of his mask.

Strucker shrugged, then clicked his heels and neatly executed a mocking half-bow, making a traditional sign of respect one of faint derision instead. "As you wish, Baron. To business, then," he said. "I requested the honor of your presence here so that we could discuss common interests and goals, and consider also the wisdom of a strategic alliance to achieve them."

"An alliance? You are not known for possessing a sense of humor," Zemo said. "If this is your idea of a joke—"

"There is the issue of competition to consider, to be sure," Strucker continued implacably, as calmly as if the other had not spoken. "We are enough alike that, ultimately, we will doubtless contend for the same prize. But today, in the here and now, we can use that commonality in our favor and accomplish more by working together. The total can be more than the sum of its parts, at least for the nonce."

"I do not believe you," Zemo said flatly. "I did not believe your emissaries when they brought me your initial overtures, and I do not believe you now. You cannot expect me to believe that you would seek an alliance with me, after our previous encounter."

During the early days of the Thunderbolts operation, when the masquerading Masters of Evil had worked to prove themselves to a hero-hungry public, Zemo's operatives and Strucker's had clashed. The Thunderbolts had won the battle handily enough, and Zemo himself, in his guise as Citizen V, had issued an ultimatum to Strucker.

In a reasonable approximation of Zemo's own tones, Strucker said, " 'Either you leave us alone, and suffer the attention any crime figure attracts from super heroes—or you can escalate this, and we'll make it our top pirority to shut you down.' You dared much, saying that to me. Or, rather, 'Citizen V' dared."

"You have a good memory," Zemo said, with grudging admiration.

"A mere matter of self-discipline, like most skills. My memory serves me well because I require it to. It served me equally well on the day that your deception was laid bare to the world. I knew then, of course, why your voice had been familiar when last we spoke, knew just who had been behind the crimes against Hydra."

Zemo tensed, as if in anticipation.

Strucker laughed then, an indulgent chuckle that was less reassuring than it was dismissive. "Be at ease," he said. "I am here today to talk, not to do battle."

Zemo did not relax.

"Of course," Strucker continued, "I did not always feel so. First, there was fury, as I realized that you had fooled my staff intelligence analysts, none of whom had penetrated your scheme and all of whom have now paid the ultimate price for your success. Then there was laughter, as I realized the complexity of the jest you had played on S.H.I.E.L.D. and SAFE and Interpol and all of the other so-called authorities."

Strucker paused, and gazed at Zemo with a speculative look in his eyes. "And then," he said, "there were memories."

"Memories?" Zemo asked, obviously confused now.

Strucker nodded. "During the war and after it," he said, "I knew your father."

He told the rest of the story quickly, in brief sentences that set forth the facts without dwelling on their implications. He told of two noblemen, both scions of long lines, who had risen to prominence in Hitler's service.

Strucker, the proud Prussian, had led campaigns in all theaters of operation, and carried out many secret missions against the Reich's most hated enemies. Heinrich, the current Zemo's father, had been a scientific genius, conceptualizing new weapons systems and overseeing their construction.

The two men had met more than once as they pursued their duties, and become friendly, if not friends. After the war, after Germany's fall, they had gone their separate ways. Strucker had overseen the buildup and establishment of Hydra, as the world's premier terrorist organization. Heinrich Zemo, for his part, had withdrawn to a secret sanctuary in South America, there to pursue his own agendas.

"Three times, I visited your father in his jungle redoubt," Strucker said, concluding his tale. "Once on Hydra business, but twice for old times' sake. The world had become a very different place from the one of our youths, and it was good to see a familiar face." Strucker smiled slightly. "You may have been there during one of those visits."

"I doubt that very much," Zemo said slowly, still considering Strucker's words and their import. He had spent his formative years studying in schools in Europe, and had not seen much of his father until well into his adult years.

"It matters not," Strucker said, shrugging. "Ultimately, the end came to Heinrich, as it comes to most. The news reached me in Budapest, where I was pursuing certain initiatives of my own. Since then, I had thought of Heinrich only rarely, if at all. Learning that 'Citizen V' was his son served as a rather emphatic reminder and brought him to mind again, along with his accomplishments and legacy."

"And now that I have brought my family to your attention, you wish to bring me into your service?" Zemo laughed derisively. "I think not. If you truly knew my father, you know that a Zemo follows his own star."

Strucker's reply was to reach into one of his coat's deep pockets and draw forth a small, leather-bound notebook. Without a word, he handed it to the other man.

The pages rustled as Zemo thumbed through them, slowly at first, and then more quickly, staring in evident disbelief at the cramped handwriting that filled their yellowing surfaces. Long blocks of text were interspersed with equations and diagrams, drawn with a sure hand in ink that had scarcely faded with age.

"This is one of my father's laboratory notebooks!" Zemo said. "They have been lost for years!"

"One of ten that survive, to my knowledge," Strucker responded. "I assure you that the remaining nine are quite safe in my custody, along with certain other personal effects that might be of interest to you."

"Explain yourself," Zemo said crisply.

He made no move to relinquish the notebook.

"When your father's organization collapsed, and well before you chose to take up the reins of power, certain representatives of mine happened to be on the scene," Strucker said.

"You had infiltrated his operations," Zemo said flatly. "You had agents on site, in South America."

"Another way of phrasing it," Strucker said, smiling again. "Those operatives secured what they could and brought them to me."

"You robbed my father's grave, before his corpse was even cool."

"I kept his legacy safe," Strucker said. "Away from the jackals and dogs who could not hope to appreciate it."

"In the doubtless vain hope that *your* jackals could."

For the first time since their conversation had begun, genuine irritation sounded in Strucker's voice. "Have a care, young Zemo," he said. "I have extended much to you already, and I am prepared to offer more. I demand courtesy in return, at a minimum."

Zemo opened the book again, and studied one page. "It's

in cipher,'' he said. ''A multilevel encryption he taught me. That must be why you need me.''

''*Need* is too strong a word,'' Strucker said, still annoyed. ''Can you read it?''

''With some effort,'' Zemo said. ''And given time. But why should I do so, for you? Tell me that.''

''Your father was a protean genius, Zemo, the Reed Richards of his day. A catalog of his achievements would feature entries in many fields—chemistry, biochemistry, nuclear physics, astrophysics, and rocketry, to name but a few. I rather imagine his studies had something to do with your own vitality and resilience.''

''That is none of your concern,'' Zemo said. ''And you still have not answered me. Give me a reason to support you in this.''

''My people tell me that your father's work was severely limited by the technology of his day,'' Strucker continued. ''Like da Vinci before him, Heinrich's vision exceeded his grasp. Some of his greatest triumphs were achieved in an age of vacuum tubes and adding machines. Even in later years, he worked under the constraints of available technology and resources. Many of his greatest creations, he could conceive, even design, but never construct, at least not with the tools at hand. My analysts are reasonably certain that his journals outline projects that were a generation or more beyond the technology base of his time.''

''But today . . .''

''Today, we can do much more. Since his unfortunate demise, entire new technological capabilities have emerged. They can give form to his vision, and you can help make his most magnificent conceptions real.''

''Help Hydra, you mean,'' Zemo said.

''And allow Hydra to help you.''

''Help, and then betray, no doubt. Even you acknowledge that such an alliance cannot sustain itself.''

''Alliances form and alliances dissolve,'' Strucker said, almost murmuring. ''Treaties are written to be broken. Allies become enemies, foes become friends, and the cycle begins anew. An endless quadrille through the catacombs of time.'' He gestured at the dusty bookcases that surrounded them, at the bound histories of all the wars that humanity had fought, and then at the lifeless form of David Erskine. "That is the story of life, of mankind, of war, and this sodden mass of flesh is its conclusion, for winner and loser alike. What matters is not the end of the day, but the day itself. The day is here for you to seize, Zemo."

"A temporary alliance, then," Zemo said flatly.

"Temporary, or perhaps more enduring—but certainly not permanent. One day, we will war, of course," Strucker said amiably, even cheerfully. "That is inevitable, but not imminent. For now, for the moment, your father's memory unites us. I have the most complete written record of his genius, and you can read that record. I have the assets to make his dreams reality, and you have the vision to implement them. Together, we can work miracles. Will you turn your back on such an opportunity?"

"I would never turn my back on you, Strucker," Zemo said, speaking with a degree of humor for the first time.

"Wise," Strucker said. "And I can provide another point for that wisdom to consider. You have already committed crimes against Hydra, transgressions that I would be quite willing to forgive of an ally, but not of an adversary. You have many enemies already; do not hasten to add me to their number."

"Offer the olive branch first and then the spear," Zemo mused. He was still holding the leather-bound notebook. Now he nodded, and slipped it into his own pocket. "Agreed then," he said. "We will work together on this."

"Excellent," Strucker said, the very embodiment of Teutonic geniality. "Your father would be pleased."

"Perhaps; perhaps not," Zemo continued. "A former associate of mine would be useful in such an endeavor. You have no objection if I choose my own second?"

"Of course not," Strucker said. "We're allies now, after all."

"Yes, now," Zemo said softly, but not so softly that Strucker could not hear him.

Chapter One

New York, New York

Some ninety-three minutes had passed since she had entered Madison Square Garden, and Wanda Maximoff was getting a bit bored.

Granted, much had happened in that hour and a half. For openers, a local rock band with the cryptic name of DQYDJP had performed five songs. None of those tunes had been to Wanda's taste, but all were played, she had to concede, very loudly indeed.

Then, three costumed clowns had frantically raced around a miniature track, each driving one of three tiny vehicles—the Kree Coupe (a blue hardtop with fins), the Sinister Skrullmobile (a pickle-green convertible), and the Shi'ar Ca'ar (complete with a winglike spoiler). Supposedly, the competition's stakes were the "fate of humanity itself," so Wanda had been vaguely pleased to see it end in a draw.

Next up, the so-called Fabulous Duff Beer Babes, barely clad in stripe-and-star-spangled bikinis, had executed a series of choreographed maneuvers that were not dance so much as they were rhythmic gymnastics, and which ended in an unnecessarily suggestive finish that rained *faux* beer foam on their appreciative (mostly male) audience.

Finally, Fearless Fireball Fred himself had sent his modified Harley-Davidson motorcycle flying from one ramped platform and through the air a moderately impressive distance above twenty-three polished Lincoln Continental Town Cars (borrowed from a local dealership), and then brought it to ground again, apparently without damage. The surrounding seats were filled with Fearless Fireball Fred's cheering fans, and the air was filled no less with the thunder of internal combustion engines than with the whoops and applause of adoring spectators.

Not for the first time, Wanda had to wonder at that. She lived in a world filled with costumed super heroes and invaded by space aliens with near-clockwork regularity. How could anyone who shared such a world find any diversion in the antics of bikini-clad "spokesmodels" and jerry-rigged special effects? She had asked herself that question more than once, and now, she turned to her date to ask him for his view.

He spoke, instead.

"Isn't this great?" Simon Williams said, seated next to her and grinning broadly. He tightened the muscles of the arm he already had draped across Wanda's shapely shoulders and drew her closer to him. Ordinarily, Wanda was ambivalent about embracing in public, but the private box they occupied was empty but for them, so she leaned against him comfortably.

Wanda felt the impulse to shrug, but stifled it. Simon had been a very accommodating escort today. Without protest, he had watched and waited while she tried on one designer outfit after another, each time taking pains to explain to the salesgirl with persistent good humor that, no, she was wrong, and that red *was* Wanda's color. He had even accompanied her to Zaboli's, New York's finest Hungarian restaurant, where an intense-looking young waitress had regaled them with tales of her childhood in the tiny village of Baktakek. For Wanda, who had spent much of her youth in that part of the world, the waitress's stories had been enchanting; for Simon, they must have been—

At least as interesting as a monster truck rally is to me, Wanda thought.

Well, there were much worse ways to spend a day. Besides, she supposed that the point of doing things together wasn't doing things—it was being together.

"When Ben gave me the tickets, I was thrilled," Simon continued enthusiastically. "I went to a couple of these when I lived in California. Those were different though, not as spectacular. More laid back."

This time, Wanda let herself sigh, but didn't say anything. Simon was a sensitive, caring, and intelligent man who came from a moneyed family, and he had led a life at least as adventurous and unusual as her own. In many ways, however, he was, in the purest sense of the word, a guy, and guys liked cars. That was a lesson Wanda had learned soon after coming to live in America.

"It's great," she said gamely. "I'm glad Ben gave you the tickets."

"Ben" was Benjamin J. Grimm, a mutual friend and respected professional colleague, better known as the Thing, strongest member of the Fantastic Four. He had not so much given the tickets to Simon as he had surrendered them grudgingly, following an unlucky hand of cards. The third Friday of each month, Ben and some cronies met to play serious poker, a running competition that Simon had only recently rejoined. It was dealer's rules, but even by Ben's standards, a straight flush beat four of a kind, so he had honored the terms of the game and handed Simon his prized admission passes for Fearless Fireball Fred's Monster Truck Rally, hosted by the Fabulous Duff Beer Babes.

Wanda was generally in favor of her man winning, but in this case, she couldn't help but wish he hadn't gotten that last two of diamonds in the hole.

The background noise was getting louder again; even as the cheers and applause faded, the canned music echoing from the PA system increased in volume. It was a generic fanfare that made the air itself throb as it boomed out from the facility's gigantic speakers. The Fabulous Duff Beer Babes had come out on the main floor again, wearing different bathing suits this time, brightly colored outfits that featured the brewery's famous logo. Marching in time to the music, they formed two lines, facing one another, like a military gauntlet or honor guard. One end of the paired line faced the shadowed alcove of an access tunnel, and two by two, the twenty dancers turned to face the dark opening.

"*Lay-deez and gentlemen!*" an electronically amplified voice called out. "*I direct your attention to the center stage!*"

The house lights dimmed as the announcer spoke, and Wanda looked at Simon, who was staring raptly at the area enclosed by the track. His eyes seemed to sparkle in the gathering darkness, as if lit from within, and he smiled again while obeying the announcer's prompting.

"Get ready for a treat, Wanda," Simon said. "I promise you, you've never seen anything like this!"

She had a hunch he was right.

"*The terror of three continents and our star attraction,*" the booming voice continued. "*Fearless Fireball Fred proudly presents seven tons of fuel-injected mechanical muscle! Twenty-three feet of high-octane horsepower!*"

Wanda could barely see now, as her eyes adjusted to the

darkness, but she could hear quite well. She could hear motors roar to life, muffled as if by intervening barriers, and more. She could hear the thunderous impact of metal against concrete, not once, but twice, and then a third time in an ominous sequence that had a familiar cadence.

The cadence of footsteps.

"He puts the 'monster' in monster truck rally!"

The music had begun to play again, more softly this time, in eerie counterpoint to the pounding footfall sound that grew louder. Despite herself, Wanda felt a sense of anticipation as she stared into the access tunnel's darkened confines. Inside that blackness, a patch of even deeper darkness grew larger.

"Now taking center stage!" the announcer continued, his voice rising to a fever pitch. *"Behold! I give you the star of our show—Carzilla!"*

The sudden glare that came when the house lights snapped back to full power was almost enough to blind Wanda. When her vision cleared she saw something standing in the open area that looked like it had been produced in collaboration by a junkyard owner and an insane sculptor, both of whom had seen entirely too many monster movies.

Vaguely—but only vaguely—dinosaurish in contours and build, the bizarre figure was composed of various car and truck components, riveted and welded to an articulated steel armature. The construction job looked rough and ready; large gaps in its sheet metal hide allowed rust-colored steel support members—bones—and other components to show through. Wanda's knowledge of automotive mechanics was limited to the point of nonexistence, but she had seen enough giant robots in her day to recognize that most of Carzilla's "works" probably didn't—instead, they were nonfunctional chunks of apparatus chosen less to operate than to impress. The thing's motive power seemed to derive from a simple series of pushrods and pulleyed cables, linked to a central power source, and operated by some hidden puppeteer.

Carzilla's exterior was somewhat more outré.

Its torso had been shaped from some kind of oversized package van, with much reshaping and welding to force the vehicle's shell into a rough approximation of abdomen and thorax. In a previous life, its forelegs had been motorcycle bodies, with chromed handlebars remade into pinching claws, and its rear legs and tail looked to have been custom-crafted from other vehicles' frames.

Its head was a vintage Volkswagen Beetle, with the hood opening hammered and bent into a rough approximation of an alligator's jaws, while two red-lensed spotlights glared out from behind its windshield, representing the creature's eyes. Ragged, chromed teeth sat behind "lips" that parted briefly to release bluish flame, presumably derived from a concealed torch.

For the sake of argument, Wanda might have been willing to stipulate that someone, somewhere, would find Carzilla impressive—even if she couldn't imagine who. Her own life, however, had been filled with sufficient spectacle to give her a somewhat different perspective.

Wanda turned to look at Simon, who was starting raptly at the low-tech spectacle unfolding before him, as Carzilla moved around in the central area of the Garden's main floor. Simon's eyes positively glowed now, and he watched every move the ersatz dinosaur made, with the kind of hypnotized rapture that he had doubtless viewed his first Christmas tree. After a long moment, however, he seemed to feel Wanda's gaze upon him.

"You hate this, don't you?" he asked. "We don't have to stay—I mean, it *is* pretty dumb, really."

Wanda sighed. She was touched by the gesture. He was obviously having a wonderful time, but had gone to the trouble of offering to leave, and even bad-mouth the show.

So she couldn't say anything but, "Don't be silly. I'm having a wonderful time."

"Look out, folks! He's out of control! He's on the loose!" the announcer's amplified voice cried, as the show's next act began. *"Nothing can stop Carzilla when he's on a rampage!"*

Carzilla was moving faster now, supposedly out of control, and supposedly on the loose. As it moved, the limitations of its improvised design became more apparent. Though they moved, its rear legs seemed to provide no real motive power. Instead, as Carzilla taxied about on hidden wheels, its legs and feet flapped futilely, but they hit the floor hard enough to make the sound of footsteps that Wanda had heard earlier. Nor could

Carzilla move very fast; the creature's star-spangled honor guard was easily able to keep out of its path and dodge the occasional gout of flame breath. They gave sporadic squeals of mock horror, but they really didn't seem very frightened.

As menaces went, Carzilla seemed to Wanda to be fairly weak tea. Other attendees were more impressed, however, and the air fairly shook as spectators hooted and hollered.

One of the girls had slowed down enough to allow Carzilla to catch her, and had levered her own squirming body into the creature's handlebar embrace. She pretended to struggle and screamed unconvincingly as she forced the "claw" shut around her waist, and then held on for dear life.

Wanda rolled her eyes again. Around her, the appreciative audience made noises that verged on ecstasy, while the announcer uttered some more sounds of dismay.

Carzilla lifted the girl.

"He's got her now, folks!" the announcer cried.

The girl shrieked, pretended to struggle. Carzilla's jaws opened, gaping wide. This time, no fire spewed forth. Instead, a thunderous roar echoed from the pseudomonster's hidden loudspeakers, with enough decibels to make Wanda's ears ring.

She hoped that the Fabulous Duff Beer Babe (solo) was wearing appropriate ear protection.

As the monster raised her to its open mouth, trying to place her where grocery and luggage had once no doubt traveled, she reached out and touched its metal snout.

"But wait a minute, folks," the announcer announced. *"Something strange is happening!"*

Wanda agreed with the assessment, though probably not with the reasoning.

Carzilla's jaws closed in response to the girl's touch. The blazing red spotlight eyes dimmed slightly, took on a warmer hue. Concealed joints twisted the mechanical monstrosity's lips into the semblance of a smile.

"It's true, folks!" the announcer continued in less anxious tones as Wanda rolled her eyes yet again. *"Beauty can tame the beast! We're all safe now!"*

He was wrong.

Wanda realized it first, perhaps because of her disinterest

in the show, perhaps because a lifetime of adventure had made her sensitive to any clues of impending danger.

Clues, such as the new, rumbling vibrations that swept though the floor beneath her feet. No, more than vibrations; actual, rippling waves of force that were strong enough to make the reinforced concrete flex.

Earthquake? Wanda thought, then rejected the idea. That was impossible, or nearly so. Manhattan was built on very stable bedrock.

She stood, only to tumble back into her seat as the tremors grew stronger, strong enough to make the mezzanine structure swift and sway. Applause gave way to genuine shouts of fear as ceiling tiles tore loose and rained on the crowd. The announcer was pleading for calm when Simon's strong fingers dug into Wanda's forearm, and he pointed with his free hand.

"Wanda!" he said, pointing at the main level's floor. "Look!"

The floor was falling away.

Many things happened then, in such swift succession that they flowed into one another. Piece by piece, starting at the outer perimeter and working inward, the floor vanished from view. It broke and fell in great chunks and slabs that were irregular in shape and erratic in size, but many in number. Performers and technical personnel alike fled the rapidly crumbling expanse even as more and more of it fell away. The plummeting debris kicked up clouds of obscuring dust as it fell, disappearing into parts unknown. Beneath the Garden, Wanda knew, were ample hollow spaces for the disintegrating foundations to fill—specifically, subway tunnels and Penn Station.

But why? What was happening?

As if in answer, the quaking thunder continued and built on itself. With surprising speed, the vast center section of the main level fell into the darkness below, taking Carzilla with it. The refugee from a Detroit giant monster movie plummeted into the newborn abyss, and was hidden by clouds of rising dust. Despite herself, Wanda felt an odd twinge of sympathy as the mock menace fell from sight.

More importantly, she wondered about the well-being of the many civilians who were doubtless thronging Penn Station and the associated subways. Would the reinforced roofing protect them from the worst of the wreckage? Or was the disaster she witnessed now only the smallest part of the catastrophe?

And then another figure took Carzilla's place, smaller by far, but more ominous, too. It came rocketing up from the churning clouds of dust that had swallowed the mechanical monstrosity. The newcomer was humanlike, but not human. Nearly nine feet tall and sheathed in dark steel, it was armored in plates that approximated the contours of human musculature. Cruel spikes studded its body, and its faceplate was a metal parody of a fleshless human skull. Bootjets lifted the robot from the rubble and chaos below, lifted it, and let it hover scant meters below the Garden's ceiling.

Wanda recognized it, by general make if not specific model. "It's a Dreadnought," she said urgently to Simon. "Killer robot, originally built by Hydra to—"

"I know, Wanda, I know," Simon said crisply as he stood. The fire in his eyes was burning more brightly now, and the air surrounding him wavered and sparked. "I've seen them before."

Wanda nodded, accepting but unsurprised. She had been in the business longer than Simon, but she knew that Simon had seen his share of action, too. It wasn't surprising that his experience included Dreadnoughts; sometimes, she wondered if there were anyone in her line of work who hadn't encountered one version or another of the things. Lately, they seemed to be very nearly standard issue for criminal cartels.

Above, the thing's head rotated on its center axis, and it gazed out over the crowded auditorium, as if taking in the lay of the land.

"But what's it doing here?" Wanda asked the question but knew that she would receive no answer. One of the more tragic aspects of the super heroic life was that there was almost always time to ask questions, but almost never time to get any answers.

There was always time for battle, of course.

"Don't know. Can't be good, though," he said, displaying his sometimes-endearing grasp of the obvious. The air surrounding him blazed abruptly, and then he was transformed. A moment before, he had been the very embodiment of athletic, casual elegance, clad in jeans, shirt, and a sports jacket; now, he was sheathed in form-fitting darkness, with a scarlet letter *W* emblazoned on his muscular chest.

W, for Wonder Man.

Not for the first time, Wanda wished that she could change into her work clothes so quickly.

The Dreadnought had directed its blank gaze at them now—directly at them, Wanda was reasonably certain, and not merely in their general direction. That was entirely possible, even likely, considering Simon's and her shared profession. The robot's hollowed eyes found her gaze, and locked with it, and then something unsettling happened. The robot's head remained in place, and its body rotated below it until their alignment matched, so that the Dreadnought seemed poised to move in Wanda's direction. Instead, it raised one steel hand in a motion that could have been a salute, or a gesture for quiet.

Time, already slowed, seemed to stop. Even the civilians in the crowd paused in their panic, as if struck by the novelty of what they saw. Then—

"Nobody moves," the Dreadnought announced. Its harsh, mechanical voice carried well in the momentary near-silence. "Nobody moves, and *everyone* gets hurt."

That was when ten more Dreadnoughts, each identical to the first, rose from the ruins of the Garden's collapsed sublevels.

Inevitably, people moved then, and, equally inevitably, the screaming started anew.

Isabella Federal Penitentiary, California

In recent months, Franz Gruber had come to the conclusion that the world had forgotten him, and also to take a cautious comfort in that thought. He had spent long years insulated from the world at large by heavy stone walls and thick steel bars, sharing a ten-foot-by-ten-foot cell with no one, and sharing a maximum security wing with perhaps thirty other inmates. During the previous five or so years, the names and faces of the men in the neighboring cages had changed, as the others escaped or were paroled or simply died behind bars.

New inmates took their place, and without exception, none of the newcomers had ever heard of Franz Gruber, or remembered how close he had come to ruling the world.

In a curious way, his anonymity pleased him. Gruber had enemies on the outside, men of great power who had ample reason to hate him. If they too had forgotten him, and it seemed to him they had, he saw no reason to remind them that he yet lived.

"I will not cooperate with you in this thing," Gruber told the beefy-looking man who sat across the table from him. "Say what you wish, make what promises you wish, but I will not cooperate." His words hung in the still, cool air for a long moment, before being swallowed up by the padded walls and acoustical tile ceiling of the interrogation room.

"That's unfortunate. Your participation would make things much easier," said the man, whose card had identified him as Mark Evanier. He was a big man, broad and heavyset, and his wide features bore a studiously amicable expression as he spoke. He had dark, slightly curly hair that he wore in a shaggy cut.

Gruber had studied Evanier's card long and hard before agreeing to accompany two guards on the long walk from his solitary cell. Gruber was quite accustomed to being presented with official credentials, ID cards for S.H.I.E.L.D. and SAFE and Interpol, and business cards from cash-hungry lawyers. Evanier's was different; below the neatly set letters of his name, more embossed lettering identified the man's employer as a major Hollywood studio. That had piqued Gruber's interest, and concern.

What possible interest could a studio have in him?

"Talk, then," Gruber said. "I will not."

Evanier shrugged. A zippered case made from leather as limp and fine-grained as silk lay open on the table before him, revealing a sheaf of typed contracts and a spotless notepad. Now, with smooth, precise moves that seemed incongruous for one of his build, he opened another compartment in the case and drew forth several pencils, each tapered to a needle point. As he arrayed the writing utensils next to his pad, Gruber felt a twinge of apprehension—not fear, but apprehension. In the right hands, sharp pencils could be deadly weapons; it had been some long years since anyone had placed them so casually within his easy reach.

Why here? Why now? More importantly, what bribes had the big American paid for permission to bring his own case and accessories past the facility's stringent security measures, when most visitors satisfied themselves with prison-inspected, prison-provided tools? And why?

He was beginning to have his doubts about Evanier.

"We'd like very much to have your cooperation," Evanier continued. "We're prepared to pay handsomely."

"There is nothing you can pay me that would make my stay here any easier," Gruber said. He snorted dismissively, making the same sound he had heard the Master make so many times, in years so far gone.

In the years before he had made himself into the Master.

"I don't think you understand what I'm offering," Evanier said, with an air of weary patience about him. "You're a public figure, Franz—"

"Gruber," Gruber interrupted. "Address me properly."

"Gruber, then, or *Herr* Gruber, *ja*?" Evanier said, with more than a faint note of mockery. "You're a public figure and a part of history, however small."

Gruber made no response.

"With or without your input," Evanier continued, "we'll proceed with what we have in mind."

"Your precious television program," Gruber said.

"Miniseries," Evanier corrected. "A dramatic recounting of the life and times of one of this century's most infamous intellects, told by the testimony of those knew him."

"Told, if I cooperate."

"Whether you cooperate or not," Evanier repeated. "You weren't alone in his service, Gruber. We have other testimony, eyewitness accounts, declassified records—"

"You have nothing from me. You will have nothing from me. I will not sacrifice my privacy and bring myself again to the attention of the world, merely for the amusement of my inferiors."

The amusement of my inferiors. Gruber savored the phrase. The words were ones that the Master might have spoken.

Evanier sighed. "Look at it another way," he said. "This

is your chance to tell your version of events. You can tell Zemo's story as it was meant to be told—''

Zemo. The name rang like a bell in Gruber's mind, and its echoes stirred memory that were never far from his thoughts.

Heinrich Zemo.

The Master.

Gruber's master had been Heinrich, the Twelfth Baron Zemo, among the most notorious war criminals to survive the fall of the Axis Powers. A brilliant scientist and master tactician with his own dreams of conquest, Zemo and his agents had struck again and again at the forces of order from a base hidden in the South American jungles. Ultimately, Zemo had fallen in final combat against his greatest foe, the so-called super hero Captain America. Through the long years leading up to his death, Gruber had served the baron as his personal pilot.

And then, for a shorter but altogether more enjoyable span of time, Gruber had become Baron Zemo.

The audacious ploy had been astoundingly easy to execute, helped along by the deceased Zemo's comprehensive planning and the considerable resources of his outlaw organization. First, Gruber had sowed doubt about Zemo's death and fabricated convincing evidence of his survival. Then, appropriately disguised, he had seized the reins of power that the true Zemo's untimely demise had left unattended. After that, it had been merely a matter of implementing one of Heinrich's more grandiose plans, a program of global blackmail using an orbiting, solar-powered death ray. Gruber had reveled in his role, enjoying a heady draft of power beyond his previous, wildest dreams.

Until, once more, Captain America had put an end to yet another dream of conquest, aided this time by another hero, the Black Panther, and agents of the American espionage organization, S.H.I.E.L.D. Severely wounded in the ensuing firefight, Gruber had been nursed back to health in the Panther's state-of-the-art medical facilities before being remanded to American custody and deposited here, in a California prison, where he had languished ever since.

''If Heinrich Zemo's tale is to be told, there is another who will tell it,'' Gruber said slowly. The whispering hint of concern he had felt earlier returned, stronger this time, strong enough to make him uneasy. He had spoken little of his crimes since his apprehension, and even less during his imprisonment, and he suspected that his silence was one of the reasons he was still alive. There were topics and individuals that it was wiser not to discuss. His master, though long dead, was one.

Another was the man who shared his master's name.

"Helmut?" Evanier smiled tightly. "He'll have no objection to my queries, I assure you."

Gruber was less certain.

After Gruber's fall, Heinrich's son had belatedly stepped into the world's spotlight, eager to succeed where his father had failed. Moving with the ruthless efficiency of a true Zemo, Helmut had reconstituted his father's organization and extended it. He had battled Captain America on a one-to-one basis, and assembled small armies of super-powered criminals to wage war on his father's other enemies, the super hero team known as the Avengers, surviving each time to tell the tale. Perhaps his most famous, most brilliant ploy, Gruber knew, had been a vast program of deceit and misdirection, using a squadron of ersatz super heroes to gain the world's trust—and, very briefly, the world's control.

During all of this, Franz Gruber had done nothing to bring himself to the new Zemo's attention. It was his understanding that Helmut Zemo was extremely dangerous to cross. Certainly, he did not sound like the sort of man who would look kindly upon one who had taken his father's name in vain.

"Besides," Evanier continued. "You know things that he doesn't. Things that I need to know."

"Eh?" Gruber said, started. Evanier's voice sounded different now, less amicable. Gruber blinked, as startled by the new tone as by the words the other man spoke. "What could you—"

"Specifically, I wish to know the disposition of certain pieces of prototype equipment," Evanier interrupted. "The items in question disappeared from Heinrich Zemo's private laboratory during the months following his death and prior to the discovery of your own foolish imposture. My other sources tell me that some items were sold, to raise funds and bankroll your endeavors. I wish to know who purchased them."

"Why?" Gruber asked flatly. He had heard inquiries like these before, from representatives of the world's law enforcement and intelligence organizations. They weren't the questions that a researcher would ask, and they certainly weren't the kind that he would answer, no matter what the circumstances. His years behind bars had taught him well the virtues of silence and discretion. "Explain yourself," he said. "What possible need do you have of such information?"

"I'm not here to answer questions," Evanier said, an ominous new note of steel in his voice. "That is your role."

Gruber laughed at that. "Never," he said. "The secrets I hold, small though they are, are mine alone. I have no more time to waste on you. Go back to whoever it is that truly employs you and tell them—"

His word trailed off into silence. Concern and irritation suddenly became genuine fear as his mind processed what his eyes saw. The supposed Hollywood producer had opened another section of his zippered case, revealing a second, padded compartment. It held a glass-barreled hypodermic needle, flanked by a pair of glass ampoules. The compartment's contents hardly looked like the tools of a show business executive.

Apparently, Gruber realized, his doubts about Evanier had been well justified.

"Enough foolishness, then," Evanier said. "Enough wasted time."

"What—you are—what are you?" Gruber gasped, the words coming to his suddenly uncooperative lips in no particular order.

Nearly paralyzed with shock, he watched Evanier methodically fill the hypo from one of the ampoules, drawing the plunger back in a slow, steady motion until the calibrated cylinder filled with straw-colored fluid. Evanier then tested it by pointing the needle straight up and depressing the plunger slightly, and nodded in evident satisfaction as a fine stream of fluid erupted from the needle's beveled tip.

This was wrong, all of this was wrong. Evanier's actions, like his questions, were utterly out of keeping with his alleged identity, and more befitting an intelligence agent's interrogation techniques.

"You're going to tell me what I wish to know," Evanier

said. ''And this will ensure you tell me the truth.'' He paused. ''After that, you will be punished.''

''Never! Never!'' Gruber shouted the words. He had regained some control of his muscles, and, desperate to get away from his visitor, squirmed backward in his seat. ''You can't do this to me! I—I have rights!''

''You have nothing. Soon, you will have less,'' Evanier said, reaching for him. ''Now, give me your arm.''

''No! No!'' Gruber cried. The two guards stationed outside the interview room's doorway were posted there to protect his visitor, but that didn't matter; they could protect him, too. ''Guards!'' he shouted. ''You must help me! *Guards*!''

''Scream if you wish. It will avail you not. There is no one to hear you,'' said the man who claimed to be Mark Evanier. Steel hard, his fingers dug deeply into Gruber's wrist and pinned his arm to the worn tabletop. Evanier's other hand, the hand that held the hypodermic, came closer.

No one to hear? Gruber considered the words desperately. Had more bribes been paid? Were the required guards absent, or simply dead? Did it matter?

Would he ever know?

''Who—who are you?'' he asked, as he felt the needle stab his arm. It was only a slight pain, like the bite of an insect, but its effect was immediate. A sudden sensation of warmth and well-being rushed through him and seemed to sweep his cares away. He barely managed to put forth the question again before the lassitude became overpowering. ''Who sent you? Interpol? S.H.I.E.L.D.?'' he asked drowsily, even though his curiosity was fast fading.

Evanier leaned closer, his lips pulling back in a sardonic smile. ''Don't be absurd,'' he said. His broad face rippled and flowed, ruddy cheeks and grinning lips, softening, losing definition. Already, he looked nothing like the man who had sat, a moment ago, across the table from Franz Gruber.

Then another moment passed, and he looked like nothing human.

The face that confronted Gruber now would have been more at home in a nightmare than on a human being. Evanier's new visage was little more than scar tissue, a mass of seared flesh, puckered and ruined beyond Gruber's worst imaginings.

It clung only intermittently to the bones of his face, most of it hanging in long, looping folds that had an almost liquid look to them. Here and there, tufts of hair and other stubble were visible, blond in color and sprouting through the ruined flesh, but nothing else remained of Evanier's dark locks. The revealed damage to his lips was especially evident; little of them remained, so little that most of his teeth were exposed, and Gruber had to wonder how the other man could shape his words.

By far, the worst parts of the nightmarish visage, however, were the eyes.

They were horrific and familiar. Nearly lidless, with the surrounding flesh pulled back from them, Evanier's eyeballs seemed ready to bulge from their sockets. Now, even as the drug took hold, Gruber felt a frisson of sheer terror as their angry glare transfixed him.

He knew those eyes.

He recognized them with a feeling of sick horror. He had felt that searing, penetrating gaze before, glaring out at him from another face, a masked face that had belonged to his master. The Master was long dead, Gruber knew, which left only one man in all the world who could be seated before him now.

Despite the tranquilizing effect of the drug that coursed through his veins, Franz Gruber suddenly wanted very much to scream. Instead—

"His eyes," Gruber croaked, in sick recognition. The choked words were the best he could do as desperate panic made one last stand against drug-induced obedience. "You have your father's eyes."

"Precisely," came the response, in tones that were almost—but only almost—amiable again. Then, the man who had claimed to be Mark Evanier set aside the needle and picked up a pencil instead. He jotted a few words on his note pad before speaking again.

"Enough foolishness," he repeated. "I am Helmut, the Thirteenth Baron Zemo, and the son of the man whose legacy you despoiled. Now that we are properly introduced, we will begin. There are so many questions you must answer." He paused. ''And so much you must answer for.'' His tattered lips pulled back in a smile.

Gruber's, however, did not.

Madison Square Garden was now the scene of more thunder, more destruction, more screams of pain and terror. The thunder roared from the jets that drove the attacking robots through the dust-filled air; the destruction came from the blue-white force blasts they fired into the crowded spectator sections in not-quite-random fashion.

The screams came from the targets that the nearly random blasts of hammering energy found.

Like roaches surprised by a sudden kitchen light, the men, women, and children crowding Madison Square Garden whirled and raced in all directions as the echoes of the first Dreadnought's words faded. They fled without consideration of which exit was nearest or who might be in their paths, and the erratic disorder of their flight demonstrated both the worst and best of human nature.

A woman jumped up and ran as one of the flying Dreadnought robots swooped down in her general direction. It raised its hands and fired blue-white energy at her. She dodged the bolt just in time; the plastic seat she had occupied only seconds before exploded into shrapnel that caught and cut others less fortunate than she.

A big man with two chins too many and a waistline to match dropped his seventy-two ounce ''Super Slurper'' of Duff Premium and platter of nachos, then headed for the nearest exit. He didn't make good speed, but his bulk was enough that he managed to knock down and trample three diminutive nuns from New Jersey. He gathered himself together and kept running, neither rendering aid nor taking notice. Then he fell, too, as more blue-white energy rained down from above, smashing into the small of his back and driving him, face-down, to the concrete floor.

A reed-thin teenager with buckteeth tore himself free from his date's clinging embrace and charged desperately for cover as another Dreadnought swooped close. He seemed concerned only with his own safety, and nothing else—until some random heroic urge prompted him to leap *between* another blue-white force bolt and shield an elderly woman with his own body. For her part, the old lady paused only for the briefest of moments, then stepped over his fallen form and into the sheltering shadows of an exit stairwell. Above her, the Dreadnought who had taken that sector of the Garden as its own flew on, looking for new targets.

"They're attacking without rhyme or reason," Wanda shouted. "It's like they're trying to cause a panic!" She had to shout, to have any chance of being heard amid the din. Even so, the volume of her hasty words was insufficient to the task.

Simon was already out of earshot.

He had launched his muscular, athletic form from their luxury seats, throwing himself into the empty space beyond the guardrail. As he leapt, the air surrounding him sparked and crackled with a sudden flare of ionic energy. It was the same energy that had effected his wardrobe change mere moments before, displacing his civilian outfit in favor of his working clothes, and the same power that bore him aloft now.

Simon Williams—Wonder Man—had powers and abilities far beyond those of normal men. Clandestine experiments by a brilliant scientist in the South American jungles had supercharged his tissues with seething ionic energy, raw, crackling power that he could express in a variety of modes—flight, super strength, durability, and others. Those experiments had changed his life, as well. They had been his first steps on a long and winding path that, after many detours and missteps, had brought him to the side of Wanda Maximoff and to the ranks of the Avengers.

The ranks of heroes.

Now, he raced upward in a long, looping trajectory that carried him toward one of the Dreadnoughts. As he came near, the thing turned its attention from the still-fleeing civilian spectators and blasted energy at Simon.

The blue-white force splashed against him and Simon Williams laughed, a deep, rolling basso profundo rumble. As he laughed, he swung his left fist forward, driving it deep into the robot's chest, smashing easily through its armored hide. Metal skin split and metal ribs broke, and then the Dreadnought's body hung limply from Simon's grasp, its central processor destroyed beyond repair.

"It's not that easy, Robbie," Simon said, shaking the ruined automaton free so that it fell. Almost instantly, it vanished into the debris-choked pit that once had been the Garden's main level.

In the audience below, those few of the spectators not caught up in the chaos and panic cheered and applauded, at least as appreciative of Wonder Man's heroism as they had been of Carzilla's antics. Simon took no notice of the acclaim, however; already, a second robot was hurling itself at him, steel fingers suddenly glowing with white heat as they reached for his throat.

Wanda took no notice, either. She had worries of her own. Some twenty yards to her left, two more Dreadnoughts were attacking a dozen or so Shriners, harrying them forward with a series of closely placed force blasts. The group of overweight men soon found themselves with nowhere to run, and cowered in a corner as the death machines drew near. They were screaming for help, and no one seemed ready to give it.

Except Wanda.

There was no time for anything fancy, Wanda knew, but she didn't see any need for sloppiness, either. She took a single split second to compose herself, and to put her mind through a mental exercise so brief that it was almost instantaneous. Even as she finished, the fingers of her right hand were swiftly inscribing a complex geometric pattern in the dusty air, and then they pointed themselves at the first Dreadnought.

Something flowed from the tips of those fingers.

It was light but not light, color but not color. It was a rippling, cascading, twisting ribbon of something that was almost painful to consider too closely. It was mystic energy and chaos given form, then bound together by the force of Wanda's will. Now, it leapt from her and found a new home in one Dreadnought's head.

Almost instantly, the robot crumbled. Gray steel turned to red rust, lost its structure, collapsed. The oxidizing rot raced through the humanoid like lightning, devouring and destroying and aging all that it touched. In seconds, the robot's metal form had fallen beneath the crushing weight of centuries, as the eldritch energies Wanda had unleashed aged it. The radioactive core of the robot's power system aged, too, and to an even greater degree; forced through countless half-lives in seconds, its plutonium pellets fell to the floor in leaden lumps as their casings disintegrated into red dust.

As the first Dreadnought fell, the second one turned from its previous targets and trained synthetic eyes on Wanda. A panel on its chest slid back, to reveal the black mouth of a gun barrel trained in Wanda's direction.

That was new. In Wanda's experience, Dreadnoughts relied primarily on physical might and thermal weapons. This one's ballistic capabilities, along with the force bolts the others had demonstrated, suggested a new step in Dreadnought evolution.

She pushed the thought from her mind. There would be opportunities to consider such things later.

Wanda gestured again. This time, she didn't bother with the mental exercise or the geometric gestures. This time, she used her power instinctively, without deliberation or skill. She simply allowed the primal power to flow from her and find its target.

The Dreadnought stiffened, then shook. It fell to the concrete floor with a thunderous thud, convulsed once, and lay still. Without a detailed examination, there was no way to tell precisely what had happened to it, but Wanda suspected that every module of its internal operating system had suddenly encountered one or more programming glitches.

"Geez, lady," the lead Shriner said, dumbfounded. "What are you, some kind of magician?"

More like a witch, Wanda wanted to say.

Specifically, the Scarlet Witch. The Shriners would have known that, had she been able to take the time to change into her distinctive costume.

Wanda Maximoff's heritage was a complex one. Born a mutant, she was the heir to one of the world's most infamous bloodlines. Moreover, due to the site of her birth and early childhood, her body had been suffused by magical energy derived from an ancient Earth deity. That energy, in turn, had conditioned the development of her own mutant abilities. Now, her mutant "hex" could effect a variety of occult effects. With concentration, she could impose a degree of control on those effects; without concentration, they took somewhat more random form.

Random, but beneficial to Wanda.

A troubled childhood and a career path nearly as tangled as Simon's had led her to the Avengers, where she worked with some of the world's other most powerful super heroes as the Scarlet Witch.

"Wanda!" Simon roared from above. He was in the process of tearing off a Dreadnought's head as he called to her. "Behind you!"

Wanda spun. Another pair of Dreadnoughts had risen from the collapsed floor. The reinforcements were headed in her direction.

How many of these things are there? she wondered. *And what do they want?* They didn't seem to be pursuing any evident goal. From the first one's initial ominous pronouncement to the seemingly random series of attacks, all they were succeeding at was sowing panic.

Maybe panic was what whoever controlled them wanted. Panic, or a diversion.

More concentration, more gestures on Wanda's part, and then the complete kinetic energy contained in the molecular structures of the two Dreadnoughts was abruptly realigned on a single axis.

One axis, but two vectors, in mutual opposition.

The two robots rushed together, as if driven by irresistible force. There came a ringing metallic thunder as they smashed together and shattered like brittle glass, since the sudden diversion of energy had extended to the molecular level, chilling their bodies to the point of brittleness. The chips of frigid shrapnel that rebounded from the sudden collision flew in all directions, but struck no one.

"It's a miracle," someone said, loud enough for the words to reach her ears.

Wanda disagreed; it was no miracle, no luck—just skill. She didn't make any comment however, but looked instead for another target.

That's when it happened.

A throbbing, flickering glare of actinic light pulsed briefly through the Garden, throwing every aspect of the chaotic melée into stark relief. The flash seemed to come from everywhere at once, but lasted only an instant, flaring into and out of life so quickly even Wanda was dazzled. It blinded less than it stunned, as if the strobe effect had been keyed to interfere with the operation of the human nervous system.

The glare was followed by yet another explosion that thundered through the auditorium's interior, this time from above. Still stunned, still trying to focus, Wanda blinked in shock as a massive section of the roof fell free, revealing a patch of the evening sky.

She was still staring upward, dumbfounded, as one Dreadnought rocketed up through the gap, and she gave out a cry of alarm as she recognized the unconscious form cradled in the death machine's armored arms.

Simon.

The robot had taken Simon.

Then, even as that terrible realization dawned, both her man and the machine were lost to sight.

Six monitor screens presented six televised images for Tony Stark's consideration, while six paired cameras and microphones noted his every gesture or word. He was seated behind his desk in Stark Tower, the New York headquarters of Stark Solutions, in his private office. Like the office, the monitors were there for his use, and his alone. The sophisticated units hovered in the cool air of the suite, held aloft by miniature antigravity generators and oriented for his viewing comfort. They were responsive and obedient mechanisms, programmed to accomodate his every move. In other, better times, they had followed him about the suite as he paced and watched and talked; now, like Tony himself, they remained nearly motionless as he considered them from his desk chair.

Just now, four monitors showed the faces of various civil-servant types, relatively anonymous but no-nonsense countenances of men and women who toiled for the federal government; screens five and six displayed an annotated pie chart and timeline, respectively. The timeline was a three-dimensional projection of the type that Tony found more irritating than informative, with incremental segments flagged for special consideration. From even the most cursory glance, however, one thing was obvious.

Someone was running seriously behind schedule.

"We appreciate your meeting with us on such short notice," the oleaginous Archibald Nathan said from the first screen.

He was an especially anonymous-looking individual of average build, complexion, and demeanor, so resolutely nondescript that Tony suspected he cultivated the effect. Nathan worked for the government, after all, holding a Special Projects Director title within the General Services Administration's ramshackle organizational strucure. It was Tony's experience that more career bureaucrats got that way by fading into the background and hoping no one noticed them than by actual accomplishment. Nathan, however, seemed to combine both approaches.

At any rate, the average-looking man was proving dedicated to his job, and remarkably tenacious, as well.

"I'm happy to make time, Mr. Nathan," Tony said, "I'm only sorry it has to be via teleconference."

Neither observation was completely true.

"Logistics and schedules are difficult taskmasters, even for the best of us," Nathan said. This was apparently his idea of a humorous aside.

Tony shrugged, and restrained the impulse to wince. He was stiff and sore from physical therapy, and still recovering from some fairly recent, fairly serious injuries. "I hadn't expected to be in the city today," he said. "Or on the East Coast, for that matter. But something came up." That something had been an appointment with a medical specialist, but there was no need for Nathan to know that.

"I know you're a busy man," Nathan said.

Tony doubted that the other man knew just how busy. Had he been able to convince Nathan of just how many organizations and individuals demanded shares of Tony's time, the current conversation would never have taken place. As it was . . .

Nathan had been rather aggressively courting Stark's company for some weeks, and Tony had wearied of dodging his calls. This time around, however, Nathan had pushed the right buttons, or called in the right favors. His most recent invitation had promised the participation of several agency heads who were too important to ignore out of hand—especially for a company as new as Stark Solutions. With a bit of reluctance, Tony had agreed to a meeting, if only to put an end to the matter.

"I'm flattered that you're all so interested in securing my services," Tony continued, "but I'm not at all certain that I'm the right man for the job. My services don't come cheaply—except in distress cases—and what you've outlined could be accomplished by at least a dozen other engineering firms." He paused. "I could recommend a few, if you'd like."

Again, Nathan responded, and none of the others. Nathan had taken the lead throughout the meeting, with the various agency representatives deferring to him. That was another surprise; those other three faces belonged to some heavy hitters indeed, major players in espionage and law enforcement arenas.

"We tried that route," Nathan said. "That's what brought about our present situation. No, Mr. Stark, your company is uniquely qualified to do what needs to be done and," he paused, smiling slightly, "undo what has been done."

Tony glanced at the fifth and sixth screens. They, along with a synopsized report provided earlier, told the story. For some years, the Federal Bureau of Prisons had maintained a special facility in Colorado, a state-of-the-art penitentiary that rejoiced in the rather unlikely name of the Vault.

Until recently, the Vault had been the home to some of the worst scum on Earth, super-powered felons (and worse than felons) who had used their more-than-human capabilities to wage war on the forces of law and order. Dr. Octopus, the Wrecking Crew, Klaw, Speed Demon, the Radioactive Man—at one time or another, all those individuals and many more besides had taken up residence within the Vault, however temporarily.

Emphasis on *temporarily*.

As a proving ground for major advances in surveillance and restraint technology, the Vault had been a success. As a prison, however, the facility had been of note mainly for a high escape rate and security breaches almost without number. Most recently, a mass breakout had wrecked the place completely. After some consideration, Congress had decided to find other ways of detaining super-criminals, which left a sizable chunk of federally owned real estate available for other purposes.

"—secure evidence repository," Nathan was saying. "The need becomes more pressing every day. We just have too much stuff piling up in existing spaces, especially with the current court backlog, and the recent increase in criminal activity that has followed the fall of the Vault. There are only so many places to store death rays and mind-control machines, after all."

Tony nodded at that. The proposal at hand called for converting the former Vault site into a repository for the weapons and tools that had been used by the same kind of individuals who had once occupied it. He wasn't sure it was such a great idea, but he understood the reasoning.

"Even with the botch the incumbent contractor has made of things, we're already storing some items on site—"

"Is that wise?" Tony interrupted, suddenly concerned. Nathan hadn't mentioned this before. He was personally familiar with a dozen bits of criminal hardware that belonged just about anywhere *other* than in a still-under-construction warehouse, no matter how glorified that warehouse might be.

Nathan nodded. "We're limiting ourselves at present to the storage for damaged, depowered, or otherwise nonfunctioning apparatus and equipment that present no apparent hazard," he said. "And Colonel Morgan's people have taken responsibility for site security."

"Is SAFE's involvement a problem for you, Stark?" Sean Morgan said from the third television screen. He spoke politely, but the tone in his voice suggested less concern that curiosity, and even that sentiment was low key. By nature, Sean Morgan was not a very expressive man, even though, paradoxically, he sometimes seemed quite intense. Now, his wintry gray eyes stared out from the phosphor image, with a gaze as direct and penetrating as if he were there in person.

"On the contrary, Colonel," Tony responded. "You're one of the reasons I agreed even to consider taking on the project. I know that you wouldn't involve your personnel without thinking the project justified."

The colonel blinked, perhaps the first sign of surprise that Tony had ever seen him from him.

Morgan was the head of SAFE, or Strategic Action For

Emergencies, a quick-response espionage/law-enforcement agency that answered directly to the president. SAFE was the youngest agency of its kind, but Morgan had already crossed paths with Tony Stark, and not under particularly amicable circumstances. Despite their disagreements on certain points of protocol, however, Tony Stark had considerable respect for Sean Morgan's capabilities.

Occasionally, he wondered if the reverse was true.

"Be that as it may," Nathan continued, obviously irritated at the interruptions but unwilling to say so, "we have a lot of high-tech work that needs to be done quickly. If you're not willing to take over the project completely, would you at least consider serving as a security consultant?"

Tony thought about that for a moment. Judging from Nathan's summary, most of the problems with the current project were pretty obvious—simple matters of time management and component integration. He couldn't say it was tempting, but . . .

"The job needs doing, and you're the one to do it," Morgan said. "And we wouldn't keep you long."

It was Tony's turn to blink in surprise.

"Why, thank you, Colonel," he said. "I—"

An electronic chime sounded, a distinctive two-note tone that Tony knew well. Screen five, the one that presented the pie chart, suddenly displayed a modified *A* logo, instead.

A, as in Avengers.

"I'm sorry, Colonel, gentlemen," Tony said. "I have another call I have to take."

Sean Morgan's features relaxed enough to show his irritation, but any comment he made was lost as the word MUTE appeared in one corner of his screen. Simultaneously, the same indicator flashed on the screens of Nathan and his other associates as their audiovisual pickups shut down in response to the priority signal. The only signals that the teleconference units sent to Nathan and the others now were a Stark logo and recorded classical music—specifically, Handel's *Blacksmith.*

Screen five moved now to the center of Tony's field of view. Its monitor flickered, faded, changed. Tony knew who he would see before the image reformed; the color of the *A* insignia had told him that.

The Scarlet Witch came into view, her image relayed by the miniature flat screen communicator in her Avengers ID card. She was an attractive woman, but now, worry and concern undercut that beauty. Tony thought he knew why; even the relatively low-resolution image relayed from her ID showed some kind of commotion going on in the background.

"Tony, thank God!" the Scarlet Witch said. "You're the first to answer!"

"What is it, Wanda?" he asked urgently. He didn't bother asking where she was; the sixth screen provided a readout of that information.

"Madison Square Garden," Wanda said, answering his unspoken question anyway. "Dreadnoughts. They've got Simon!"

That, in itself, was amazing. Wonder Man was among the most physically powerful of the Avengers, pound for pound as tough as any foe he was likely to face—certainly, far tougher than any Dreadnought robot.

In fact, given the Simon's remarkable physiology, Tony would have thought him almost impossible to capture, period. Anyone strong enough to do that . . .

"I'll see what I can do," he said. "And I'll see about finding you some support, too." He broke the connection and, after a moment's thought, broke the other connections, too. Nathan and Morgan and the others would be furious, but they could wait. Tony Stark could make his excuses later.

Iron Man was needed now.

Chapter Two

The Vault, Colorado

Joshua Ballard didn't like Colorado. He didn't like the weather and he didn't like the too-blue, too-big sky and he especially didn't like his first and third ex-wives, whom he knew were still lurking in Denver and Boulder, respectively. He didn't like his latest assignment, and when Sean Morgan had handed it to him, Ballard had read the particulars, rolled his eyes, and done his best to get out of the job. His best, however, hadn't been good enough.

That, in itself, was extremely unusual in Ballard's experience. He was accustomed to succeeding at any task (other than marriage) he set himself, or any assignment he was offered, whether he liked it or not—and he didn't much like the duties he had been handed here.

"Interim Site Security Officer," Morgan had said. "Responsible to me, overseeing a staff of twelve. Coordinating with the construction crews and the technos installing the electronics."

"I don't like site security work," Ballard had responded.

"I don't know how long the assignment will last," Morgan had continued, ignoring him. "But you'll be there until the last of the main alarm and surveillance systems ship, and that won't be for at least six months, at the rate things are going."

"I really don't like site security work," Ballard had repeated. "I have problems with site security work. How about a nice undercover slot, instead? I hear that A.I.M. is up to something in Belize, and I always did look good in yellow."

"I want you to keep a close eye on the construction and management contractors," Morgan had continued. "They're spending too much money and showing too few results, and I want to know why. Technically, it's not SAFE's beat, but as long as you're in the neighborhood—"

"The last time I served as Site Security Officer, I got most of my bones broken by robots," Ballard had said. "I saw my second in command disintegrated into gray ash, and I had to sucker punch a mad scientist who was working on our side."

Morgan had shrugged at that, and given one of his rare smiles. "We'll try not to let that sort of thing happen this time,'' he had said, and then continued outlining Ballard's new duties.

That was the problem with Morgan, at least as far as Ballard was concerned. The SAFE chief wouldn't ask more of his people than he would of himself—but he wouldn't ask less, either.

Ballard thought about that as he sat behind a cluttered desk that was not his own and opened one buff-colored folder after another. To his left was a heavy-duty file cabinet with a combination lock, the kind that was used to store classified files. Originally, this office had belonged to the Vault's warden. Nowadays, the management firm overseeing the site renovation used the space, at least during normal business hours.

Just now, however, the place was Ballard's.

Breaking only a few laws and using only a representative sampling of his many skills, Ballard had liberated and was busily reviewing six months' worth of facility reports. As he worked, he wore a sour expression on his face, the mirror of one he had seen Morgan make more than once.

He didn't like what he saw.

The clues were small, but they were obvious to a trained eye—excessive overtime, orders for incompatible hardware and software, purchases from unauthorized vendors, buying tools when it would have made more sense to rent, invoices without matching requisitions. Something stank at the former Vault; the only question now was whether the smell came from incompetence or fraud.

Ballard was hoping for fraud. Finding evidence of willful fraud would make him feel more like he had done his job. He hadn't joined SAFE to conduct audits and push paper; he had signed up to make a difference in the world, and make some headway against the various scum who did so much to make it a bad place. Scum like A.I.M. and the Secret Empire, like Hydra and URSA. That, and to get away from his various ex-wives. Unfortunately, this assignment seemed to have little to do with either of those goals.

Ballard's cell phone rang then, the insistent chirp breaking his concentration. His sour look deepened to a scowl. He had given strict instructions that he wasn't to be interrupted.

He unfolded the little device and thumbed a switch. "Ballard," he answered. "Better be important."

"It is, sir," returned a voice that he recognized as belonging to Chaz Clemdale, one of the dozen agents assigned to his command. "We've got a situation, we've got—"

Situation?

The connection broke, but not before Ballard got an earful of a buzzing sound in the background, a sound that he recognized all too well—the sound that energy weapons made.

What the hell is going on down there? The thought raced through Ballard's mind even as he tucked the phone back in his belt and stood. This was just a construction site, after all. Nothing of value had been consigned to the erstwhile Vault yet, just odds and ends that couldn't do anyone any good.

Then those considerations fled as the door to the office swung back. A man wearing a too-familiar and much-hated green and yellow uniform stood framed in the opening. His presence was a shock and a surprise, but the energy pistol he held in one green-gloved hand was not.

Hydra agents tended to be armed.

New York, New York

Seen from far above, Manhattan was mostly straight lines and clean angles, a pleasing sight to an engineer's eye. Right now, however, Tony Stark had no time for such considerations. Presently, he was viewing the world through the eyepieces of Iron Man's gold-and-red helmet, and from a vantage point high above the city streets that he had attained via the pounding power of Iron Man's bootjets.

Tony Stark was a man whose life was more complicated than most, with multiple aspects that seemed contrary to one another, but that added up to a remarkably complex whole. One of the Western world's most brilliant engineers, he was equally well known as an playboy and man-about-town, with a social calendar so full that many wondered how he spared even a moment for lab work. Not content with the considerable fortune he had inherited, Tony had parlayed his genius into a successive series of technological innovation firms, each with more substantial achievements than the last, and each bearing his name. The most recent, Stark Solutions, was an essay in niche marketing that reflected one of his key interests—finding the solution to problems.

Other people's problems—and his own.

The high-tech, high-powered armor he wore now had begun its existence as one such solution. Terrorist actions by foreign nationals had left Tony with a piece of shrapnel embedded in his chest. At the time, his means to address the problem had been limited, but his solution had been elegant and effective: he had crafted an external pacemaker chestplate that kept his injured heart beating.

Naturally, Tony being Tony, he had been less than satisfied with mere survival. Thus, the chestplate had become merely the central component for a complex, integrated array of surveillance, analysis, tactical, and weapons systems.

In short, for the armor that made him Iron Man. Today, even long years after surgery had corrected his damaged heart, and after countless upgrades to his signature creation, he continued in the role.

Solving problems. His own, and other people's.

Now, rocketing above the city split seconds after his launch from the Stark Solutions tower, Tony's cobalt blue eyes focused less on the streets below him than on the high-resolution surveillance display that had sprung to life in the lining of his steel mask. He was flying northwest from his base; Wanda's hasty report indicated that the Dreadnought assailant was heading southeast. Assuming the thing hadn't changed its trajectory, any moment now—

Bingo, Tony thought, as his in-suit surveillance systems registered a find.

Tony gave a mental command, cybernetic relays processed it, and the armor's remote imaging system kicked in, then presented a familiar profile. It was a Dreadnought, all right, one of the mechanical shock troopers so popular with various criminal organizations. Iron Man had fought them in many settings, on many continents. This one was headed in his direction, and Tony frowned as he realized that the robot was empty-handed.

There was no sign of Simon.

A hasty external scan showed that this particular Dreadnought's general configuration didn't deviate much from standard design—except in terms of scale. It was a good twenty percent larger than any Dreadnought unit he had seen before, at least twelve feet tall.

Tony frowned. That much extra volume suggested additional capabilities. Certainly, it bore investigation. He sent another command and activated a remote subsurface scan.

Something smashed into him. It struck with enough force to overcome the forward thrust of his bootjets, and send him tumbling backward, head over heels. System alerts screamed a warning, and the visual display gave way to a threat assessment report.

Kinetic force blasts, Tony thought. That was a new Dreadnought feature, one he had never encountered before. Even as he considered that fact and its implications, autostabilizer overrides took control of his bootjets and did their job. In slightly less than two seconds, the suit he wore had righted him again. As it did, Tony took conscious control of the steering jets and amended his trajectory slightly.

He banked, swooped, and let gravity pull him down slightly, until the Dreadnought passed overhead. As it did so, he fired his palm-mounted repulsor beams. Essentially miniaturized particle beam accelerators, they spat twin plumes of coherent neutrons at his target. The beams chewed a hole through the intervening air and made it glow red with heat and ionization as the atoms comprising it either got out of the beams' way, or tore themselves apart under the withering onslaught. His repulsors were Tony's primary offensive weapon and devastatingly effective against most threats. At this intensity, at the range, they should be enough to make any Dreadnought pause and take notice, if not simply explode.

The energy streams smashed into the machine's gray hide, blasting free chunks of armor but apparently doing no significant damage. Even as the heavy shielding tore away in ragged chunks, segments of the surrounding metal extended themselves to heal the breach.

High-speed autorepair, Tony thought. That was new, too.

The Dreadnought turned in midflight, trained the optical receptors that served as its eyes in his direction. Impossibly, the rigid, stylized death's-head mask seemed to twist slightly, and smile at him. Then the robot's blank eyes receded into its steel skull, and something else took their places.

Instinctively, Tony dodged. Even as he did, his armor detected a burst of wide-band energy, scarcely more than a second in duration, that radiated outward from the Dreadnought's new eye sockets and passed over the armor's left arm.

When that second passed, so did all control and functionality for the affected limb's motors. The flesh and blood within were fine, but powerless to move a steel exoskeleton that was suddenly locked rigidly in place.

I'm not getting anything on the arm at all, Tony thought, annoyed. The effect was similar to that of an electromagnetic pulse, like those associated with nuclear blasts, but an EMP would be omnidirectional. Besides, his armor was proof against such. The armor's computer had been unable to identify the energy.

No doubt about it—someone, somewhere, had made some remarkable advances in Dreadnought design.

Locked in an awkward position, the deadened and paralyzed arm almost halved his offensive capabilities and made maneuvering difficult. Tony compensated as best he could, shifting his body's orientation, angling himself to present his right side rather than his left as he raced directly towards the Dreadnought, as if preparing to ram it. He gave another mental command, and grinned in tight satisfaction as his ears filled with the high-pitched whine of charging capacitors.

Its generators take some time to recycle, he thought. *I should be safe for a moment, but only a moment.*

Artificial lightning exploded from Iron Man's right hand. It unfurled in a rolling, jagged ribbon of radiance that seared the Dreadnought's head assembly and burned gray steel into black slag. Caught in midflight, the robot faltered, shook. The bootjets that drove it flickered briefly, but continued to fire. Even so, the death machine paused in its flight, as its own inboard systems struggled to reboot themselves after the massive electrical jolt.

Tony moved closer again, tensed the muscles of his right arm, concentrated. A panel on the wrist assembly of his armor's right glove opened and a diamond-edged rotary saw emerged, its outer perimeter spinning at more than the speed of sound.

This was going to be messy, Tony knew; messier than he liked. It was a measure he had used before, but not one to his liking, and the stuff of desperation. He brought the saw closer, moved to let it bite into the Dreadnought's skin.

The robot moved, too.

Its right hand reached out, and its oversized steel fingers dug into the armor covering Tony's left shoulder, embedding themselves knuckle-deep in the super-tough alloy. They dug deep enough that Tony could actually feel them through his armor, feel their crushing pressure grind into the flesh and bone of his shoulder.

Wincing with pain, Tony pressed the saw home, and cut a gash across the thing's thorax plates. He felt some satisfaction as he saw the blade do its work, but that satisfaction faded fast.

Almost as swiftly as the gash healed itself.

Behind Iron Man's mask, Tony Stark's eyes blinked in astonishment. The effect was like nothing he had ever seen before. He took another swipe with the blade, only to watch the effect repeat itself.

The robot seemed to smile again.

The fingers of its left hand, moving with unbelievable speed, grasped the extensor that held the saw blade, pinched and twisted. The cobalt-steel mount broke like balsa wood and the robot tossed it aside with casual contempt. Even as the ruined tool fell down and away, panels on the Dreadnought's right arm opened. Jointed probes reached out, each tipped with a drill bit. Red metal shavings flew as they cut deeply into Iron Man's dead arm.

Turnabout is fair play, Tony thought, not really believing it. He struggled to tear himself free, first pressing his free hand against the robot's chest and pushing hard. The flat-armature motors that gave his armor its strength still worked, but the gesture didn't give quite the effect that Tony desired. He didn't have the proper leverage. He couldn't apply force from the appropriate angle, and the force he could apply was having more of an impact on his suit's structural integrity than on the robot's. He was only hurting himself. Alarms sounded as seals gave and metal tore.

A display above Tony's left eye presented the good news and bad news about his left arm assembly. The inboard processors were recovering from the odd energy blast, but a full breach of the outer armor layers by the grinding drills was imminent. By the time his armor was fully back online, the Dreadnought's probes would have achieved full penetration.

He had to get loose.

Muscle power hadn't worked, but maybe applied physics would. Iron Man's hand was still pressed flat against the Dreadnought's chest plate, and pushing hard enough to deform the tough metal there. The seal between the two metal surfaces was a tight one. If he fired his repulsor at this range—closer than point blank, really—the full force of the blast would be trapped between the metal of the robot's chest and the metal of his right hand. It might just be enough to tear him free.

Or the robot's armor might give.

Or Tony's might.

At his shoulder, the probes dug deeper.

Tony shrugged. He didn't seem to have much choice.

The Dreadnought's probes were in now. He could feel them, metal snakes, sliding along the skin of his arm. He struggled and twisted inside the metal confines of his suit, futilely trying to avoid the intruders, but they would not be denied. Further and further they extended, until he could feel them pause at the perimeter of his chestplate, the section of the armor that contained the primary operating computers and system controllers. The suit's alarms were shrieking now, a complex cacophony of alerts that demanded his attention.

Desperately, he sent the mental command to the right repulsor array.

No response. No blast, no ignition at all, not even the typical cybernetic feedback that should have acknowledged the receipt of his command.

Then, abruptly, the alerts fell silent.

Tony directed his gaze again at the systems report display, and felt his blood run cold. His suit systems were going offline. Navigation, surveillance, telemetry, targeting, weaponry—one by one, but in alarmingly quick succession, their telltales went red, then dark, as system after system shut down and ceased responding to his commands.

That was impossible, or should have been.

Life support, communications, motor control—the shutdown protocol continued, as the impossible continued to take place.

More than a few times in the past, outside forces had taken control of his armor. Indeed, they had made such a habit of doing so that Tony had installed increasingly complex safeguards against such action, specifically keying the internal command processor to his personal electroencephalographic brain wave signature, and integrating aspects of his mental architecture into the suit's operating system. As configured now, the armor should be blind and deaf to any commands but his.

Energy manipulation systems down, propulsion . . .

No.

If the bootjets failed, the fight was over. He would fall, like any other material body in a gravity well, and be reunited rather forcefully with the asphalt streets below.

He couldn't let that happen.

Tony concentrated, focusing every erg of his considerable will on the unblinking red of that last, lighted telltale. He had to drive back whatever it was that was wresting control of his greatest, most personal creation from him. He concentrated, shutting out everything else but that single, red light.

The light flickered.

Tony concentrated. As long as he was alive, there was hope. To lose now was to lose forever. He knew that. All that mattered was keeping that single red light lit.

The light flickered again, and his boot thrusters coughed. They didn't fail, merely coughed. Tony ignored the troubling sound. The boots didn't matter. The red telltale representing the systems that drove them did.

He mind was perfectly attuned now to what remained of his suit's operating system. He could actually feel the deadness that had invaded his circuits, sense dead numbness where control should have been. That much, at least, was reassuring. The Dreadnought hadn't so much taken control of the armor as disrupted it.

That suggested possibilities.

Tony's entire being was focused now on the system status display. The propulsion indicator was lit brightly now, no longer flickering, and burning an intermittent green instead of red.

He felt the invading deadness pull back slightly.

The air he breathed was no longer fresh, and heat was piling up as the cooling systems continued to refuse to function. Sweat formed on his forehead, trickled down to sting his eyes. Tony ignored it. All that mattered was the system status display, the now-stable green light that represented his bootjets.

That light, and the one next to it.

The bootjets were roaring now, driven by self-contained stabilizing subroutines that had recovered sufficiently to take control of them. As the Dreadnought holding him rocketed through the twilight air, Tony's suit kept pace with him, running on something very much like a super-advanced automatic pilot. The war wasn't being fought out there anymore; the only battlefield that mattered now was the interal circuitry and processors of his suit's workings.

The green telltale burned brightly now, brightly enough that Tony could turn more of his attention to the one next to it. Tony let himself smile as it flickered to intermittent life in response to his insistent prodding.

It was the weapons system indicator.

Dark, then flickering red, then steady red, then flickering green, then steady green. Those were the steps he had to make it take.

A red-lighted system was in danger of imminent failure or shutdown. Green meant fully operational. It was a simple coding system, and served now as an excellent tool for creative visualization. Tony kept the sequence of colors in the forefront of his mind as he concentrated on forcing the deadness back some more, on guiding the weaponry telltale back to full green. It was still lit in red, but stable now. Two more transitions remained until he could safely fire the locked repulsor, then only one, then—

Completely without warning, something moving at only slightly less than the speed of sound smashed into the two steel forms that hovered high above the city. Specifically, it struck the Dreadnought, hard enough break the death grip it had on Tony's armor. The robot gave what could only be called a yelp of pain as it exploded into a cloud of metal shrapnel and other components.

Trails of friction-fire erupted on the skin of Tony's chest and left arm as the shattered Dreadnought's grip broke, and its extended probes were yanked back out along the path they had followed. It felt like a series of rope burns, but worse. Tony ignored the pain and blinked in astonishment as his suit systems came back online *en masse*. Among those systems, the one most eager to make its presence known just now was the damage assessment program module; his left epaulet had been ruptured and needed sealing. The self-repair modules enabled themselves again, so that miniature nozzles emerged and sprayed the breach with quick-setting plastic.

As his armor repaired itself, Tony blinked again and took stock of the situation. All systems were back online, as if their service had never been interrupted. Diagnosis and threat-assessment routines were running automatically, preparing reports regarding internal and external status alike. For the moment, however, Tony looked past them, and peered through his eyepieces to take advantage of the situation with his own eyes. Contradictory feelings flooded through his mind as he assessed what he saw.

He saw Thor, his fellow Avenger, perched on a rooftop below, waving the open hand that must have, only a moment before, released the instrument that had destroyed the Dreadnought. Tall and muscular, blond hair and red cape waving in the twilight air, Thor looked every inch like the master of all he surveyed. Even in his present, relaxed stance, he was the very portrait of godly majesty.

It had taken Tony some years to accept that Thor, was, in fact, the Norse thunder god of legend and that Mjolnir, the hammer he wielded, was truly magical in nature. Now, as the enchanted mallet smashed a twelve-foot armored behemoth into fragments, Tony had to wonder fleetingly how he had ever been a doubter.

"Ho, Iron Man!" Thor bellowed, his voice scarcely less loud that the thunder that was his to command. "Well met, my comrade!" Having passed through, shattered, and gone beyond its target, the hammer he had thrown now reversed its course. In moments, it would return to its master's hand.

Well met, indeed, Tony thought. He liked doing things himself, but sometimes it was good to have friends. Obviously, Thor had answered the general alert that Tony had broadcast, and, equally obviously, he had spotted Iron Man's plight and paused here instead of proceeding to Madison Square Garden.

There would be time for official thank-yous later, however, and more to see now than just Thor. There was a cloud of metal components that had once been a flying Drednought robot, raining to Earth. Tony's glimpse of the shrapnel was necessarily brief, but telling. Even as the fragments fell, they reached out to one another with segmented probes like the ones used on him. As he watched, the pieces of metal began pulling themselves back together, using articulated feelers to do the job. Tony blinked again in astonishment.

The Dreadnought's capacity for self-repair had been amazing enough, but this was ridiculous.

Ridiculous, and easily resolved.

Tony raised his hands, snapped them back so that their palms were directed in the general direction of the falling Dreadnought parts. A targeting sight superimposed itself on his field of view, and he prepared to fire the repulsors again. A wide-angle, high power burst should be sufficient to—

He paused.

Something had caught his eye. Even as the smaller chunks of robot reached for one another, a larger, central mass was revealed. Like the Dreadnought, it had arms and legs and a human form.

Unlike the Dreadnought, it was human.

The largest of the remains was a black-clad human body. For a second that seemed to last much longer, Tony stared at the plummeting body. A familiar scarlet *W* was emblazoned on its chest.

It was Simon Williams. Somehow, Wonder Man had been inside the Dreadnought, in effect, wearing the robot like Tony wore his own armor; the aberrant automaton's ability to reassemble itself suggested how *that* little trick might have been accomplished. He could wonder about that later, however. Now, rendered unconscious either by Thor's hammer or by the Dreadnought itself, Simon was falling fast.

That left Iron Man.

With a shrug, he cancelled the repulsors' priming sequence and headed after Simon. He didn't see any other choice. Thor's power of flight depended on his hammer—still on its way back to him—and Simon would smash into the street before the thunder god could reach him. That meant Iron Man had to act, now.

Simon was remarkably durable, but he was falling far, fast, and there was no way to be certain of his present physical status. It didn't make sense to put matters to the test.

In Iron Man's book, at least, rescues took priority over most other matters.

Wanda was wearing down fast. Her breath came in ragged gasps and every fiber of her being throbbed with fatigue—but there was work yet to do. Mere moments after Simon's abductor vanished, and after her frantic call for help, yet another wave of Dreadnoughts had erupted from the churning chaos that had been the Garden's floor. Of those, she felled five in reasonably quick succession, by paralyzing their systems or forcing elements of the surrounding structure to collapse on them. Literally hundreds of the panicking spectators owed their lives to the hex bolts that she fired in swift succession, and into which she had poured so much of her own vitality.

Through it all, however, one small part of her mind remained focused on the man who had brought her here, and who had been so cruelly taken from her side.

Who had sent the Dreadnoughts? Why had they taken Simon? They were good questions, but ones that would have to wait until later.

Now, another of the robots headed in her direction. Moving with relentless mechanical speed, it raced towards the mezzanine level where Wanda was still holding forth against its fellows. Yet again, she raised her hands, and yet again, she unleashed the arcane energies that were her birthright.

This time, however, the hex faltered, flickered as it spanned the distance between her fingertips and the robot's structure. This time, the sparkling bolt of radiance was more distinct and easier to see, as if it had become more a part of the material world, and this time, when it struck, it flowed along the metal surface and dissipated. In slow response, patches of the gray steel turned reddish with rust but did not crumble.

The robot kept coming.

Wanda made a worried sound, concentrated. She reached deep within herself and accessed the last reserves of her power, and released it again. More energy found the robot, enough to make its progress slow as interior systems failed, but not enough to make it stop.

"Do something, lady, f'gosh sakes!" a terrified bystander called from where he huddled behind her. "It's still comin'!"

The Scarlet Witch tried again.

There was no response, no effect. No more of the eldritch power answered her call, and no mystic radiance flowed from her hands. Her last reserves had fled.

The robot reached for her.

Something reached for the robot.

It was a yellow-gloved hand at the end of a green-sleeved arm, and when its questing digits found the Dreadnought's gray steel hide, they brushed its surface—and then passed through it.

"Vision!" Wanda said, making the name a cry of relief as more of the green-costumed figure came into view.

The Vision's hand penetrated deeper into the robot's structure, passing through tempered steel armor as easily as it might through morning fog. The Vision waited until his arm had penetrated the thing's chest to his elbow's depth, then—

The Vision's form seemed to waver, and gain new definition. Something happened to the green and yellow of his costume that made the colors not brighter or darker, but somehow more intense, nonetheless. At the cleanly defined boundary between his body, a faint flare erupted as some kind of energy found release.

The Dreadnought fell.

"Their central processors are in the thorax segment," the Vision observed in his characteristic near-monotone. He was an artificial human being, a specialized class of android, or synthezoid. Among his abilities were complete control of his body's density and tangibility. By reducing them to minimal levels, he could actually penetrate other physical forms—and then reassert his own solidity.

The resulting disruption could have gratifyingly effective results.

"That would appear to reflect a design change," the Vision continued.

Wanda nodded. "Tell me about it," she said. "They're all manifesting new abilities." She gazed carefully at the Vision's composed features, trying to read their expression—but to no avail. The android's face was as neutral as his voice.

She wanted to sigh, but did not. The Vision had played many roles in Wanda's life—teammate, protector, lover, and even husband. Now, however, there was a distance between them, bridged only by tangled emotions and shared memories. They had not been a couple in some time, but since she had taken up with Simon, Wanda had learned that the Vision still harbored feelings for her.

How strong were those feelings?

"Are you well?" the Vision asked.

Why did he ask? To be polite? Or out of genuine concern? Wanda couldn't know.

"I'm fine," she said. "Worn down. They keep coming."

"They kept coming," the Vision amended, stepping closer to her. His yellow cape billowed as he moved. "Their ranks are thinning now."

Part of the reason for that, Wanda realized, was that the Vision had not arrived alone. With him were Justice and Firestar, the two young super heroes who were the newest active-duty members of the Avengers. Both were mutants, like Wanda, gifted with super-human powers by a random roll of the genetic dice.

Justice's powers were all variations on psychokinesis, the ability to move matter through the application of mental energy. In his case, that energy took the form of a magenta nimbus that achieved a variety of effects. Right now, as Wanda watched, a hovering Justice shaped that field into a pointed ram, and forced it into the juncture where one Dreadnought's neck segment joined its thorax section. The young super hero gave a whoop of exultation as the joint shattered, and the robot broke into pieces.

Firestar was enjoying similar success, but not being as demonstrative about it. She could fly, and generate microwave bursts that induced enormous heat. Just now, she was using one of those bursts to liquefy one Dreadnought's still-firing boot thrusters. For a brief instant, the robot hung in the air like a cartoon character, remaining aloft only thanks to its upward momentum—then it fell, tumbling backward and down, into the rubble-choked pit that had been the Garden's ground level.

No more robots rose to take its place. For whatever reason, the onslaught had come to an end, and even now, the last straggling spectators were fleeing the ruined facility.

When Ben lost those tickets, he won, Wanda thought.

It really hadn't been a very pleasant evening.

"That's the last of them, I think," Firestar said, in a voice that was remarkably businesslike, given the carnage she had just created. Angelica Jones could be a very pragmatic young lady.

Justice, alighting beside her, agreed. "I took out three," Vance Astrovik said, "then there weren't anymore. What's next? Crowd control? Police reports?"

Wanda shook her head. "We can leave that for the regular authorities," Wanda said anxiously. "I want to find out what happened to Simon."

Chapter Three

The Vault, Colorado

"Turn around," the Hydra agent said by way of introducing himself. "Hands behind your head. Slowly."

Ballard obeyed, moving slowly and deliberately. There was no need to give his captor any reason to act.

Sean Morgan's words came back to him now, from a thousand miles distant: *"We'll try not to let that sort of thing happen this time,"* SAFE's commander had said.

Didn't try hard enough, Ballard thought. No doubt about it, he realized, he was at least partly to blame for his current predicament. Simply put, he had allowed himself to be lulled into a false sense of security by his surroundings, and had reacted to the distress call with more irritation than anything else.

Did Morgan ever make mistakes like that?

"Proceed," the newcomer continued. He was a tall man, with a muscular build that was evident through the loose green tunic he wore as part of that organization's signature uniform, but Ballard was reasonably sure he could take the guy, given the chance. Unfortunately, the Hydra agent apparently felt the same way, and was being careful to keep all the chances to himself. He stood well behind Ballard, close enough to do major damage with his energy pistol, but far enough that Ballard could not hope to disarm him.

"Refrain from moves that I would find displeasing," the other man continued. "And you may be among the survivors here today."

He was lying, Ballard knew. He had spent time doing undercover work in Hydra's ranks, and he knew how the organization operated. As the ranking officer on site, even a site as trivial and unimportant as this one, Ballard was a much-coveted target for Hydra's attack agents. Ballard's death would earn this man a commendation, and maybe a promotion.

"Slowly," the Hydra agent said. "Through the door, down the stairs. We'll join the others in the main dining area." Ballard heard him snap open the folding communicator that hung from his belt, whisper coded words into it, then close it again. "Your associates are waiting for us," he continued. The timbre of his voice changed now, rising slightly in a way that Ballard recognized. It was the slight shift in tone that came when lips pulled back and up, changing the mouth's volume.

The Hydra agent was almost certainly smiling. That wasn't likely to augur well.

Nothing about Hydra did.

Hydra had been founded in the closing days of World War II, and had flourished in the economic boom that had swept the post-war world. The brainchild of Baron Wolfgang Von Strucker, Hydra was, simply put, a substantial representative sampling of the very worst people the world had to offer, operating under the guidance of a madman, and dedicated less to world domination than to simple chaos. More than once, Strucker's people had held the world in an iron grip of fear, using a variety of weapons to terrorize the populace and issuing demands that were grotesque beyond imagining. Only the best efforts of S.H.I.E.L.D., SAFE, and other organizations like it had fought back the mad German's crazed initiatives, and most of those battles had been close calls, indeed. Hydra set its sights high, and fought tenaciously to make its grasp match its reach.

Which raised a simple question.

The new elevators still weren't working properly, so it was to the stairwell that his captor directed him. The winding shaft was well lit, but littered with construction supplies.

Fire code violation, Ballard thought. *A guy could trip and fall.*

The thought prompted others.

"What is it you want?" Ballard asked.

"Silence," the Hydra agent snapped. He was a good three paces behind Ballard.

"Me, too," Ballard said. "That's why I'm not married these days."

"I said, silence!" his captor repeated, all traces of humor gone from his voice. "And keep moving."

Ballard moved. He took the first half-flight of stairs to the first cluttered landing, stepped past a bucket half-filled with sealing compound, executed two right turns, and then began trudging down more stairs. The maneuver brought him parallel to the Hydra agent for a single brief moment, when the green-clad goon finished the first leg of descent as Ballard began the second one.

Enough separation on the straightaway, Ballard thought. *But not on the curves. Sloppy.*

Sloppy could be good.

Seven steps, landing, two turns, seven more steps, and another sideways glance at the Hydra agent's green leggings through the intervening rails.

Very sloppy, Ballard thought.

Six full flights of stairs—twelve half-flights and landings—separated the former warden's office from the new commissary area. Ballard waited until the fourth to make his move. As he made the second turn, during the brief moment that his hands were out of the Hydra agent's line of sight, he unlaced his fingers while keeping his hands where they were. Then, as his right foot came down on the second step, he lashed out and up and grasped his captor's gun hand in an iron grip.

"Hey," the Hydra agent said, abruptly sounding more like a nickel-and-dime thug than the masked operative of a world-spanning terrorist conspiracy. "You can't—"

Ballard could. Both hands clamped down now on the other man's forearm, he pulled, twisting the limb in its socket as he did. The Hydra operative slipped, stumbled, and the fingers of his gun hand opened, releasing the weapon they held instead of firing it.

That was good.

The energy pistol fell, hit the edge of a stair riser, bounced, fell again, and skittered away until it came to a stop well beyond either man's reach.

That was bad.

You work with what you get, Ballard thought grimly.

He yanked some more. The Hydra agent tried to resist the pull, but with no success. He fell forward and sideways, and his feet went out from under him. As he fell Ballard brought one hand down on the back of his head.

The Hydra agent gave a sound like deflating balloon, and fell silent.

Ballard retrieved his sidearm from the Hydra agent's belt, and then the other man's gun from where it had fallen.

Things are looking up.

Or maybe they weren't. A muffled thunder reached his ears, and he felt vibrations sweep though through the flooring at his feet.

Explosion, he thought. *Big one.*

That, plus the fact that uniformed Hydra agents, like cockroaches, tended to travel in large groups, suggested that discretion might be the better part of valor, at least for the moment. Certainly, he couldn't count on making it to the communications shack.

His cell phone was still in the Hydra agent's belt. He retrieved it now, and punched three keys in quick succession.

"Police," a flat, midwestern voice said politely.

Ballard disliked involving civilian authorities, but no other options presented themselves just now. He said, "This is—" then quit speaking.

The line had gone dead.

Then the door to the stairwell swung open, and Ballard found himself once more confronted by more pressing concerns.

Somewhere in Colorado

KRAD-FM out of Boulder was a classical station, and whoever wrote the playlist liked Aaron Copland's music. The opening movement of "Fanfare for the Common Man" was just fading from MACH-1's helmet speakers when he saw the goose approaching him and decided to get out of its way.

He tensed the muscles of his back and swung his arms forward another fraction of a degree of arc. Sensitive feedback relays situated along his arms and shoulders noted the move, reduced it to digital code, and relayed it to his suit's control surfaces and jet thrusters, where circuits integrated that data with the mental directives noted by his headset assembly. In near-instant response, his wing ailerons changed the angle at which they bit into the clean Colorado air, the jets flared, and the world seemed to turn over and over as he executed a series of midair lateral rolls. Another series of mental commands, another flex of muscles against feedback relays, and he came out of the last roll and entered into a steep climb. Somewhere far below him, the goose no doubt honked its protest as he left it far behind.

Abe Jenkins loved flying.

He wondered how he would ever live without it.

That was one reason that he had designed the black-and-silver suit he wore now, the integrated assemblage propulsive and tactical systems that would respond to his every directive. Years before—a lifetime ago—he had worn their prototypes during his career as the criminal Beetle. Later, upon joining the Thunderbolts, he had worked with a teammate, Techno, to revise and update those systems, but the core concept had remained his own: a fighter jet so small, so light, that a person could literally wear it. The new suit had led to a new name—Mobile Armored Cyber Harness-1, or MACH-1 for short. It had also led to a new role in life for him, working on the right side of the law, first as a ruse, and later for real, when he found the role of a hero appealing.

Unfortunately, it was also dangerous. The armor had taken a pounding lately, and Abe's expertise wasn't enough without Techno's help—at least, not without proper facilities—to effect complete repairs. Still, the patchwork job he'd done seemed to be holding up. That was part of the reason why he was out flying now.

First you play the game, then the game plays you, Abe thought with grim humor. Sometimes, he had to wonder at how he had changed since that fateful day when Zemo had brought him together with the other men and women who would comprise the Thunderbolts. His name, his appearance, his abilities . . .

His very self?

That was something he had to think about. Certainly, the Beetle could never have embarked on his current course of action.

One of the miniature scanners lining his helmet flashed. The goose was long gone, but now he had another visitor—or, rather, someone was within visiting range. "Mute," Abe said softly, and his radio receiver complied. Copland's eloquent thunder faded into silence and something else took its place.

"Very impressive roll, Abe," Moonstone's voice sounded in his headphones, relayed from her lips by the microphone she wore in her own masking helmet. Even filtered twice through communicator circuits, the tone of her words was distinctive—an odd mix of indulgence and condescension, with a dose of arrogance thrown in for good measure. "I'm sure the wildlife is impressed."

"Glad you liked it," said Abe, lying. He really didn't care. Moonstone—Karla Sofen—wasn't his favorite person in the world, and he didn't spend much time these days trying to impress her. Karla was, more or less, the Thunderbolts' deputy leader, and usually acted as if the qualifier didn't apply.

"Do I detect a note of disdain?" Moonstone continued. She was some twenty feet to his left, her trajectory mirroring his precisely in angle and speed. Her golden form cut through the air even more easily than his own streamlined gear, despite the evident absence of any conventional propulsion system. That was because Karla could fly under her own power, and was immune to various hardware limitations that were inherent in the MACH-1 armor—especially damaged as it was.

Abe didn't reply. For the moment, at least, Karla's little digs weren't having much effect on him. He had other things to ponder.

"Abe? MACH-1? Do you read me?" That was Karla again, and the mocking note in her voice said she knew full well that he heard her. She was still keeping pace with him, maintaining the same flight path.

Parallel, but apart—and MACH-1 wondered if that was to be the story of his life.

Still racing upward, Abe watched as the big sky got bigger. The red lens of his helmet downshifted the pellucid blue a bit, making it a sullen purple, but he knew that was only an illusion. With a bit of effort, he could look past that illusion, see the tranquil open spaces and the infinite possibilities they seemed to offer.

Infinite for other people, but not for him.

Abe was going back to jail. The Beetle had committed many crimes, and MACH-1 had made amends for most of them, but now the time had come to expiate the blood crime of murder.

The Beetle had killed a man, and the man he had become now was going to pay for that crime. If things went as Abe expected them to, it was entirely possible that MACH-1's last act as a super hero would be to turn in the Beetle, one of America's most wanted criminals.

The thought was absurd, even ironic, but Abe didn't feel like smiling. He had embarked on this course of his own free will, but that certainly didn't mean there were no misgivings or doubts.

MACH-1 cut his jets a bit and let his trajectory level off, then raised his wingflaps and added the force of his engines to gravity's pull. The world seemed to rush up at him as he raced downward; hills and woods and the first ragged outcroppings of the Colorado Rocky Mountains.

Moonstone was keeping pace with him on the power dive, too, he noticed, and doing fair (if technically incorrect) justice to the other name she had used: Meteorite.

"What's it to you, Karla?" he asked, with some irritation. "I came out here to run a systems check, and to be alone. I've got some stuff to think about."

"I just wanted to make sure that you were all right," Karla said, suddenly sounding solicitous.

She was good at sounding that way, but not so good that Abe believed her. It was barely possible she felt some concern for him, but he knew that scientists were quite capable of worrying about the rats that ran their mazes, too. Karla's civilian career had been as a behavioral psychiatrist and to say she took a clinical approach to interpersonal relationships would be putting it mildly.

Abe could think of other words to describe her, however, shorter words that were considerably more to the point. Either way . . .

"And?" he asked, snapping out of the power dive and resuming a more level flight path.

Moonstone did the same. "And Hawkeye said to see how you were doing," she acknowledged, naming the Thunderbolts' current leader.

That, Abe could believe.

Currently on detached service status from the Avengers, Hawkeye billed himself as the world's greatest archer, and Abe could believe that, too. Certainly, he had enjoyed far more success as a super hero than MACH-1 would have believed possible, considering that the other man's chosen tools were a bow and a quiver filled with trick arrows. Even in their brief association, Hawkeye had struck him as a right guy, someone who could say, *"I just wanted to make sure that you were all right,"* and mean it.

Which was funny, considering that it was Hawkeye who had suggested MACH-1 turn himself in, and that Hawkeye's current project was pulling the strings that would facilitate that return to a life behind bars. As an Avenger, and with his connection to the Thunderbolts not generally known, he was uniquely qualified to make such negotiations.

Before joining the Avengers, however, Hawkeye had enjoyed a brief outlaw career of his own. That taste of the lawless life had been enough to give him sympathy for the various members of the Thunderbolts, and an understanding of the mixed sentiments that Abe felt now.

"I'm fine," he said. "I just have some stuff to sort out. Tell him thanks."

"Are you sure that you—"

"I said, I'm fine," Abe interrupted, then he sighed as his communicator buzzed again and a familiar voice called along the Thunderbolts' private scrambled frequency.

"MACH-1, I—" Hawkeye said.

"I'm all right, Hawk, really," Abe said testily. "Honestly, can't a guy go off by himself for a little?"

"Never mind that, Jenkins," Hawkeye said, the sound of command suddenly entering his voice. "You and Moonie are gonna have to adjourn your meeting of the Breakfast Club. We've got work to do, and fast."

Jenkins sighed again, and turned off his FM tuner. As KRAD-FM's call letters faded from his receiver's display, he cut his jets, banked, turned, and dropped. In moments, he was headed back to the rented hunting lodge that was serving the Thunderbolts as their current, temporary HQ ever since their last temporary HQ was destroyed. A glance at his proximity scanner confirmed that Karla had done the same. He was preparing to land when he saw that it wouldn't be necessary.

The other Thunderbolts were coming up to meet them.

Other than Karla, only one of Jenkins's teammates could fly—but she did so in a way that made up for the others' inability. That was Melissa Gold, better known these days as Songbird.

He looked at her as she approached, smiled as she looked back. Neither of them said anything. Neither had to.

Melissa was a very important part of Abe's life these days.

A former lady wrestler, Melissa had undergone a series of surgical augmentations, some performed by Techno, that had left her with a variety of sound-based super powers. Most dramatic among them was the ability to project elaborate constructs composed of a pink force that amounted to solidified sound—a concept that still made Abe's head hurt sometimes, no matter how many times he had seen Songbird's powers in action. Right now, she was generating a pair of light pink wings to carry her aloft, and an open platform that bore the rest of the team. Beside Hawkeye stood Atlas and Jolt.

Atlas, Erik Josten, was a man who had operated under many aliases—Power Man, the Smuggler, Goliath. Abe supposed that Josten had found it easy enough to change his identity yet again when Zemo first put together the Thunderbolts. Whatever his current label, Atlas's present powers were similar to the ones he had wielded as Goliath—growth, strength, and durability—albeit with some new strings attached. Josten had spent most of his adult life as a mercenary, being paid good money to do bad things. In recent months, he had shown a surprisingly kinder, more considerate side, and Jenkins thought he knew at least part of the reason why.

Jolt, for her part, was the only Thunderbolt without a prior criminal career, something that set her apart even from Hawkeye. Orphaned during the Onslaught disaster, Hallie Takahama had been abducted by a rogue geneticist named Arnim Zola. His experiments had induced—or awakened—new powers in Hallie. Now, as Jolt, she wielded a variety of powers that were mostly extensions of normal human attributes. She had super-enhanced reflexes with agility and speed to match, and at least a smidgen of extra strength. That strength was helped along a bit by what some called her "jolt-effect" punches—stinging bioelectric discharges that underscored the physical impact of her blows.

Atlas and Jolt had settled into an odd big brother/little sister dynamic. Odd especially in view of how widely their backgrounds differed—but welcome, considering how much Hallie had done to ameliorate the more abrasive aspects of Atlas's approach to life.

"What's up, Chief?" MACH-1 asked, cutting his jets enough to keep pace with the elevated platform, but not stepping onto it. There was no need to add to Melissa's load, and he preferred doing his own flying, anyway.

"Picked up a funny trouble call on that communications matrix you rigged," Hawkeye said. He was tall and muscular, with body language that spoke both of great grace and great confidence. That wasn't surprising; once upon a time, he had been a carnival performer.

"Funny?" Moonstone asked.

Hawkeye nodded. "Yeah, but not funny ha-ha," he said. "It's just a nine-eleven call, but considering where it came from, it should have been on a dozen different secure frequencies, too. It wasn't, though."

" 'Where it came from'?" Abe quoted.

Again, Hawkeye nodded, a puzzled expression on his face, despite the disguising mask he wore. "Yup. Familiar territory for some of you guys. The Vault."

The two words, uttered with such casual finality, had an effect on MACH-1 that surprised even him.

He smiled.

Looks like I'm going back to prison a bit ahead of schedule, he thought.

"Any more details than that?" Moonstone asked.

"Not much," Hawkeye responded. In quick, clipped tones, he told of intercepting an aborted emergency call for help, relayed along police scanner frequencies—point of origin, the Vault. A quick check with his Avengers communicator, however, had revealed no activity along the frequencies reserved for federal authorities, specifically for those agencies most likely to play an oversight role for the former prison site.

No activity at all, not just an absence of significant messaging.

"The air's dead, huh?" Atlas asked. "That can't be good. Feds love to hear themselves talk."

Hawkeye nodded. "I thought it might bear investigation," he said. "The Vault is pretty isolated. Thanks to Songbird, we can get there a lot faster than any of the conventional authorities and get away too, if need be.'' Even with Hawkeye among their number, the Thunderbolts still operated as outlaw heroes, wanted desperately by most law-enforcement organizations.

''But I thought they had closed that place down,'' Jolt said. ''At least, that's what I read in the paper.''

''Message to Hallie,'' Hawkeye said with a smile. ''When you've been in this business a bit longer—on either side of the fence—you'll learn that nothing gets closed down forever. The Vault might not be in the prison business anymore, but it's still a federal enclave, and the government will find a use for it.''

''So something's up, and something's up with whatever's up,'' Abe said sourly. He modified his trajectory a bit, and fell into line near Songbird. ''We've got two mysteries, then.''

Hawkeye nodded again. ''Or two opportunities,'' he said.

Then Melissa picked up the pace a bit, until they were all moving fast enough that the landscape below merged together into a green blur, and he could lose himself again in the pleasure of flight.

Abe Jenkins loved to fly.

Twenty men and women huddled together in the approximate center of a large open space that once had been the Vault's cafeteria. Ballard recognized all of them, by sight if not by name—they were members of various installation teams and of the skeleton security staff assigned to the facility.

Skeleton staff. Ballard repeated the thought, wishing he had used a different turn of phrase. Even unvoiced, it had a grim resonance.

Surrounding the clustered civilians were a similar number of Hydra agents, weapons drawn. Three of those agents had brought Ballard here, after capturing him in the stairwell.

''There's no point in doing this,'' Ballard said. ''There's nothing here for you and no point in killing these folks.''

He said the words not because he thought they would be believed, but because he could think of no others. Whatever had happened while he was in the warden's former office, it had happened fast, and there seemed little he could do to reverse the situation.

"Spare me your foolish appeals," came the response from a man taller than Ballard, a man who carried himself with a curious athletic grace and who wore the uniform of a Hydra section leader. Just now, he had a plasma pistol trained at a point somewhere between Ballard's left and right eyes. "You would do better to give me a reason to let them live. Tell me where my agents can find what I seek, and I will allow your charges to survive. If you cannot, then be silent and await your fate with the rest of them."

Ballard made no reply, but studied the other man carefully. The stance and cadence of the section leader were naggingly familiar, which was something of a surprise; Hydra troops prided themselves on a lack of individuality. Despite that, Ballard was reasonably certain he had seen and heard this man before.

Where? In person or in televised images?

The section leader made an annoyed sound, muffled by the concealing drape of his mask. Ballard had to wonder about that; most Hydra hoods left the lower part of the face exposed, but not this one. That might be a function of rank—the variation was one he had seen before—but it might have another cause.

"Bah," the section leader said. "I weary of this."

His trigger finger pulled back.

"Hail Hydra!" someone yelled.

The section leader did not return the ritual salute, more anomalous behavior that Ballard noted carefully. Instead, he uttered a single word.

"Report."

"We recovered the processor," the newcomer said. He was a stocky man, with a beer gut that his baggy green uniform did little to conceal. He stepped closer. "It was precisely where you told us it would be, *Herr—*"

The section leader shot him. He made the shot with remarkable speed and accuracy, changing his aim, squeezing the trigger, and then training the laser on Ballard once more, all in less than a second.

Herr? Ballard wondered, even as the hapless operative fell to the floor in a crumpled heap. What name would have followed the honorific? Or what title?

And why hadn't the masked man wanted it heard?

The section leader gestured with his free hand. Another Hydra agent approached, trembling, and handed him something. It was a plastic case of a type used to protect circuit boards from inadvertent electrical discharge.

"It would appear that your services are no longer of any use," the section leader said to Ballard.

"His, too," Ballard responded.

"Just so," his captor said, and nodded slightly.

Then Ballad saw the green-sheathed trigger finger tense again.

New York, New York

"Did something to me," Simon Williams said. His words were slow and tentative, and his eyes had a dazed and unfocused look to them—odd in and of itself, since Wonder Man's eyes were typically blank orbs, unless he willed them to look normal.

"Well, you seem all right," Iron Man said. *Emphasis on "seem,"* he added silently.

Moments before, Iron Man had caught Simon's plummeting form and laid it gently down in a convenient parking lot. Now, he knelt beside Simon, using sensors hidden in the armor's gloves to assess his fellow Avenger's condition. It was difficult to draw any definitive conclusions, however. These days, Wonder Man was little more than a living mass of ionic energy, and to say that his physiology was mysterious was to put things mildly.

" 'Twould take more than a mere tap to fell a doughty warrior such as good Simon," Thor said. His words brimmed with confidence, but his tone of voice did not. For Thor, a warrior born, it was a terrible thing to have struck an ally, no matter how inadvertently, Tony knew. True, the god of thunder had not known that Simon was enclosed in the oversized Dreadnought, but—

"Did something," Simon repeated. He blinked his eyes once, twice, producing an odd strobe effect as they flashed from normal to blank and red and then to normal again. "The whole world went away."

"What's the last thing you remember?" Iron Man asked.

"A bunch of flying robots," Simon said, his voice almost normal now. "A whole flock of them. They attacked—"

He paused, then stood, so forcefully that he shook off even Iron Man's solicitous hand. "Wanda!" Wonder Man said. "Wanda was with me! Where is she?" He seemed ready to launch himself into the air in search of her, only to be held back by Thor's gently restraining hand.

"Hold," the thunder god said. "You fret for naught."

"Wanda is fine," Iron Man said. "I've already received her all-clear transmission. Vision and the others helped her put down the last of the Dreadnoughts, and she's on her way here. Now, tell me what happened."

Simon shrugged, and the crackling discharge surrounding him suddenly flared again. When it faded, he was clad once more in civilian attire. "One of the Dreadnoughts was tougher than the others," he said. "Lots tougher. It zeroed in on me early in the match. I kept hitting it, and it kept coming back for more."

"Did it seem to—heal?"

"Heal?"

"Put itself back together," Tony amended. "Some kind of self-repair function, but faster than any I've seen before."

Simon blinked, then shrugged again. "Can't remember," he said. "Its hand came up, reached for me. There was a flash, and then the whole world went away."

Tony nodded. "That fits," he said. "Your energy waveform matrix shows signs of having been destabilized. The effects are fading now, though. You should be okay in a minute or two."

"I'm okay now," Wonder Man said. "What I want to know is, what happened to the thing that grabbed me?"

"I sought the varlet in all directions," Thor said, "and of signs, I found none. The metal scoundrel hath fled."

After putting itself back together, Tony thought. That aspect of the encounter continued to nag at him. He had no doubt that it merited invstigation; in fact, in Tony's view, anything that could still function after being smashed by Thor's hammer bore further study.

Of course, Simon had survived that same hammer blow.

"We can worry about that later," he said aloud. "We—"

"Worry about what?" someone demanded.

Wanda and two of the others had arrived. They arrived as a group, with Justice and Firestar flying under their own power, and Justice carrying Wanda in a PK grip. As the three figures came closer, she wiggled from his grasp, dropped a few feet to the ground and ran to Simon's side.

"Worry about what?" she repeated anxiously. "What's wrong with Simon?"

"Fear not, fair Wanda. Thy beloved is unharmed," Thor said.

Iron Man glanced at the two younger Avengers who stood before him.

"We finished up early," Justice said in answer to the unasked question. "And traced your ID signal."

"Good call," Iron Man said. "If Thor hadn't shown, I would have needed the help."

Justice very nearly blushed.

The next few minutes were filled with hurried reassurance and hasty explanations. While Simon and Wanda each reiterated to the other that he or she was just fine, really, Iron Man quizzed Justice and Firestar on the doings at the Garden.

"Robots," Firestar said simply, with the matter-of-fact tone that characterized her approach to Avengers business. "Lots of them. Vance ID'd them as Dreadnoughts."

Justice nodded. "I've been doing my homework with the Avengers files," he said. "They looked like standard issue, but their weaponry was all wrong. I mean, I know that a lot of Dreadnoughts can fly these days, but most can't—"

"I'm familiar with Dreadnoughts," Iron Man said dryly, interrupting. "You'll find most of us are."

That was putting it lightly. Since their original design by Hydra scientists, the killer robots had been very nearly ubiquitous. Justice looked so chagrined at the comment, however, that Tony smiled under his helmet and asked, "Any idea what whoever sent them wanted at a monster truck rally?"

The younger super hero paused a moment, thinking. "Not

really," he said. "By the time we got there, it was mostly a cleanup operation." He paused again. "And there was a lot to clean up."

Firestar nodded. "They fought hard, but not particularly well," she said slowly, "and if it was a smash and grab, they did more smashing than grabbing. Much more."

"I would surmise that they had taken their prize," another voice said. It was a familiar voice, but detached and neutral to the point of coolness, and it came suddenly enough to make both Justice and Firestar give soft gasps of surprise.

"Vision," Thor said. "I did not hear your approach. You are as silent as an evening breeze."

"Unsurprising," the Vision said. "Since that is what brought me here." The Vision's method of flight was different from any used by his teammates. He could reduce his body's density and tangibility to negligible levels, and drift on available air currents. The technique wasn't as speedy as the more directed flight of Justice and Firestar, hence his later arrival.

"Anything else you can add to the assessment of the situation?" Iron Man asked.

The Vision glanced to one side, where Simon and Wanda were speaking softly to one another. The calm expression that was almost always present on his artificial features briefly became one of sadness.

Of loneliness.

He looked back in Iron Man's general direction. "I believe they wanted Simon," he said. Impossibly, he spoke even more coolly now than before. "I believe that the point of the incursion was to neutralize and secure him, and the remainder of the attack was of a diversionary nature."

"That fits," Iron Man said. Quickly, he told the others of his brief battle with the lead Dreadnought, and the surprising discovery of its internal cargo. "We're definitely up against something new here," he concluded. "And I'd like very much to know who is behind it."

"What happened to the one you fought?" Firestar asked.

"Thor happened to it," Iron Man.

"Or, in truth, Mjolnir did transpire," the Thunder God said cheerfully. With evident pleasure, he laid one hand on the magic hammer that hung at his belt.

"I don't mean that," Firestar said doggedly. "What about the pieces? There must be something left to analyze."

"No," the Vision said. "I surveyed the area quite carefully on my approach. There is nothing to be found."

"This is something new," Iron Man repeated. "That machine had self-repair capabilities like I've never seen before. It acted almost like a living thing."

"The others couldn't do that. The one you rumbled with doesn't even sound like a Dreadnought," Justice said.

"Precisely," came the Vision's observation.

The Vault, Colorado

"Just so," Helmut Zemo said, his trigger finger tightening. He took no special pleasure in killing, but nor did he shrink from it. The execution of the captured American intelligence agent fit well with the Hydra section leader role that he was playing. Even if it had not, he saw no reason to allow the agent to live.

It was Zemo's experience that loose ends tended to cause problems later.

Abruptly, something hit the weapon he held and sent it spinning into the distance. Zemo gave a cry, less from pain than from surprise, as the weapon spun away into the distance.

"Didn't your mother teach you *anything*?" a voice called.

It was a voice he had heard before.

Hawkeye, another arrow already notched in his bow, stepped from an open doorway, behind which two of the least-incompetent agents assigned to Zemo should have been standing guard.

"Aw, the heck with it," Hawkeye continued. "Everyone's heard that line!"

A cold thought swept through Zemo. If Hawkeye were here, could the rest of the Avengers be far behind?

More costumed figures abruptly entered the room, appearing from all directions, from each of the cafeteria's four entrances, as if in answer to his unspoken question.

But the *wrong* answer.

That didn't matter now. There would be time for investigation later, and for punishment and for execution. All that mattered now was salvaging the mission, and evading—

"The Thunderbolts!" someone yelled. "It's the Thunderbolts!" Then, surprisingly, "But whose side are they on?"

Zemo knew that they weren't on his.

In seconds, the former cafeteria and erstwhile holding area had taken on a third role, as the field of battle. Even as chaos erupted around him, Zemo took note of his former underlings' current skill levels.

They had gotten better, he had to admit.

Atlas, far from his maximum height but still several heads taller than anyone else, reached out with oversized hands, clamped them hard on the shoulders of two Hydra agents and slammed their heads together, making a sound like hammer on wood. When he released his grip, both men fell to the floor, unconscious.

Atlas reached for two more.

A red and yellow form, shapely and feminine, oozed through the floor as if it were not there, and raised one perfect hand. Yellowish energy erupted from Meteorite's—from Moonstone's—fingers and struck one of Josten's targets. The Hydra agent gave a cry of pain, collapsed.

"Hey!" Atlas protested. "I was—"

"Don't get greedy," Jolt said. The younger woman half-bounced, half-danced closer, then, midhandstand, drove one booted foot into the second operative's jaw. As she struck, there was a flash effect, and then the second Hydra operative fell, too. "We're on the same side, after all!"

"Yeah, but she got to take care of the sentries—"

"No squabbling in the ranks," Hawkeye shouted. "Pick a partner and dance!" Another arrow flew from his bow. Impossibly, it followed a curved trajectory, trailing cord of some tough plastic filament that served to bind yet another of Zemo's fast-dwindling ranks.

Why is Hawkeye issuing orders to the Thunderbolts?

That was a consideration that could wait for another time. Now, there were other matters to worry about. MACH-1, his flying powers almost useless indoors, was nonetheless making substantial inroads against the other Hydra operatives, and even the SAFE agent had found a weapon and was using it to good effect. The tide of battle had turned quickly and decisively, and it had not turned in Zemo's direction. Strucker's lackeys were falling rapidly to the invaders.

Zemo saw little hope of reversing the situation, but some change at salvaging it. He still had the processor, after all, and that was what mattered.

He dropped, scooped up someone else's weapon, and fired a few bursts to clear a path. Then, in a quick, loping run, he headed for the nearest exit. It was only twenty steps away, then ten, then—

A barrier formed of pink energy blocked his way.

"Naughty, naughty," another voice said. It was a dulcet voice, lilting and light, oddly out of keeping with the words it formed. "You don't leave until the ref says so!"

Even without looking, Zemo knew whose voice it was.

Songbird. The former Screaming Mimi, or Melissa Gold. She was physically powerful but a mental and emotional weakling. At lightning speed, Zemo considered possible ways of dealing with her, and instinctively selected the one most likely to succeed.

It was the simplest alternative, and something of a risk.

Without breaking stride, and speaking in a tone that would brook no denial, he snapped, "Drop the barrier, Melissa! Drop it *now*!"

The barrier faltered, failed. Too late, it sprang back into existence, even as Songbird's puzzled voice said, "Oh, no! I didn't mean to—"

Zemo didn't hear the rest of her words. He was already on the other side of the barricade and making for the shadows beyond it.

It took only a matter of minutes to resolve the hostage situation, but the better part of an hour for Hawkeye and Joshua Ballard to convince one another that neither was going to talk.

"So you're not going to tell me what they were doing here?" Clint Barton demanded one last time.

"So you're not going to tell me what you were doing here?" Joshua Ballard asked, in about the same tone of voice.

"You were just lucky, I guess," Hawkeye said.

"I need a better answer than that."

"Okay. The local police commissioner used the Hawkeye

Signal.'' Clint was getting edgy; Ballard's questions were both too numerous and too good—exactly the kind of questions that he would have asked, had the circumstances been reversed.

They weren't ones he wanted to answer, however.

The Thunderbolts had left the scene almost immediately after securing the last of the Hydra agents. Later, he would rendezvous with them, but for the moment, he still had some questions of his own to ask, and they could be asked most easily by the one Thunderbolt who was not a wanted felon.

''Not that lucky,'' Ballard said. ''You let the boss get away.'' The section leader had made his way to one of the various craft Hydra had used to storm the site, and used it to escape.

''You let the boss put a pistol in your face,'' Hawkeye pointed out, but the comment was halfhearted.

Churlish and ungrateful though he might be, the SAFE agent was also right. The newly captured Hydra agents were strictly cannon fodder, good for stoop work and refusing to answer questions, and little else. Their section leader, however, had been something more. Something about the way the hooded man had moved, something about his entire demeanor had seemed disturbingly familiar.

And then, there was the matter of Songbird's response to his barked command.

''Well? What are you going to do about it?'' Ballard asked, in a tone of voice that Hawkeye found remarkably demanding, considering the circumstances. ''I want an answer!''

I do, too, Hawkeye thought.

Chapter Four

Avengers Mansion, New York City

Edwin Jarvis, arguably the most famous butler in the world and certainly the best, took care of the hard stuff, as he almost always did. It was Jarvis who reviewed visit requests and checked IDs, who set appointments and received visitors and made excuses. In short, he performed for Avengers Mansion all of the drudge work that security protocols demanded and circumstances rarely permitted. By the time that Jarvis led the two men along twenty feet of lushly appointed hallways and ushered them into the similarly lavish receiving area where Captain America waited, it was a reasonably safe bet that neither caller posed a threat.

Of course, such *i*-dotting and *t*-crossing was more for the benefit of the visitors than of the visited.

"Impressive security measures, Cap," Jasper Sitwell said. He extended one perfectly manicured hand and took the one his host extended, unmindful of the heavy red glove that Captain America wore as part of his work clothes. "I haven't been here since the renovations. I assume that was a subphotonic structurescope in the foyer?"

"Something like that," Cap said. "You'd have to ask Iron Man about the details, though. He's in charge of hardware." He turned to face the other visitor, extended his hand again. "Good to see you, Doug," he said.

"Good to be here," Doug Deeley responded, then glanced at Sitwell. "The structurescope was in the doorframe, I think," he said coolly. "That was a DNA scanner in the foyer."

Sitwell glanced back at him, clearly annoyed.

Cap held back a sigh, then gestured at a pair of vistor's chairs. His duties were usually more interesting than Jarvis's, but typically no less specific. When on watch duty, he got to receive those few visitors who made it past the butler, and field their questions as best as possible. Some callers were more assertive—more aggressive—than others, of course, and some had more than questions that needed fielding, but that didn't seem likely today. Neither Sitwell nor Deeley was likely to prove to be an enemy, either to the Avengers or to each other.

Of course, they were unlikely ever to be the best of friends either, Captain America knew. That was perhaps unfortunate, but understandable. They were two very different men, working for agencies that had similar but sometimes conflicting agendas.

Seated before him, they made an odd pair. Sitwell was fair-skinned and freckled, reed-thin and bespectacled. He had an unfortunate fondness for loud sports jackets and bow ties, and an excess of nervous energy that made him fidget. Deeley, on the other hand, was a handsome African-American man with the kind of huskiness that comes from layered muscle, and had tastes that ran more to Brooks Brothers. He sat motionless in his guest chair next to Sitwell's, radiating a tranquil calm that bordered on lethal.

Captain America knew both men well. Many years had passed since he had worked directly for the U.S. government, but he often found himself allied closely with others who did. Both as a solo super hero and as an Avenger, he conferred regularly with operatives from every level of his own government, and with those of other nations. But even in those elite ranks, Sitwell and Deeley were noteworthy.

Sitwell was one of the most senior agents of S.H.I.E.L.D., the Strategic Hazard Intelligence, Espionage, and Logistics Directorate, an espionage and law-enforcement agency specializing in international threats. Cap knew him as both a shrewd administrator and a cunning tactician, despite the overeager, almost juvenile aspect he sometimes presented to the world. Deeley, on the other hand, was one of America's most decorated fighter pilots, and had recently joined the ranks of SAFE, another, younger agency chartered to address domestic threats. Occasionally, events required the two organizations to work together.

Such as now.

After brief pleasantries, Sitwell spoke first and quickly, summarizing a recent raid by Hydra forces on the federally owned site still popularly known as the Vault. "A comprehensive review of the inventory shows only one item missing—an inoperable apparatus constructed by a Hydra section leader named Burton Hildebrandt. Recovered from his Long Island facility, it was the central module in a device capable of producing duplicates of the Hulk,'' Sitwell said. He drummed the fingers of one hand on his chair arm and used the others to twiddle his bright red bow tie. ''We don't have many details on that case.''

''We do,'' Deeley interjected, his smooth tones in remarkable contrast to Sitwell's nasal ones. He slid a file folder across the table and nodded as Cap accepted it. ''You can keep this; just return it when you're done. And Hildebrandt probably didn't build that component, by the way. Our preliminary analysis says it was the work of Dr. Doom.''

''Doom?'' Cap said, startled at hearing the name of the reclusive leader of the tiny nation of Latveria, the iron-masked madman who was probably the single most dangerous individual on Earth. ''He's involved in this?''

Deeley shook his head. ''Probably not. The entire planet is littered with the debris of his various attempts to rule it—and even his failures are better than most folks' successes. It's not surprising that someone else wants to gather up his toys.''

''Whoever constructed the device in question, it's utterly inoperable,'' Sitwell repeated, making his assessment more forcefully this time. ''We had our best people conduct a complete analysis. That item's only potential utility was evidentiary.''

''Our science division disagrees,'' Deeley said. ''We don't have quite the assets of Mr. Sitwell's organization—''

Sitwell looked even smugger than usual. S.H.I.E.L.D. had always boasted a healthy budget.

''—but R.B. Hayes is pretty good,'' Deeley continued. He handed over another folder, this one with a bright red cover. ''Here are *his* preliminaries. Hayes was of the opinion that the item in question should be stored under maximum security provisions. That's why Colonel Morgan didn't make any protest when S.H.I.E.L.D. took it for analysis; no reason to believe that it wouldn't be safe. Of course, we expected to get it back when they were through.''

''You did get it back,'' Sitwell said, looking even more smug. ''The new Vault facility is under SAFE's security aegis, after all.''

''Along with three hundred and fourteen other pieces of bric-a-brac, identified only by case numbers, with no explanation as to what was what.'' For the first time, Deeley's dark eyes locked with the other man's blue ones. ''Hardly a good example of smooth interagency coordination, Mr. Sitwell. And one that begs the issue of how Hydra knew what to steal. Hydra was able to get a better inventory list than S.H.I.E.L.D. was willing to give SAFE.''

Jasper blinked. ''Yes,'' he said. ''Well—''

Deeley continued. ''The problem is, Cap,'' he said, ''this seems to be just one more incident in a flurry of Hydra activity. In the last few weeks, Hydra forces have struck at seventeen different sites in the U.S. and Canada, focusing primarily on high-tech raw base components—superconductors, waveform filters, exotic isotopes, collapsed-molecule alloys, and the like. Even setting aside the issue of Thunderbolt involvement—which seems to be a coincidence—the Vault heist is qualitatively different from any of the others. Colonel Morgan finds that mighty troubling.''

''The module in question is dead,'' Sitwell repeated doggedly, still a step or two behind the conversational curve. ''Whoever ran that Hydra operation must have been working on bad information.''

''Or knows something we don't,'' Deeley said. ''That theft is different from the others, which makes it significant.'' He smiled slightly. ''The discrepant member of a set is almost always the most promising route of inquiry,'' he said. ''Reed Richards told me that once.''

''What else?'' Captain America asked.

''What else?'' both men responded.

Cap nodded. ''It's not every day I get to play host to two high-ranking intelligence agents,'' he said. ''Doug is our regular liaison with SAFE, but you have different duties, Jasper. There must be a reason you're here. There must be something more to this case.''

''Indubitably,'' Sitwell said, a slightly prissy tone in his voice. ''There is an additional aspect to the scenario that merits discussion, but I was hoping that—''

Cap shook his head. ''No secrets,'' he said. ''I don't have time to play interagency games.'' This was one of the most frustrating aspects of his long affiliation with the Avengers—the need to work against the organizational inertia, however understandable, of the agencies that were supposed to be his allies. S.H.I.E.L.D., SAFE, the NSA, and all the rest had charters and agendas of their own, he realized, but they all had common goals, too. Sometimes it seemed to Cap that half his time was spent reminding his various allies of one simple fact. "We're all in this together, after all," he said.

"Very well," Sitwell said. He glanced again at Deeley. "Your discrepant member isn't quite as discrepant as you appear to think," he said slowly. Sitwell, despite his poor interpersonal skills, was a basically honest man, and evidently embarrassed by what he had to say now. Before continuing, he plucked a folder from his own briefcase and surrendered it to Captain America.

It held a single sheet of paper, listing a short list of places and recent dates. The places were all federal facilities—armories, contractor laboratories, evidence vaults, and similar sites. Each site identifier was followed by a series of alphanumeric characters in a coding system that Cap recognized, even if he could not read the individual entries.

They were federal court case numbers.

"What happened on these dates, Jasper?" Cap asked, certain he knew the answer.

Sitwell drummed his fingers some more, then finally seemed to relax. "Those are the dates that the listed items were stolen by Hydra forces from the listed facilities," he said. "None of those are S.H.I.E.L.D. facilities, of course—"

"Of course," Deeley said.

"—but we were called upon to help investigate, since most of the items taken were evidence in cases stemming from S.H.I.E.L.D. investigations. Our agents were able to uncover a pattern of infiltration and bribery—"

Cap cut to the chase. "What was taken, Jasper?"

Sitwell took a deep breath. "In the last few weeks, various high-tech components have been stolen from supposedly secure facilities. Some unknown agency has been collecting apparently disparate components with remarkable persistence."

"I hadn't heard anything about this," Deeley said with deadly calm. "Is there a reason for that?"

"Our case, our investigation, our call," Sitwell said simply.

The three men sat silently for a long moment.

"I take it the cases are connected," Cap said.

"That's the logical presumption, yes," Sitwell said. "But the Vault case is different; what was taken from there simply doesn't match the other thefts—thefts of prototype devices with uncertain purposes, in federal custody only because of who built them." He paused. "Heinrich Zemo."

"I see now why you wanted to meet with me in person," Captain America said softly. The elder Zemo had been one of his most persistent, deadliest enemies. They had contended during World War II—where he was responsible for the death of Cap's sidekick and best friend, Bucky Barnes—and then, after a freak accident had thrown Cap into suspended animation for long decades, they had fought again in the more recent past. Heinrich Zemo was dead now, Cap knew.

But his legacy lived on.

"There's more," Sitwell said. "All of the items in question included in their provenance one Franz Gruber."

"Gruber," Cap said softly. "Now, there's a name I haven't heard in years." Captain America had been at the forefront of the effort that captured the ersatz Baron Zemo in his hidden African redoubt.

"Unfortunately, somebody has heard it more recently. He was attacked in his cell early last week."

"By whom?" Deeley asked.

"By what is more interesting. The prison authorities were able to put him in stasis after he fell into a coma, and—after bringing in the Center for Disease Control—identified his malady as a form of the Death-Spore Virus."

"That means Strucker," Cap said, "and Strucker means Hydra."

"And that," Deeley said, "adds a second discrepant member to our set." He sounded almost cheerful.

"Or a third," Cap said, "if we count the attempt on Wonder Man." He hadn't been able to answer Wanda's call for aid that night, having been on a mission in another state, but he had been briefed about the entire incident.

Had it been part of the current Hydra initiative? The only real linking evidence was the use of Dreadnoughts, and that was hardly conclusive. But Simon Williams's super powers were, in a way, still more of Heinrich Zemo's twisted legacy.

"Two additional factors to consider," Sitwell said easily. "The presence at the Colorado raid of the Thunderbolts—"

"Under circumstances that our agent termed 'ambiguous,' " Deeley interjected.

Cap noted the comment, filed it away for future notice, but did not respond to it. The Avengers' informal arrangement with the Thunderbolts was still a tightly kept secret.

A faint hint of annoyance swept through him as he realized the he was committing an action he found frustrating in others—observing his own agenda rather than sharing data without reservation.

Sitwell, as was his wont, had continued speaking as if uninterrupted. "—who were, of course, a creation of the current Baron Zemo," he said. "Coming so soon after an attempt on one of Heinrich Zemo's operatives, one thing seems likely. Zemo and Strucker are both participants in the current campaign."

"But together or separately?" Captain America said.

Amazingly, Sitwell and Deeley answered as one. "That's for the Avengers to figure out," the two men said. Startled by the impromptu exercise in stereo sound, the two men glanced at each other, then smiled.

Cap smiled, too. Suddenly, the air seemed a little less thick.

"We'll do what we can," he said.

The *Barbarossa*, deep beneath the Atlantic Ocean

Surrounded by age-darkened oak walls and watched by stuffed and mounted hunting trophies, Strucker and Zemo sat at a dining table big enough for ten, confronted by the remains of an excellent meal for two. They were in Strucker's private quarters, patterned closely after the Bavarian hunting lodges of his long-ago youth. Zemo found the place comfortable, if a bit ostentatious, and dining here reminded him yet again of how much of Strucker's heritage was also his own.

The meal had made that commonality especially evident, and yet, had thrown some differences into highlight, as well.

Zemo, for his part, had eaten as swiftly and efficiently as he could without being too blatantly impolite. Typically, food was merely fuel to him, something to be consumed so that he could get on with the real business of his life.

Strucker, however, apparently felt differently. He had made a great production of savoring every bite of each course, and explaining the different ways that wine complemented the various elements of the menu, and why stew was better than soup, and why dessert was an indulgence for the pusillanimous. Throughout the long—too long—meal, he had interwoven the running gustatory commentary with anecdotes about his own exploits, no doubt hoping to impress his guest.

Hoping, but not succeeding.

"—then the report came," Strucker said, continuing another of his interminable war stories. "The American sergeant and his doltish underlings had established a base of sorts in the disputed territory. No longer was destroying the village a simple gesture of destruction; now, it would be an effective strike against my most hated foes." Strucker raised his glass, sipped from it. "Naturally, I pressed the button."

"And destroyed him?" Zemo asked dryly, knowing the answer.

Strucker sipped again, perhaps to hide a frown. "No," he finally said. "Total victory was denied me that day by a capricious fate. I took one lesson from that day, however, as I watched centuries-old hovels explode in a paroxysm of cleansing fire. I saw the old fall, and knew that the new would inevitably take its place." He paused, and looked expectantly at his dining companion.

Zemo did not rise to the bait.

"Destruction and chaos are the foundations of human civilization," his host finally continued, after a too-long pause. "It does no good simply to seize power. Rather, smash the old and decadent on the anvil of time, and use their remains to forge the new and strong. That is why many wars' losers have proven truly triumphant in later years. The Allies taught Germany and Japan that lesson, by smashing their infrastructures and economies, and allowing newer, stronger ones to take their place. Hydra and I will teach that same lesson to the world entire, before many more days pass."

With effort, Zemo refrained from responding. This was a lecture he had already heard from Strucker—and from his own father before, for that matter. The philosophical ramblings of the previous generation had long since ceased to enthrall him.

Now, at last, Strucker raised the last morsel of Wiener schnitzel to his thin and bloodless lips, chewed twice, and then swallowed. He nodded appreciatively. In response, the attractive, dark-haired woman hovering at his side lowered her head briefly in acknowledgement of the implied command, then took the plate and utensils, added them to the stack she held, and left the room.

Zemo, whose plate had long since been taken, felt disgust well up within him—a familiar sensation of late. To Zemo's way of thinking, Strucker's self-indulgent love of etiquette and courtly manners was wearisome at best and a waste of authority at worst—but the older baron was a dominant factor in Zemo's life these days. Thus, he watched every move the other man made with interest, if not approval.

Stucker apparently thought that he had been watching something else.

"Attractive, is she not?" the Supreme Hydra said. "Her late father headed the largest banking concern on the continent. She is heir to the seventh-largest personal fortune on record." He smiled, a humorless grimace that was as ragged as the dueling scar that marked his face. "A shame that the estate's representatives have never found her, never will."

Zemo had no response to make to that.

"The years will teach you wisdom, if you will but let them speak, Helmut," Strucker continued. "Her father would not. He denied me certain assets that were mine by right, so I availed myself of his most precious prize, instead." He smiled again. "That was twenty years ago."

"There is a tale to be told there, I am sure," Zemo replied, very much hoping that Strucker would choose not to tell it. Of late, the older man had been doing his best to play the part of avuncular, entertaining host—trying, and failing. Zemo found the façade more wearisome daily but pressed on. All recent indications were that the current enterprise showed considerable signs of success, signs strong enough to justify playing the part of the attentive partner.

For now.

"There is a tale, indeed!" Strucker said, his eyes lighting. "It began in Budapest—"

A tone sounded, low and sonorous, the sound old metal made when struck. It sounded a single time, prompting Strucker to glance at the cuckoo clock that hung to the left of a ten-point stag head. The half-hour was ten minutes hence.

"That will be Ebersol," he said, speaking with mild irritation. "Simply because he need not eat, he assumes that others do not, either."

"I directed him to let us know when he was ready," Zemo said. "So long as it was not before the hour. And he is a very literal man."

"True enough, and understandably so," Strucker said, nodding again. He rose. "Brandy and cigars can wait for later, then," he continued. "Duty calls."

Zemo stood, too, and fell into step beside Stucker as the taller man strode toward one section of oak-paneled wall. As they approached it, the dark slab of aged wood slid to one side on hidden tracks, revealing a brightly lit, austere hallway that seemed like a passage from another world.

In a sense, it was.

Strucker's private quarters would have been at home in an Alpine hunting lodge, or any of another hundred playgrounds for the world's rich—but appearances were deceiving. The oaken panels and mounted trophies hid, not stone and more wood, but reinforced steel bulkheads and elaborate life-support systems arrayed within them.

They were but one of many spaces on board the *Barbarossa.*

Hydra's nuclear-powered mobile command center, the *Barbarossa* was the size of an American aircraft carrier, but configured very differently. Mounted on huge tractor treads, the subsea fortress did not ride on the sea, but rather, below it. *Barbarossa* moved constantly through the eternal subsea night, hidden from the world above by countless fathoms of cold saltwater. More than five hundred souls lived their lives onboard the *Barbarossa*, every moment of their existence dedicated to serving Hydra and pleasing Strucker—two tasks that Zemo knew were essentially synonymous. It was here that Strucker repaired after the failure of one campaign or another, and here that he made his most elaborate, ambitious plans. Its quarters housed not only rigorously trained troops and tacticians, but also an elite braintrust of the world's most skilled criminal scientists and engineers, coupled with the faciltiies that could make their dreams reality.

Zemo could see how a resource such as the *Barbarossa* could prove useful.

Srucker led the way down the hidden passage. At its other end, two more sentries waited. Again, both came to attention and saluted.

"Hail Hydra!" they cried as one.

"Hail Hydra, indeed," Strucker said, plainly directing the words only to one of the two.

He responded somewhat differently to the other man's salute.

Strucker's right hand lashed out, with speed that bordered on the superhuman. He moved utterly without warning and without any evident reason, striking in a nearly serpentine motion that drove his fingers toward the second sentry's chest. As he struck, a halo of red energy sprang into existence around his hand, a crackling nimbus of energy that tinted his fingers red.

A split-instant later, those same fingers were another shade of red, colored now by something more material, more fluid. They stabbed through the green fabric of the guard's tunic, and then into the flesh and blood beyond.

"No!" the hapless man yelled, or tried to yell. He was unable to force out even the single syllable before it trailed off into a choking gurgle. His body convulsed, then locked up, then fell to the floor to lie in a motionless heap, smoke drifting up from the ragged hole in his chest.

Zemo watched the summary execution impassively and without comment.

Strucker looked at the first guard. "See that he is replaced," he ordered coolly. "And see that you do not repeat his mistake."

"Yes, Baron! Hail Hydra!" the remaining man said again, saluting a second time with respect that was underscored by stark terror.

Then the second set of doors opened, and Strucker and

Zemo stepped through them. As the heavy steel barriers slid back into place, Strucker paused, apparently waiting for something.

Zemo decided to indulge him.

"Was there a reason for that?" he asked.

Strucker nodded, pleased. "A simple demonstration," he said, and began walking again. "Immediate proof of my power, if you will."

"What mistake did the man make, then?"

"Mistake? He existed. He breathed," Strucker said. "That was enough."

"You slew him for breathing?"

"I slew him to make an example," Strucker amended. "And I gave him a new life in the memories of all who serve me." He smiled. "A random execution can do wonders for morale, after all."

There was more to it than that, Zemo knew. Strucker's right hand was prosthetic, one of several he could wear to replace the original, which had long since been lost in a battle with a lifelong foe. Strucker's so-called "Satan Claws" varied in configuration and capabilities, but all were deadly weapons. But Strucker's men knew that fact well, and had doubtless already seen one or more of the Satan Claws in action.

The demonstration had been less of the weapon's capabilities than of Strucker's ruthlessness, and it had not been a demonstration for the surviving sentry at all.

Zemo had been its intended audience.

He filed the bit of data away for future consideration, neither frightened nor especially impressed by his host's maneuver. Still, there had been something worth noting about the older man's strike. It had been an odd idiosyncrasy in Strucker's strike, a distinctive way that the other man had bent his elbow . . .

"Ebersol was a good choice for the task we have set him," Strucker said. "I was skeptical at first, I will admit, but his expertise has proven most useful. His history—"

"His history with *me* has been one of loyalty and trust," Zemo interrupted. "He stood beside me when others fled."

"But my reports say that your alliance with him had come to an end. And still, you trust him?"

"We did not part as foes. And as for where I choose to place my trust," Zemo said, with a sidelong glance at the other baron, "that decision is mine, and mine alone."

"Of course it is, Helmut. You are responsible for that decision, and for any consequences it might have," Strucker said. "Each of us is the same, in that."

"Greetings, Barons! Glad you could make it!" said a new voice as the two men entered a larger chamber filled almost entirely with massive banks of equipment, some of it startlingly incongruous in its current setting. Squarely in the center of the jumble of hardware, poised before a control console, stood a remarkable figure.

He looked like a man, but a man made of metal. From a distance, he appeared to be wearing a costume, but on closer examination, the red and black proved not to be fabric, but colored metal, presumably the same alloy that made up his silvery hands and face.

The metal man's face was his most remarkable feature. Silvered like his hands, it was narrow and angular, evocative of human features without mimicking them precisely. On a human, the face that his approximated might have been handsome, even dashing; cast in steel, those same features took on an oddly elfin look.

"Hello, Techno," Zemo said. "What have you to report?"

"Ebersol," Strucker said, nodding in acknowledgement.

"Actually, it's Techno these days, your Baron-ness," the metal man said, his lips pulling back in something like a smile. "I haven't been using the Norbert Ebersol handle for a while, now." As he spoke, he passed a cloth to Strucker, who took it and wiped the blood from his hand without comment.

Long years before, Techno's human incarnation had served Hydra in several interrelated enterprises. In those days, Ebersol had used the codename Fixer, and been widely recognized as an intuitive technological genius with few, if any equals. Now, however, his consciousness inhabited a metallic shell, and he operated under a new name in the pursuit of new goals, not all of them his own.

"Hope I didn't interrupt your dinner," Techno continued. Cables ran from his control panel to an open plate on his chest; now, one by one, he began disconnecting them. Spring-loaded reels made whirring noises as they drew the leads back inside him. ''I have to keep reminding myself about stuff like that, but since I quit eating—''

''We were just concluding,'' Zemo said. Techno's loquacity was one aspect of his former associate that he disliked, and he saw no reason to encourage it. ''Now, continue. What have you to report?'' he repeated.

Strucker glanced in his direction as he took charge of the conversation, Zemo noted, but neither man made any comment.

Techo snapped his chest panel shut and then wiped his own hands on another piece of cloth. ''Just finishing the backup logs now,'' he said, and turned his artificial eyes in Zemo's direction. ''You father was hot stuff, Baron. I wish I could have met him,'' he continued. ''I mean, I know I'm smart, and I've worked with some real brains in my time, but, judging from the notes he left behind, old Heinrich—''

''Yes, yes, continue,'' Zemo said, impatience verging on genuine irritation. He did not care to hear his father's name spoken so casually by metal lips.

''Your dad was onto something good,'' Techno continued implacably. He was in his element now, and clearly enjoying himself. ''He called it 'ionic mutation.' That's not the term I would use, but I guess it was his call, right?''

Neither Strucker nor Zemo made any comment.

''Well, anyway,'' Techno continued, ''his process ended up getting used on at least two human subjects we know about—Simon Williams and our old buddy Erik Josten, or Atlas. Or the Smuggler. Or Goliath. You'd think a guy would pick a name—''

''Ebersol,'' Strucker said softly, his tone of voice a warning.

''Anyway,'' Techno continued, ''Williams and Josten are both doing okay these days, but they've both had problems, too—problems I figure we can trace at least partially to the shortcomings of Zemo Senior's equipment. There was only so much he could do with the tools at hand, after all. That's one reason I wanted to examine at least one of the two survivors before I went further.''

''So you captured Williams,'' Strucker prompted, ''at considerable expense to my organization, and with only momentary success.''

Techno shook his head, an oddly human gesture for a machine to make. ''He was the easier of the two to find. And I had him long enough,'' he said. ''Sure, I'd like to have held onto him for a while longer, but I was able to get the readings I needed while he was inside me. I work fast, after all.'' With a bit of preparation, Techno had been able to reconfigure his artificial body to mimic that of a Dreadnought, and then reconfigure it again to surround the captive Wonder Man. ''And, as regards the assets issue—I think you'll be pleased with the replacements I've made for your precious Dreadnoughts.''

Techno paced the distance between his lab station and another, larger bank of machinery anchored to the *Barbarossa*'s steel deck plates. Six transparent cylinders stood in symmetrical array around a central pillar of apparatus that was linked to them by looping cables and conduits. Visible through curved crystalline walls of each cylinder was the figure of a man, shrouded by a clinging nimbus of transforming energy.

Or, rather, something that looked like a man, only better.

''These are what your father's process would have produced, if he'd had access to modern technology. I was able to combine his prototypes with the other stuff that you've managed to procure in the last few weeks,'' Techno said to Zemo. ''Most of what you see here came from old Heinrich's noodle. Oh, sure, I added a few twists of my own, and incorporated some aspects of the processor you retrieved from Colorado.'' He paused again, glanced at Strucker. ''You were right about that, by the way, your Baron-ality. That thing was just what we needed. Whoever built it knew what he was doing. It looked wrecked, but—''

Strucker was obviously ignoring Techno's words in favor of gazing at Techno's handiwork.

''Perfect,'' the Supreme Hydra said softy. His pallid face suddenly glowed with a new light, and his stormy eyes took on the awed delight of a child at Christmas. For his part, Zemo strode slowly around the strange carousel, his keen eyes assessing every detail of what they saw.

Each of the figures was identical with its fellows, in height and weight, in build and demeanor. Each was a full head taller than Techno, with a body that seemed constructed entirely of slabs of muscle and then covered with golden skin. Each had facial features so handsome that they verged on beauty, with raised cheekbones, an aquiline nose, a high brow, and blond, close-cropped hair.

"Impressive," Zemo said. No other word would come to his lips.

"The conversion process is complete. I was about to bring them online," Techno continued. "I figured you gents would want to be here for that."

Zemo nodded, then he and Strucker watched as Techo reached toward a nearby control panel. He extended an articulated probe from his left index fingertip and inserted it in a convenient receptacle. In instant response, the six cylinders rose, and so did six pairs of golden-hued eyelids. They revealed six sets of eyes that were perfectly blue and perfectly blank.

"I've already loaded them with a series of test sequences," Techno said cheerfully. "That was easy, once I erased their original personalities. The hard part was reprogramming them for higher-level command processing. I finally created one personality I liked and copied until I had enough. That makes for a certain amount of redundancy, since they're physically and mentally identical, but—"

"They will be obedient?" Strucker interrupted.

"Absolutely," Techno said. "They literally don't know how to be anything else."

"Good," Strucker said. "Too many times, I have granted great power to operatives, only to see them pursue their own agendas instead. I am certain that Helmut has had similar experiences."

Zemo heard Strucker's jibe, but ignored it. Instead, he watched attentively as the first of the six superhuman figures approached a test bed holding a massive girder.

"I requisitioned a few odds and ends from General Supplies for demonstration purposes," Techno explained. "Nothing that can't be replaced."

The first golden man paused, plucked the girder from the clamps that held it. There was a shrieking, groaning noise as he bent the heavy slab of metal at its midpoint, then bent it more, again and again. When he paused, the steel beam had been tied into a knot.

"Super-strength," Techno said cheerfully.

"Impressive," Zemo repeated. He had seen displays of raw physical power that were greater, but not substantially so.

The first golden man still held the deformed girder. He spun on one heel and threw it at one of his fellows. The second of Techno's creations caught the lump of metal effortlessly and then clutched it, his strong fingers digging deep into the structural steel. Then, those fingers began to glow, and an electrical, burning stink made itself evident as the metal softened, then flowed. White-hot rivulets of liquefied steel trickled along the second golden man's hands and arms, before splashing down to sear the floor at his feet. The test subject showed no sign of injury, or of pain. He gazed impassively at nothing in particular as blast-furnace heat bathed his flesh.

"High-energy discharge capacity," Techno said, ticking off the attributes one by one on extended metal fingers. "And greatly enhanced durability."

In the cluttered space surrounding the trio, the rest of the golden men were going through their programmed paces, using the props that Techno had provided for them. Golden hands crushed stone blocks and smashed through foot-thick slabs of seasoned oak. Golden biceps bulged as they strained against massive weights, and golden skin remained unmarked as it bathed in one corrosive acid solution after another. Through the entire demonstration, the six remained utterly calm and expressionless, giving no sign of pain or even effort.

"These are the programmed routines, of course," Techno said. "These boys can fly, too, but there's no way to demonstrate that effectively onboard."

Strucker nodded. "And they are all equals to Wonder Man?"

Techno's mechanical head pivoted on his steel neck. "Nope," he said. "I would assess these units at about eighty percent of Wonder Man's current power levels, or equal to Josten at his prime."

Both barons gazed at him. Neither looked pleased.

"Hey! Hey!" the former Fixer said, raising his hands in a

gesture of mock resignation. "Give a guy a chance to explain!"

"I'm waiting," Zemo said. "You said that you had duplicated my father's process."

"No. I said I've done what he would have, with access to modern technology," Techno said. "I didn't duplicate his so-called ionic transformation process; I perfected it."

"Explain," Strucker said, his voice making the single word an angry whip-crack of command.

"Your own files tell the story," Techno said. "Look at all the changes that Wonder Man and Josten have been through since receiving their powers. Mental instability for Josten, deathlike comas for Williams, radical physical mutations for both of them—are those *really* the attributes you want for your super-soldiers? Either of you?"

Zemo made no response, but he recognized the truth in his associate's words, and assumed that Strucker would, too. Neither of the previous survivors of the ionic transformation process had enjoyed particularly stable careers afterwards. Josten had also suffered periods of impaired reasoning ability, and was sometimes prone to psychotic episodes. Another consideration that had troubled Zemo, one that Techno had not mentioned, was that Williams's and Josten's powers had proven inconsistent, changing over the years. These days, for example, Wonder Man could fly without aid; originally, he could not. And Josten's initial enhancements of strength and durability had given way to size changing, but his body was still fueled by the same ionic energies of Heinrich Zemo's creation.

"That's because your father couldn't stabilize the process," Techno continued, speaking as if he knew what Zemo was thinking. "He didn't have the tools he needed, so he tried to make up in power what he couldn't accomplish in precision. With modern equipment, I've been able to remodulate the fourth-order waveform completely, and create absolutely stable platforms that are suitable for further enhancements."

"Enhancements?" Strucker demanded, his cold blue eyes glinting.

Again, Techno nodded. "Now that they're stable, I can incorporate some other features I think you'll find attractive. But even as they are now, they should be enough for most jobs—eighty percent of Wonder Man is eighty percent of a lot of power. As a combined force, the prototypes give you six times that, already.''

Zemo glanced at Strucker.

''True,'' the Supreme Hydra said. ''But I will require a demonstration.''

''They're more than ready for a field test,'' Techno said cheerfully. ''And I can make some suggestions along that line, too. Will six be enough, or do you need more?''

''More?''

''Now that I've worked out all the bugs, the conversion process takes only a few hours,'' the mechanical man responded. ''As long as you keep providing me with human subjects, I can keep upgrading them to superhuman levels. Trained agents or rejects, or even prisoners—it doesn't matter. Once I get done with them, they'll all be the same. I'll have an army up and running in no time.''

''An army?'' Strucker mused, smiling. ''No, not an army. Not yet. Until I am convinced that they can perform as you claim, and that they are loyal, a mere squad will suffice.'' His smile widened. ''My Blitz Squad.''

''Blitz Squad?'' asked Zemo, who wanted very much to question the use of the word *my*, instead.

But that could wait.

Strucker nodded. He gazed at the six enhanced Hydra agents, who now stood in perfect formation before him.

''My Blitz Squad,'' he repeated, a not entirely new note of nostalgia in his voice. ''During the war, in your father's day, Helmut, I had in my command an elite squadron of special operatives who were the terror of Germany's foes. They were the Blitz Squad.'' He gestured. ''These are the inheritors of their title.''

As he gestured, the standing figures responded. As if prompted by some residual trace of their original identities, all six members of the newly christened Blitz Squad came to rigid attention, and their hands raised in perfect unison.

''Hail Hydra!'' the six transformed men thundered, their voices sounding as one. ''Hail Hydra, immortal Hydra! We shall never be destroyed! Cut off a limb, and two more shall take its place!''

Strucker beamed, but Zemo merely glanced at Techno, a baleful look in his eyes. He did not put his question in words, but he did not need to.

"Hey," the former Norbert Ebersol said, shrugging and smiling, "so sue me. I thought it was a nice touch."

Chapter Five

Avengers Mansion, New York

Tony Stark had personally designed the teleconference facilities, not only in his own offices, but in Avengers Mansion, as well. The respective systems were similar in concept but quite different in execution, partly because they answered differing needs and partly because their maker liked to check out new gadgets personally before providing them to anyone else. Thus, the twenty-four video displays that confronted him now did not hover on antigravity modules but were firmly locked in wall mounts, instead.

"I'm glad you could brief us personally, T'Challa," Captain America said, speaking from behind a rostrum at the front of the small auditorium. Iron Man stood beside him. The video teleconferencing center served double duty as a meeting hall and could seat up to fifty easily. Just now, however, the space was less crowded. The assembled Avengers—Justice and Firestar, the Scarlet Witch and Wonder Man, the Vision and Thor—had plenty of room to spread out as they listened attentively to the conversation.

The handsome black man whose face filled the active monitors smiled, revealing perfect teeth in an open, sincere grin. "My pleasure, Captain America. It is always good to speak with friends."

In the front row, Firestar leaned close to Justice, whispered something in his ear. Acting on automated subroutines, the audio receptors in Iron Man's helmet caught the words and relayed them to Tony's ears. He had only a few of her words before he muted the eavesdropping function.

"—studied him in school," Firestar was saying. "It was such a thrill to meet him. He negotiated the Latverian settlement—"

Tony had to smile at that. T'Challa's renown as a statesman was considerable, but he had other, more immediate claims to fame as well. T'Challa, son of T'Chaka, was another of the elite group of heroes who had served as Avengers. He was the ruler of Wakanda, an African nation rich in mineral wealth and possessed of a fantastically advanced technology. As the Black Panther, he had been at Captain America's side those years long ago when Franz Gruber's schemes had met their timely end. That was the case that had led him to join the Avengers. Firestar and Justice had met him—and most of the rest of the still-living people who had ever been Avengers—shortly before they joined the team.

"Regrettably, there is little more that I can tell you that you do not already know," T'Challa continued. His voice was like mellow thunder, and he spoke with the musical rhythm of a born orator. "When my own royal forces apprehended the false Zemo, we impounded his property, as well. Later, we forwarded most of that hardware to S.H.I.E.L.D., which, in turn, allocated it for further analysis and for use as prosecutorial evidence."

"T'Challa has already provided us with a copy of his inventory," Captain America told the others.

"It is a near match for your Mr. Sitwell's list of stolen properties," the Black Panther continued. "The exception is a single item—an apparent protoptype for some manner of energy manipulation system. It was incomplete and unfinished, and would be of uncertain use."

"Or of use only to someone who knew how to make it work," Justice chimed in. "And if this false Zemo guy had it, why didn't he use it?"

Iron Man glanced at him, mildly irritated. The kid's keen grasp of the obvious was sometimes endearing, sometimes annoying.

Seated beside Wanda, Wonder Man brought his hands together silently several times, pretending to applaud his teammate's insight.

Justice didn't seem to notice. "And who was this false Zemo guy, anyway? I mean, I've heard of Heinrich, and met Helmut, but—"

"I'm coming to that, Vance," Cap said. In quick, concise words, he told his attentive audience about the late Franz Gruber, the false Zemo, and his failed attempt to conquer the world.

"So that's what happened to old Franz," Wonder Man said, when Cap had finished. Simon had been part of Zemo's organization briefly, in the earliest days of his career. "Talk about a social climber. From pilot to potential potentate."

Cap nodded. "That's an important thing to keep in mind, too," he said. "Heinrich Zemo was a protean genius, and one of the deadliest foes the Avengers ever faced—but Franz Gruber was just a clever opportunist. When he appropriated Zemo's African arsenal, he ended up with a lot of equipment he couldn't understand, much less use. He apparently sold some of it to raise money, and kept the rest."

"But you keep saying that stuff didn't work," Firestar said.

"Experimental prototypes often don't," Iron Man said. "But even failures are instructive."

"And, in truth, with the scientific wonderment that such as our own Iron Man and good T'Challa have accomplished in recent years, e'en yesteryear's failures may prove of value now," Thor said.

Again, Tony grinned. Leave it to the Norse god of thunder to make a point about technological progress.

"Which might explain the other thefts," the Vision said coolly. "Who knows what Heinrich Zemo might have accomplished, had he been able to make use of more modern technology? Who knows what others might accomplish, working in his name?"

"My thoughts precisely," Cap said, nodding. "It's a bit of a jump, but we have to work on the assumption that an individual or individuals within Hydra are trying to finish something that Heinrich Zemo started. Presumably, they shook a shopping list out of Gruber before infecting him. The prototype T'Challa mentioned was probably part of his list, too."

"But what's the ultimate goal?" Wanda asked. "And what does this all have to do with the attack on Simon and me?"

"ShellHead's got some ideas about that," Cap said.

"I had a video chip open, recording a lot of what happened during that little skirmish," Iron Man said. "Restricted to line-of-sight, but useful. I analyzed the feed last night."

"And?" Simon prompted. "Am I as photogenic as ever?" Wonder Man had worked briefly as an actor.

"When that Dreadnought broke up, it revealed what looked like diagnostic probes attached your body," Iron Man said. "They were torn loose by the impact, but we have to assume that they'd done at least part of their job. And, remember, your own powers originated with Heinrich Zemo." That was a delicate subject, and one that he didn't like bringing up; when the Avengers and Wonder Man had first met, it had not been entirely as friends.

"So I'm on the shopping list, too," Simon said. "Or was. I wonder whose list? And I wonder why?"

"I've got some ideas about that, and some more ideas on how to verify them," Cap said. "Who's available for some surveillance duty?"

The Fonesca Complex, North Carolina

For Hallie Takahama, boredom was a Barnacle Burger Supreme with cheese-flavored tartar and large fries, accompanied by a medium beverage of the customer's choice. Of course, that was simply the most popular source of boredom; there were seven other great combos on the Frying Dutchman's plastic menu board, each consisting of several perfectly reasonable foodstuffs, processed and combined into arteriosclerotic time bombs.

How could anyone make eating *fish* unhealthy? That was what Hallie wanted to know, but pondering that eternal question was not enough to keep more than a small corner of her mind occupied.

"That's one Cod'n'Kaboodle, one Barnacle Burger, no cheese, and a Titanic-size Sargasso Fries," the rest of her mind ordered her lips to say. "Would you like a nice Skipper's Grog or sugar-free Grog with that?"

"I'd like a better attitude from you, little lady," a familiar voice said.

Hallie blinked and gathered her wits hastily. She hated fast food and hated fast food work more, but this job was important, at least for now. "I'm sorry," she said, "I—"

Then she blinked again, as she realized who stood before her.

"Oh! Oh, hi, Erik," she said, smiling for what felt like the first time that day.

"Hello, kiddo," big, buff, and muscular Erik Josten responded. He was wearing a dark coverall, the uniform of the food court's maintenance staff. "Thought I would see how you were doing. Want to split a catch o' the day?"

Hallie shook her head. "No way. Bad enough I have to sell this stuff. I'm not going to eat it! But—"

She looked at the wall clock, then gestured at a man wearing a simplified pirate costume. "Mr. Oglodytes!" she called as she waved at him. "Mr. Oglodytes! May I take my break? It's almost time!"

Mr. Oglodytes, a beetle-browed balding man with tufts of white hair sprouting from his ears looked at her, nodded. "Argh," he said amiably. "That ye may, little miss."

"Good, good, good, good," Hallie murmured to herself as she handed Atlas his food, rang the sale, closed her register and locked it, then leapt gracefully over the counter to join her teammate. Several coworkers applauded the effortless gymnastic maneuver, but Mr. Oglodytes scarcely seemed to notice.

"Take me away from here," she told Erik eagerly. "Even if only for a federally required thirty minutes, take me far away."

Unfortunately, far away proved to be only about twenty yards distant. A moment later, once the two were seated at one of the many tables shared by all the food court's outlets, Atlas offered her some of his fries.

Hallie shook her head again. "I don't think I'll ever eat fast food again," she said. "Every time we go undercover, you guys fix me up with a smock, name tag, and hairnet. Why can't I be the rocket scientist for a change?"

"Because there aren't any teenage rocket scientists," Erik responded. He opened his mouth, inserted his sandwich, bit, and chewed. "If there were, they'd be here, though."

Here was the Fonesca Complex, a high-tech research center comfortably ensconced in the North Carolina Piedmont, where a surprisingly elaborate food court took the place of a an employees' cafeteria. The Fonesca Complex, in turn, was a federally chartered (but not federally funded) research complex, where private corporations engaged in advanced scientific studies, encouraged in their labors by a special tax-free status. It was laid out vaguely like a shopping mall—a broad, low structure with several levels, each divided into office and work spaces, all of which opened on common corridors linked by escalators.

Hallie had never heard of the place before, but once it was described to her, it made a lot of sense—lift taxes, streamline regulations to encourage research and industry, and, ultimately, revitalize the local economy. She was reasonably certain that there was a catch somewhere, but she hadn't found it yet.

Unless maybe it was her job at the Frying Dutchman.

"We need to be on the scene," Erik continued, with implacable logic, but speaking more softly now. "And there are limits to the roles we can play, no matter how many fake IDs and credentials Abe and Karla whip up." He ate some more. "You don't see me hanging my hat near the supercollider, do you?" One of the Fonesca Complex's higher-profile projects was an advanced particle beam generator, powered by a geothermal tap that drew magma heat from below the North Carolina Piedmont.

"They could try harder," Hallie said darkly. She didn't say what was really bothering her—that she didn't like pretending to be someone else, for any reason. Subterfuge struck her as an evil—sometimes necessary, sometimes not, but never desirable.

She wondered how the Avengers managed situations like this.

"Maybe. Maybe not. It doesn't matter, in the long run."

"I guess not," Hallie said. The Thunderbolts had used this ploy before, assuming still more identities to fade in with their surroundings. She and Erik were the most problematic to place, Erik because of his muscleman demeanor, and Hallie, because of her age. Abe and Karla could pass themselves off as an engineer and a counselor, respectively, since that's what they were, and Melissa had lucked into a receptionist's slot at Osborn Chemical's on-site offices.

Heaven only knew where Hawkeye was, or what he was doing—capitalizing on his real ID and hobnobbing with the local gendarmes, maybe. The most recent addition to the Thunderbolts, the nearly legendary Avenger, was at once a part of the team, and apart from it. Hallie liked him, but she didn't know him nearly as well as any of the others.

"Have you heard anything? Seen any signs?" Erik asked. He had finished his Sargasso Fries and Barnacle Burger, and was making good progress on the Cod'n'Kaboodle.

Hallie didn't have the heart to tell him what the Kaboodle part was.

"Nah. I probably won't, though, unless Hydra decides to get takeout." Frustrated, annoyed, and, despite her protestations, hungry, Hallie spoke more loudly than she had intended.

Erik shushed her, looking genuinely irritated. "I know you're bored, Hallie," he hissed, "but this isn't a game! We're undercover! You can't spout off like that!"

Hallie nodded, chagrined. She reached for the cardboard trawler that had held Erik's Sargassos and found a last, lost fry. She put the greasy morsel in her mouth and chewed slowly.

She was nervous and edgy, not sensations to which she was accustomed.

Some delicate inquiries by Hawkeye and Abe had yielded promising hints about Hydra's current interests. Friends of friends had passed the questions along, and then, like the returning tide, those same secondhand acquaintances passed back the responses.

They were troubling. Sources on both sides of the law had mentioned North Carolina and the Fonesca Complex.

That struck Hallie has being a bit too convenient for comfort and was one reason for her current edginess. Since joining the Thunderbolts, she had encountered one lie after another, and more than one attempt at manipulation.

What if Hawkeye's and Abe's oh-so-convenient "leads" proved to be more of the same?

"What if this is all some kind of trap?" she finally asked, voicing her doubts for the first time. "I mean, the whole thing feels like a setup."

Atlas shrugged, raising his muscular shoulders then lowering them again, in an eloquent, easy movement that suggested an earthquake sweeping through a mountain range. "If it's a trap, it's a trap," he said. "You're just antsy from waiting. When you've been in the business a while, you'll get used to it."

"You sound resigned."

"Just realistic. There's folks who issue the orders, and folks who follow them. I'm used to being in the second group."

• • •

Kintnerburg, New Jersey

In a federal building so minor that it had no name, Fred McDowell unclipped his plastic ID badge from his shirt pocket, waved it at the time clock on the break room wall, and then put the badge back in its normal riding place.

The clock made no response. It was supposed to chirp, but it didn't.

Fred scowled at the piece of digital hardware for a moment, chewed his lip, and wondered what to do.

''You're supposed to give it a full second to read the chip in your card,'' Roger Stevens said. He spoke easily, even amiably, but something about his words set Fred's teeth on edge, nonetheless.

Stevens was one of the new feds that had been making Fred's life a living hell the past few days, and Fred didn't like him. Fred was honest enough with himself to recognize he probably wouldn't have liked Stevens under any circumstances. The guy was just too darned perfect—big and muscular, with blond hair and piercing blue eyes, he radiated absolute confidence, a confidence underscored by an athletic build that strained against the lines of his tailored black Brooks Brothers suit.

Fred glanced at him now. Stevens stood—not sat, stood—behind the break room desk, leafing through what looked to Fred like personnel files.

Fred wondered whose names were in those files.

''Huh?'' he asked.

''The clock,'' Stevens repeated. He spoke pleasantly, but with the voice of authority. ''You've got to give it a full second to read the badge, or it won't register.''

''Huh,'' Fred said, and repeated the three-step operation. This time, he allowed enough time, and this time the clock chirped merrily as it acknowledged his presence, recorded his name and time of arrival, and filed the information away for future reference.

What Fred didn't know was that the chirp also meant that the DNA scanner hidden in the clock had taken his measure and found it not wanting.

''See?'' Stevens said. He smiled, and sincerity fairly oozed from his pores as he nodded. ''Not so hard, is it?''

Fred hated him, not just for who he was, but for what he had brought with him. In the three days since Stevens and his associates had descended upon the facility, it had become a remarkably less pleasant place to work. Whereas in the past, Fred's effective duties had consisted of punching the (old) time clock, initialing his time card, then reading comic books in the guard station until his relief arrived, now he found himself working for a living.

Now, he actually had to make his rounds, verifying that the seals on various storage cubicles were intact, noting time and temperature readings, and otherwise spending his time productively.

He had to. If he didn't, Stevens or one of his flunkies—maybe that snot-nosed kid with the faint Bronx accent—would ask him why he wasn't working, and Fred knew full well that any answer he made would be recorded and forwarded Upstairs.

''We're here to make your job easier,'' Stevens had said, during their first briefing session. ''We're not going to get in your way.''

Fred hadn't believed him then, and he could derive a certain satisfaction from knowing that he been right not to. That satisfaction wasn't enough to offset the displeasure of his new drudgery, but it helped.

Something else bothered him about Stevens, too—a nagging sense of familiarity that wouldn't go away. Fred had seen the blond man's face before, seen that flawless smile, in a televised image if not in person.

He paced down the first floor's main corridor, past heavy steel doors set in concrete walls and held there by even heavier steel frames. Each door bore a number-letter code—A7, A9, A11 on his left, A8, A10, A12 on his right. These were mid-security evidence lockers, holding stuff that was valuable but not dangerous, and Fred paid them little attention. On this floor, in this wing, all that he was expected to verify was the each door was closed, and that nothing was overtly amiss.

Upstairs, in the higher-security levels, things got a bit more complex.

Twenty more paces brought him to the main elevator bank

and another guard station. This one was staffed by another of Stevens's associates, a chilly looking character with eyes so dark and deeply set that they seemed to be holes bored into his head.

"Good evening, Fred." The words were polite, but the tone was something else—neutral to the point of coldness.

"Good evening, um—" Fred realized that he had forgotten the SAFE agent's name again. To cover his embarrassment, he unclipped his badge a third and repeated the identification ritual, this time with the guard station's clock.

The SAFE agent—what *was* his name?—seemed to look completely through Fred as the second clock chirped and the left elevator door opened. Despite himself, Fred smiled slightly.

"Got it right on the first try," he said.

"Commendable," said the SAFE representative.

Fred shrugged and stepped past the other man and into the elevator.

"Wait," the dark-eyed man said. Even as the elevator doors slid shut, he lifted a metal-cased clipboard from his work surface and passed it to Fred, reaching into the elevator car to do so. "You'll need this."

"Uh, thanks, uh—" Fred said, taking the board that held his log sheets. The doors were closing as he took the cool metal in his hand, and he looked at the control panel, trying to find the OPEN button before the doors closed on the guard's arm.

He wasn't fast enough.

Fred felt his eyes try to leave their sockets as the two gleaming metal slabs came together on the other man's fore-arm—

—and passed through it.

It was impossible. Even more impossibly, there was no resistance as the metal edges met, no blood, no gore, no cry of pain. Its apparently severed end still flush against the metal doors, the arm hung motionless in mid-air, and then fell as the elevator rose.

"No," Fred murmured. Nausea swept through him. His own fingers, suddenly nerveless, opened and let the clipboard fall to the floor. "No, no, no, no." He had seen some things in his day, but nothing like this.

Then the arm vanished, receding through doors and floor and disappearing from view. Forearm, wrist, palm, fingers, fingertips—step by step, the last of the SAFE agent receded and disappeared.

Except Fred was beginning to think maybe, just maybe, the man hadn't really been just a SAFE agent.

Or maybe not even a man at all.

Steve Rogers closed the last of the personnel folders, returned it to its place in the file cabinet—fourth drawer, K–M—then slid the drawer shut and spun its combination lock.

Nothing. He was extremely skilled at reading between the lines in such files, and he had seen nothing worth worrying about. None of the folders had held any suggestion of wrongdoing, no hints of excessive income or aberrant behavior. Certainly, there was room for improvement, but SAFE hadn't arranged his cover identity so that he could conduct a standard security review.

No; his reason for being here wasn't in any of these file folders, but in cubicle C17, two floors above his head. That was where the federal courts system had seen fit to store the orphaned brainchild of Heinrich Zemo, and doubtless a goal that Hydra's agents would try to reach.

But when?

Then a shattering explosion both underscored his question and answered it.

At his guard station, the Vision heard the blast. It came from above and behind him. He whirled as he heard it, moving faster than his disguise could accommodate. As he moved, he relaxed for a moment the degree of his interaction with the physical universe, and let his government-issue identity fall away. Clothes, flesh-colored plastic mask and gloves, the very semblance of humanity—all fell from him as he turned to face the source of the explosion. As he completed the turn, however, and with a similar lack of effort, he reversed the process, so that his body achieved its maximum density once more.

Just in time, too.

Frederick McDowell had taken the third of four elevators; now, one other set of sliding steel panels crumbled as something tore through them.

Two somethings, actually, and both of them were golden.

Metal shrieked as it tore into shrapnel, then into less than shrapnel. Golden fists smashed through the barriers, driving chunks and chips of metal into the foyer. The impromptu missiles moved at bullet speed, fast enough to punch through human flesh as easily as through the air, but not fast enough to damage the Vision's super-hardened body. The force of the barrage was enough to make him rock back, however, and he very nearly fell as the first of the gleaming titans forced its way through the sundered frame of the elevator number two.

"Hail Hydra!" the behemoth roared. He was several heads taller than the Vision and had to duck to step out of the ruined elevator. Golden of skin and hair, surrounded by a flickering nimbus of energy, he wore a modified version of an easily recognized uniform.

A green uniform, marked with an *H*.

"Immortal Hydra!" the familiar oath continued.

"I doubt that," the Vision said, his voice even grimmer than usual. Another transient instant's worth of concentration, and his physical outlines wavered again. He reached for the newcomer's chest, plunged his hands through the boundaries of the golden creature's body, then solidified himself again.

"We shall never be destroyed!" the gigantic Hydra agent thundered.

The Vision screamed as pain, white-hot and impossible, swept through his circuits. Desperately, he reverted to intangible form and withdrew his hands.

The gloves that clothed them were charred black, seared by the unknown energies contained within his antagonist's body. The Vision stared at them, feeling something very much like shock.

A backhand blow smashed into him, lifted him from the floor, threw him against a wall.

"Cut off a limb and two more shall take its place!" the giant yelled.

As if on cue, the other golden figure, identical to the first, made its way from the shattered elevator car and into the corridor.

"Hail Hydra!" they yelled, in perfect unison.

Fleetingly, the Vision wondered if they knew no other words—but then a golden fist smashed into his face and that thought, like all others, fled.

The hand that pointed at the armored door C17 wore the green glove of a Hydra uniform; the hand that smashed through that same door was sheathed only in energy. The metal split and tore, and the concrete blocks of the surrounding wall broke under the impact, and then the door wasn't a door anymore, merely rubble.

Zemo led his escort into the room beyond. The space was only dimly lit, and tall shelving units blocked much of what light there was. Despite that, Zemo did not pause. His moves were confident and assured as he stepped into the shadows between two of the bookcaselike fixtures. The information that Strucker's personnel had purchased from an anonymous second-year law clerk included specific inventory numbers, numbers that matched the digits and letters painted at the end of each shelving unit.

Zemo worked quickly, scarcely taking note of his surroundings. The shelves were divided into compartments and subcompartments, and locked behind glass doors, but he could still see the impounded evidence that crowded them. Pistols, surveillance cameras, communicators, computer components, and a hundred other sundry items competed for his attentions, but to no avail. He had eyes for the single item that Techno had specified.

Finally, he saw it, neatly arrayed in one of the glass-doored evidence cases—a flat metal disk perhaps a quarter meter in diameter, bounded by a golden filament network perhaps twice that big around. Just now, the spiderweb mesh was folded beneath the disk, but its complexities were still easily visible and embodied design principles that were as recognizable as fingerprints to the trained eye. Zemo drew a dagger from his belt, reversed it, and drove its hilt though the cabinet's glass.

Something else broke, too, at the same moment.

Startled, Zemo glanced to his left. The towering figure of his Blitz Squad escort had tried to follow him into the space between the shelves, only to bump another of the locked cabinets and shatter it. The oversized brute scarcely seemed to notice, but continued to approach. More glass broke.

Zemo frowned. The thing's assignment had been to escort him, and never leave his side, and apparently, the creature was doing its best to obey. Hydra agents in general were slavish in their subservience, but Techno's enhancements had escalated that tendency to an extreme.

"Back," he said curtly.

The golden brute looked at him. The fact that Zemo still wore the uniform of a Hydra section leader seemed to attract it.

"Back, Drei," Zemo repeated, scooping his father's handiwork from the evidence locker and dropping it in the bag he carried. The dense metal mesh, though as fine as lace, was surprisingly heavy. Despite that, it seemed oddly reluctant to leave his gloved fingers.

The Blitz Squad agent nodded, and retreated. "Hail Hydra," the creature that Zemo had addressed as Drei said. His face was blank and his eyes were blanker. "Immortal Hydra," Drei continued. "We shall never be destroyed."

Zemo wanted very much to disagree, but that seemed impolitic at the moment. Instead, he made a mental note to discuss certain matters with Techno upon return to *Barbarossa*.

Before the walls quit shaking but after the alarms started sounding, Captain America turned off his Avengers communicator. Even as his left hand's fingers returned the tiny device to the pocket hidden in his belt, he charged down the hall that led from the break room to the elevator lobby, his red-white-and-blue shield on his arm.

This was bad, very bad. A glance at a convenient security monitor array had told him that. Two oversized monstrosities on the ground floor, wearing an approximation of Hydra's colors; two more on the second, and a final pair on the floor above, apparently the personal escort for a Hydra section leader.

This was worse than the Avengers had expected. Hydra had

used superhuman forces at Madison Square, true enough, but that had been a trap for Wanda and Simon. To send creatures like these to raid a mere evidence storage site . . .

Hydra had to be planning something more.

Only two of his teammates had been able to respond to his alert—Firestar and Thor. The others were busy elsewhere, or simply too distant for the local summons. As with so many things in life, the main strength and main weakness of the Avengers organization were closely related. The strength came from the ability to use only the very best members of the super hero community, and the weakness came from the fact that those same individuals had duties and challenges of their own, and sometimes could not heed the team's call.

The problem at hand, however, seemed to require additional reinforcements.

Cap forced the thought from his mind; as he turned one corner, dropped and rolled in a perfect somersault to confuse his foes, he righted himself in a low crouch and leapt for the golden figures manhandling the Vision.

"Get away from him!" Cap roared, as he sprang to his teammate's aid. Even as he moved, however, a worried thought flickered through his mind.

What kind of creatures could humble the Vision so swiftly? The android Avenger was among the team's toughest members, and he possessed powers more than adequate against most physical threats.

Why, then, was he apparently unconscious now?

As if in response, a more-than-human form threw itself at him.

Cap moved fast; the monster moved faster.

"Hail Hydra!" the golden creature roared, swinging one clenched fist at Captain America's red-white-and-blue form.

His shield caught the blow, absorbed most of its force—but only most of it. Even blunted, the hammering impact was enough to lift Cap from the floor and send him tumbling backwards.

That's impossible, Cap thought. The shield's special nature made it proof against almost any physical force, and able to protect him from nearly any impact.

Then he saw the rippling aura of energy surrounding the

golden creature, and realized that he was no longer dealing with purely physical force.

"Hail Hydra!" the titan bellowed, coming for him again.

The elevators were useless now, their cables and cars demolished. The Blitz Squad had stormed the facility from above, smashing through the rooftop elevator shacks and working their way down from there. Now, Drei, Zemo's personal escort, was able to make even shorter work of a stairwell door, and the two of them made their way to the floor below.

"Hail Hydra," Eins said by way of greeting and salute as he beheld Zemo.

"Immortal Hydra!" roared Drei.

Zemo was more than a little tired of the ritual salutes, but there was nothing to be done for the situation now. Besides, there were other factors to consider.

Eins and Sechs had finished their work. In the seven minutes it had taken him and Drei to retrieve their prize, the other two Blitz Squad members had completed their work. Strucker's organization had obtained the blueprints that identified the main load-bearing members. Hydra's ordnance experts had calculated the size and placement of charges to destroy them, and it had fallen to Techno to program the Blitz Squad members to place those charges.

Evidently, everyone had been successful.

Zemo drew a keypad device from his belt and removed one glove. The remote control detonator chirped as it recognized the naked thumb he pressed against it. Zemo entered a string of digits, then pressed a red key, making the detonator chirp again.

"Hail Hydra?" Eins asked.

Zemo nodded, then turned his attention elsewhere. A security camera hung in one corner of the elevator area. He stepped closer to it, and gazed into the unblinking lens. Reduced and distorted, his reflection stared back at him, and what was left of Zemo's lips pulled back in a smile. The disguise he wore now was less elaborate than the biodermic systems Techno had crafted for him, but it was no less effective. To the camera, and to any who watched its feed, he was a Hydra officer like any other, wearing the full mask that came with elevated rank.

And Hydra, as an organization, was notoriously fond of declarations and ultimata, and of leaving live witness to spread word of the terror it inflicted.

"If anyone remains to hear these words," he said, "I would advise you to take your leave of this place immediately. Flee, and live to tell of what Hydra's Blitz Squad has done here today. Remain, and be destroyed. Testimony or forensic evidence, it matters not to me."

He paused, then forced himself to say the hated words at last. "Hail Hydra!"

Behind him, four golden hands raised in a ritual salute, and four pairs of golden lips voiced the rest of the ritual chant.

Zemo tried not to listen.

"Give me a lever long enough and a place to stand, and I will move the world."

That was how Galileo had put it.

It's all a matter of leverage, was Cap's way of phrasing the same lesson in applied physics, as validated by countless encounters with foes bigger, more powerful than he.

He was about to validate it again.

The golden goliath with the *H* on his torso charged toward Captain America now, even as the Avenger sought to recover from the toppling blow. With a speedy grace that came without conscious thought, Cap dropped again as the behemoth approached. At the last moment, after a span too brief to be measured in seconds, he kicked up, using the long muscles of his legs to drive both booted heels into the creature's solar plexus.

"Hail!" the thing roared, then voiced less-distinct syllables as its own momentum added to the force of Cap's strike.

Even though he had braced himself for it, the impact was enough to make Captain America wince with pain, but not enough to make him forget the job at hand.

The giant's momentum was still driving him forward, but the angle of Cap's blow had diverted his path a bit, adding an upward element to his trajectory. Cap braced himself, then grunted and pushed. His knees remained perfectly straight, but his legs pivoted on their hip joints as he added his not inconsiderable muscle power to his assailant's momentum. He grunted again as he assumed the burden of the giant's weight.

The behemoth's feet left the floor and a look of bafflement washed across his vacuous features.

At the last moment, as the burden became unbearable, Captain America twisted, and pushed again, then sighed in relief as the improvised throw sent the titan tumbling away.

Toward its fellow.

"Vision!" Cap yelled, as one golden form slammed into another, and both tumbled away from the fallen android. "Vision! You've got to—"

Then the world, or at least the portion of it that they occupied, collapsed.

The ways of mortals were passing strange, and, despite his many—well nigh countless—years dwelling among humans, Thor still found source for wonder in them.

The Norse god of thunder streaked through a cloudless sky, pulled along by his enchanted uru hammer, achieving speeds that most would find unimaginable. The world that passed below him would have been little more than a blur to most mortal eyes, but to his godly ones, it was clear and distinct—skyscrapers giving way to lower buildings, to warehouses, to a river, and then to the land called New Jersey. In his long-past youth, Thor had seen this portion of Midgard as a pristine, verdant wilderness, and held mixed regard for what the mortals had done to it.

Once, New Jersey had been a rolling green wilderness, a fit place for hunt or battle. Now, here, the wilderness was gone, replaced instead by sprawling metropolises and their vassal suburbs—more warehouses, and industrial complexes, and tank farms, and low, squat structures that hugged the earth as if afraid to leave it.

Then, abruptly, one of those structures was gone, too.

It vanished in a roar of thunder no less impressive than that which Thor commanded, and collapsed in a raining cascade of wreckage.

"'Od's blood!" Thor roared, dropping to the ground, and suddenly knowing something vaguely like fear. A quick glance at his communicator confirmed his apprehensions.

This was the origin site of the Avengers distress call he had received from Captain America. If liberty's champion had been in that structure when it was destroyed . . .

Captain America, for all his valor, was, after all, but a mortal.

Then the concern was gone, suddenly swept away by something more emphatic. Rage made Thor's words into thunder as he roared, "Captain America! Vision! If you yet live, I shall do all in my power to aid you! And if your shades still haunt this place, know this—you shall be avenged!"

Kneeling atop the heap of rubble, he gripped a shattered section of wall, pulled and lifted. Concrete and steel shifted, slid, and cascaded away in an artificial avalanche as Thor began the search for his fallen comrades. He dug and lifted for long minutes without tiring, worried urgency lending even more power to his godly strenghth. He dug so rapidly that he didn't even notice additional shifting in the wreckage, and the sound of his labors masked any other noise.

Nothing hid the two golden forms that erupted from the sundered structure, however. Unscathed by whatever holocaust had destroyed the structure, unmarked by their own escape from beneath countless tons of steel and concrete block, they were almost beautiful as they came into view.

"Hail Hydra!" the giants roared, and lashed out at Thor.

With impact scarcely less traumatic than Mjolnir, Thor's hammer, four golden fists slammed into the thunder god. The impact was enough to stun but not topple him, and despite the urgency of the situation, Thor smiled with suddenly bloodied lips.

The god of thunder was a god of battle as well, after all.

"Well struck," he said, blocking a second barrage of blows with Mjolnir's head. "You have shown me your mettle, and it is not wanting! Now, taste mine!"

Thor's fist, spoken of in legend as shattering mountains, smashed into the first golden giant's jaw. The titan staggered back, stumbled, slid—then righted himself, some three feet above the mounded wreckage.

The things, whatever they were, could fly.

Thor's quick mind had only just finished digesting that fact when the creature's hand came up and lightning danced from its fingertips, to bridge the gap between him and the beleaguered thunder god. Not as potent as the true lightning he commanded, it was nonetheless enough to make his skin burn and his ears ring.

"Hail Hydra!" the thing repeated. "Immortal Hydra! We shall never be destroyed!" Then it, and its fellow, moved upward, almost as swiftly as the energies they had released.

"Nay, I say, a thousand times nay!" Thor bellowed. He grasped Mjolnir by its haft and swung the enchanted hammer in a tight circle, gathering the energy to depart. "None may so strike the son of Odin, and then escape the consequence!"

"If not escape, then at least delay," a familiar voice said.

"Eh?" Startled, Thor glanced down just in time to see a familiar green and yellow form emerge from the wreckage at his feet, passing through broken concrete as though it were insubstantial mist.

"Let them go, Thor," the Vision said, a note of concern evident in his normally neutral voice. "Captain America must have your aid."

Chapter Six

The *Barbarossa*, deep beneath the Atlantic Ocean

"Excellent," Baron Strucker said. He tasted the word, savored it, rolled it around on his tongue as if reluctant to let it pass between his lips and be heard by others. Triumph was a heady draught, and one that had been all too rare of late. No matter now; the long drought made the current draught all the sweeter.

"I'm glad you're happy," Techno said, "But there's still some room for improvement."

Zemo said nothing.

The three stood in Techno's assigned laboratory space within the *Barbarossa*. Before them, neatly arrayed on a test bench, was the golden form of Vier, one of the two Blitz Squad members assigned to ground-floor duty during the recent repository raid—the level of the building that had sustained the most extensive damage during the evidence repository's collapse. Despite that, Vier's skin was unmarked and the enhanced being showed no sign of any damage. Nor did he give any protest as Techno poked and prodded at him with various medieval-looking instruments.

"Improvement?" Strucker asked. "Our creation withstood having a building dropped upon it, and you believe that it still demands improvement?"

"*Our* creation," Zemo said, giving an ironic emphasis to the possessive, "demands many improvements. Their vocabulary alone—"

"Hail Hydra," Vier said softly, as Techno lowered a visor into place, obscuring the Blitzer's features. "Cut off a limb—"

He became silent as Techno pushed a button on the helmet and it hummed to life. A moment later, and its golden eyes were hidden behind golden eyelids.

Zemo took a short, sharp breath, but said nothing.

Strucker smiled. "The ritual affirmation annoys you?" he asked. "You are so unaccustomed to loyalty that its reminders are disconcerting?"

Zemo shook his head, obviously angry now. "It is not as simple as that. Stealth alone demands that—"

"Not a problem," Techno said. "I can enhance the discretionary logistic function without impeding the allegiance factor. You need them to be quiet, they'll be quiet."

Strucker glared at him, all good humor suddenly fled.

"But," Techno continued, "I think you'd both better watch this."

A video monitor emerged from a bulkhead recess, then filled with light. All three watched the images unfold in chaotic sequence—the elevator shack and the shadowed confines of the shaft below, rending metal and an almost abandoned corridor, a security guard who abruptly wasn't a mere security guard anymore.

Strucker cursed as the guard's uniform and flesh-colored mask collapsed and a green and yellow figure stepped out of them. The disguise, far less sophisticated than the one his partner used, had been no less effective.

"The Vision," Strucker hissed. He turned on Zemo. "You did not tell me that the Avengers were present in that facility."

"I did not know," responded Zemo, who sounded as if the admission did not please him. "I had thought Thor's advent on the scene a coincidence."

"Baron Z was on the third floor," Techno pointed out. "Vier here was one of the pair we chose for the test to destruction, remember?" That had been the secondary goal of the field test, after the primary one of appropriating Heinrich Zemo's prototype—to see just how much punishment the Blitz Squad members could survive.

No one had anticipated the presence of the Avengers.

Strucker spat, then found it in himself to grin once more as he watched the Vision fall before the superhuman blows of the Blitz Squad agent. "The android appears pained," he said. "Can we get sound on this? I wish to hear his cries of agony."

"That will have to wait," Techno said. "Audio takes more processing than the visual feed."

A minute or two passed, as the two barons and the man with the mechanical body watched silent footage unfold. The Vision fell, crumpled beneath pounding blows. Then Vier's assigned partner, Zwei, slammed into him, and the screen filled briefly with a face that Strucker hated as much as any in all the world.

"Captain America," he said, making the name a curse. Then the screen filled with a flash of light, followed by darkness. "He or the Vision must have summoned the thunder god, then. But why were they there to begin with?"

The question went unanswered.

"That takes us up to the blast," Techno said. "You know the rest of the story, Baron Z."

"There is little to tell," Zemo said. "The remainder of the team and I had evacuated by then. Vier and Zwei both survived, rendezvoused with us, and we returned here." He paused, thinking. "I saw no sign of either Avenger emerging from the demolition site."

Techno said, "The Blitzers have automated aggression subprograms. They must have recognized the Vision and Captain America as foes, and attempted to deal with them."

Strucker glanced at Zemo. "Perhaps they were successful?" he asked. "Could our agents have found the success that has so long eluded us both?"

Zemo shook his head. "It is too much to hope for," he returned. "To eliminate two enemies so easily, by mere chance—"

"Fortune favors the bold," Strucker said softly. He felt hope surge through him.

"It favors the wise even more," Zemo rejoined. "You would do wise to remember that. Captain America alone has escaped countless apparent deaths that seemed far more certain."

"And you would know, would you not, dear Helmut?" Strucker japed. He knew full well that there was bad blood between his partner and their common foe. In this one way, at least—the hatred of Captain America—Strucker was willing to concede that Zemo might be his equal.

Might.

"That is of no matter now," Zemo said testily. "What matters is that the Avengers will be ready for us next time."

" 'Prepared' is more like it," Techno interjected. His metal features had taken on a remarkably smug cast. "They won't be ready."

"The upgrade," Zemo said, in acknowledgement. "How soon can you implement it?"

"I haven't had a chance to study the prototype yet."

"How long?" Zemo repeated.

Techno cocked his head, and his burnished features took on a speculative look. "Judging from your father's notes, two days. That's my best projection."

Strucker shook his head. "*Nein*," he said. "You have one."

"Nine yourself," Techno returned. "My estimate stands. We're talking about considerable destructive potentials here, and I need time to do my work."

"We've come far," Zemo interjected. "This is no time to take a misstep."

Strucker grunted, tacitly conceding the point. "And how long to empower the additional agents?" he demanded. Vaguely defined enhancements were all well and good, but pure, brute muscle was better.

"Not long. I can do that by dinner, if I have to. There are some tweaks that could stand being made first, though." Techno gave a steel grin. "The vocabulary banks, for starters."

"Do that," Zemo said. "Make the changes, empower the new agents, and apply the system upgrade to the entire squad." Then, to Strucker, "I assume you want another field test?"

His tones suggested that he had views of his own on the matter.

"No," Strucker said. What he understood of Techno's promised "upgrade" had suggested some promising possibilities, ones that would serve Hydra's long-term goals as well as the needs of the current project. "More than that. Not a field test," he continued, and smiled again. "Say instead, a demonstration."

Kintnerburg, New Jersey

Thor swung his hammer carefully, precisely. With a grinding roar, the last of the concrete slabs that blocked his path crumbled and he stepped forward.

"Step carefully," he told Firestar, two steps behind him. "Should the tumbled wreckage shift—"

"If the wreckage slips, I'll worry about me," the attractive young woman said. As if on cue, a nearby heap of debris released a small avalanche in their direction. Without even pausing, she aimed a bolt of high-energy microwaves that caught the cascading rubble at its leading edge and fused the stuff into a solid mass. The remainder of the shifting heap surged toward the new barrier but could not pass over it.

Angelica Jones scarcely seemed to notice. Her resolute expression looked quite at home on her features, and had resided there ever since her arrival, some moments after Thor's adversaries had departed. "In the meantime," she said, "we'll worry about Cap."

"The Captain shall prevail," Thor told her, but for what seemed like the twentieth time, his keen blue eyes were searching for any sign of life. "Even collapsed, this structure is bountiful with hollows and crannies. We need but find the one that holds our comrade."

Nearly an hour before, the two had begun the search for their leader. The clouds of dust and debris had just begun to settle then.

"How can you be so calm?" Firestar asked. "I mean, sure, the Vision says—"

Abruptly, the Vision's immaterial head emerged from a slab of reinforced concrete. "A degree to your left, Thor," he said. "And perhaps three meters ahead. I've assessed the situation from within and verified relative stability here. Apply a reasonable degree of force."

"Good," Thor responded. He drove one fist forward, aiming precisely one degree to his left. The punch passed through the android's intangible form without any evident effect and into the slab beyond. With gratifying ease, the artificial stone split. Thor forced his fingers into the gap between the fragments and began levering pieces of concrete free. In a moment, he had the beginnings of a human-sized hole.

Upon their arrival, the android had told them the essentials of what had happened, and explained that he had shielded Captain America from collapse by increasing the density and durability of his own body to a near-infinite degree.

The last layer of wreckage fell away, revealing a hollow formed by intersecting steel beams, one hidden remnant of what had been the structure's first floor. A moment later, and a famous, costumed form struggled out of his cramped shelter.

"Hello, Thor, Firestar," Captain America said casually, even cheerfully. He had spent more than an hour pinned beneath tons of wreckage, trapped in the darkness and the dirt, and yet he seemed totally at ease as he greeted his associates. He dusted himself off, then clapped his hands together. "Good to see you both."

"Good to see *you*, Cap," Firestar said, her relief evident. "What happened here?"

"We can go over that back at the mansion," Cap said. "And at a full meeting. We've got some preparations to make."

North Carolina

The five trucks made an odd sight as they rolled in close sequence down the weathered ribbon of asphalt highway. Similar in size, they were different in all other particulars—make and model, number of axles, general cleanliness, and color scheme. Each bore an easily recognized commercial logo, but no two of those logos were the same. Cartoon mascots, three-letter business names, and irritatingly abstract geometrical designs labeled them as belonging to a donut bakery, a food delivery company, a plumbing contractor, a chemical supply house, and a popular package delivery service, respectively.

The logos lied.

The North Carolina Piedmont is a craggy, hilly place, a zone of transition between that state's seaboard and the mountainous regions that bound its western border. The highways in that rocky area must wind around foothills or punch through them, and it is easy to lose track of comings and goings on those rocky roads. Any driver catching sight of the five trucks for the first time might reasonably conclude that they had joined the highway from some concealed entrance ramp, during a transient moment of blocked view.

That driver would have been wrong.

The five trucks moved almost as a unit, maintaining a consistent distance from their fellows, and moving at precisely the posted speed limit as they rolled, dead center, down the right-most of three westbound lanes. One exit passed, untaken, then another, and then a third loomed. The sign that marked it read, FONESCA COMPLEX SERVICE ENTRANCE. THREE MILES.

Two and fourth-fifths miles later, five right-turn signal indicators flashed, pulsing in a synchronized rhythm.

Another two miles passed, and then, at the bottom of a steeply inclined access tunnel, the first of the five disparate vehicles pulled up to an open loading dock. Its lights flashed and its horn sounded. In response, a portly man wearing a black coverall emerged from behind a grease-stained door and came closer.

"You made a wrong turn somewhere," the loading clerk said to the driver, grinning sympathetically. "Zippy Donuts closed its outlet here a year ago." Then he fell silent and fell backward, as a hole opened in his chest.

Zemo sheathed his laser pistol and turned to the man who shared the front seat with him. "Note that," he said crisply. "When we return to *Barbarossa*, I want the name of the individual responsible for vehicle camouflage."

The Hydra agent, a thin man, little more than a boy, with blond hair and freckles, nodded. There was no fear in his voice as he replied, only obedience, and he spoke with the disturbing directness of a fanatic. "Yes, Section Leader," he said. "As you command, it will be done."

"Of course," Zemo acknowledged. His outlines were softening now, wavering, as the image inducer he wore changed modes and his concealing hologram reconfigured itself. Once more, his primary disguise, the uniform of a Hydra section leader, came into view.

The others in his convoy had less sophisticated means at their disposal. The drivers and passengers in the other four vehicles spilled forth. Following the lead of Zemo's personal companion, they shucked their outer clothes and replaced them with similar yellow and green uniforms. As they dressed, the cargo holds in all five trucks opened, and more Hydra agents spilled forth, along with fifteen of the golden titans who made up the Blitz Squad. Moments later, Zemo's task force operatives, human and superhuman alike, stood in military formation, their arms raised in silent salute.

Zemo had been quite specific about that, when issuing his

commands, back at *Barbarossa*. No more shouted affirmations, no more ritual salutes, except to impress their enemies.

"You have your orders," he said briskly. "Obey them, or face the consequences." The tone of his voice suggested that those consequences would be dire, indeed.

The assembled forces remained silent.

He gestured at two of the human agents assigned to his detail, the only Hydra agents who had remained in civilian attire, and who held polished metal equipment cases. "You two," he said. "You know what to do."

It was not a question.

"Yes, Section Leader," one member of the pair replied. "Your associate's instructions were most specific."

The second man coughed, scratched his chin, and then spoke in a quavering voice. "As to the matter of reinforcements," he said, "might I inquire—"

"Not if you wish to live," Zemo said. Then, in the silence that followed: "Be off with you, then," he said, and glanced at his watch. "The diversion will commence in precisely seven minutes."

Hallie Takahama was scooping greasy fries into a cardboard sleeve when she heard it.

"About time," she said softly, shoving the sack of food at her baffled customer, who scarcely seemed to notice. "Two days is two too many."

Then, without a backward glance, she raced for the break room, and a change of clothes.

Erik Josten was buffing a lengthy stretch of red tile floor and Abe Jenkins was carefully explaining to an engineering intern that flux modulators needed a secured ground to operate properly. Karla Sofen was telling an unhappy secretary that her complaint was not actionable, and Melissa Gold was writing down a seventh message from that annoying man who kept asking to speak to the site manager. Clint Barton was making time with an attractive Korean office-supply saleswoman who thought he was connected to site management.

All of them heard the alarm at the same moment.

It would have been hard to ignore—a loud, shrieking wail that seemed to split the air itself in a screaming call to action.

Before anyone could respond, however, the siren's wail became a human voice, and its ululation gave way to something more intelligible.

"Attention, all occupants of this facility," came the booming tones, echoing from every intercom speaker, sounding in every nook and every cranny of the vast installation. "The Fonesca Complex—and all within it—are now in the custody of Hydra. Your freedom is forfeit, but your lives need not be. Obey us, accede to our demands, and live. Resist us, and perish."

Well, they finally made their move, Hawkeye thought.

It was about time.

The operation went well, all things considered. If there was one thing that Zemo was willing to grant Strucker, it was that the older man's forces were well trained and surprisingly competent. They scarcely needed supervision at all as they swarmed through the site, taking easy charge of a vastly larger civilian population. In a matter of short minutes, they had effective control of the place.

That was good. His operatives' speed freed much of Zemo's mind to consider other issues, even as one corner of his consciousness monitored the operation itself.

Surrounding Zemo was chaos—the shouts of panicked civilians, the angry commands barked by members of his cadre, the occasional burning snarl of laser fire as Hydra agents herded their captives to a central point. All those noises and more mingled to create a dense wall of sound too rich, too complex for any single input to dominate.

He strode along the broad concourse that led from Osborn Chemical's site offices to another, smaller suite of offices that served as home for an engineering services firm. As he walked, he ignored the human cattle milling about him, herded toward the food court area by Hydra's rank-and-file members.

The site was secure, or would be, in moments. Equipment in the donut truck had overridden all site communications systems, leaving Zemo to decide what messages got in and what messages got out. The Fonesca Complex itself had seven entrances, including the loading dock; at each of those seven portals stood a Blitz Squad agent, sufficient to hold it against any and all attackers, at least until reinforcements could be summoned.

The other eight Blitzers had orders of their own.

And as for the occupants of the complex—

Fleeing, a beetle-browed, balding man whose ears sprouted white tufts of hair came racing in his direction. Zemo scarcely noticed him, or the zealous Hydra foot-soldier who moved swiftly to come to his commander's aid. "Argh," the balding man said, collapsing as a rifle butt slammed into his skull. Zemo stepped over his crumpled form and continued on his way.

Thus far, the occupants here had offered no resistance worth noting.

That, in itself, was mildly disconcerting.

A twinge of sensation cut through the near-boredom Zemo felt, a whispering hint of something like apprehension. He had planned this effort carefully, choosing the site and making clandestine plans of his own, even as he accommodated Strucker's vision. By now, Zemo thought, those efforts should have born richer fruit than this.

He had laid this trap carefully, leaking information through channels of his own, ever since the Colorado incident had offered the opportunity. The notes in his father's journals had suggested what the next step of the operation would be, and he had seen a way to combine it with achieving certain cherished goals of his own.

Where were those goals?

Where were the Thunderbolts?

Zemo's communicator buzzed and he answered it, setting all other thoughts aside for the moment. "Report," he commanded into the tiny device.

"Hail Hydra!" came the response. "Technician First Class Veitch reporting." Veitch was one of the two plainclothes operatives he had assigned to special duty. "We've secured the geothermal tap and integrated modules one and two."

"Status?"

"The nuclear device is armed," Veitch continued. "The relay is online, and cycling to full power now."

• • •

A building—any building—embodies opposites.

Solid barriers bound hollow places; walls and ceilings and floors are postioned according to the spaces they enclose. Positive and negative define one another, and never more so than in a modern structure, because modern buildings are mostly empty space. Walls define rooms and corridors, but they enclose other emptinesses within themselves—cable conduits and plumbing and dead-air spaces.

In Fonesca, they hid more.

They hid narrow maintenance and access tunnels that wound through most of the complex, with entrances and exits that were hidden equally for aesthetic and security purposes.

Just now, those same walls—or the tunnels behind them—hid the Thunderbolts.

"I hate to say it," Hawkeye whispered in the dimly lit passage. "But you did good, Moonstone."

Karla Sofen's response was to use her phasing powers to extend her face slightly beyond the wall's boundaries, and take a peek at the scene beyond. She was careful to take only the briefest of glimpses before pulling back and making her report.

"They've corralled the civilians in the food court area," she said. "And you don't need to whisper; they can't hear us."

She was the one who had discovered the passageways, and worked with Abe to circumvent their alarm systems, so she was well aware of what shelter they offered. Most importantly, for the moment, those hidden corridors offered a tactical advantage that promised to be essential.

"I say we bust some heads," Atlas said grimly. "Hit fast and hit hard."

Hawkeye shook his head. "Too many hostages," he said grimly. "Too many guns. We go charging in before we know what's what and there'll be a bloodbath."

"This is Hydra we're taking about," Atlas said. "If we *don't* go charging in, there'll be a bloodbath, too." His previous career as a mercenary had taught him much about the organization.

"No," Hawkeye repeated. "This isn't something you can solve by slamming a few heads together—at least, not unless they're the right heads. We've got to know more before we act. If we can capture their leader—"

"I think he's the same guy we ran into at the Vault," Songbird said. "He's wearing the same kind of mask."

"Might not be any time to worry about stuff like that," MACH-1 said, with grimness equal to Hawkeye's. "I'm getting a consistent feed on a wide range of frequencies. Listen." One of his suit's external speakers, ordinarily used for PA purposes, clicked to life.

Zemo placed himself carefully in the broad open area that had been the food court's dining space a few moments before. His agents had cleared away the tables and chairs, and leaving him an arenalike area from which to speak his piece. He stood in the center of that area now, apparently alone, with two operatives waiting some twenty feet to his left.

"Satellite override engaged, sir," a Hydra communications expert before him announced. He made some adjustments to his equipment. "Ready in five, four, three, two, one—now!"

Zemo gazed at the camera's lens. His own hooded visage gazed back at him, reflected by the polished glass. He knew that the same image filled every television screen on the Eastern Seaboard, thanks to Hydra's considerable technological resources. More importantly, he knew that his words would be heard on any radio or television served by any of five primary communications satellites.

That was good. Ultimata demanded audiences.

"Attention, America," he said, speaking without preamble or greeting. "The Fonesca Research Complex for Alternative Energy Resources, home of the much-vaunted nuclear particle supercollider, now belongs to Hydra. Our agents have secured the facility against any attempt to retake it. More, all within its walls are hostage to the American government's compliance with Hydra's demands.

"Those demands are simple—the sum of ten million dollars, payable in gold bullion. Should that sum seem excessive, consider that this facility draws its power from a geothermal tap. My operatives have attached a nuclear device to that tap, sufficient to trigger volcanic and seismic activity that will be felt throughout the surrounding five states. Meet our demands, or pay a terrible price. You have six hours to agree.''

He paused, allowing his audience to consider his words. Zemo knew that he was speaking not merely to the human cattle who comprised most of this hated nation's populace, but also to their leaders, and to the Avengers, the Fantastic Four, S.H.I.E.L.D., SAFE, and all the other so-called forces of order who had contended with him in the past. He knew the effect his words would have—shock, disbelief, outrage, panic, and fury.

And Strucker's beloved chaos, as his audience acted on the emotions he invoked now. Hydra wanted the money, true enough, but the terrorist organization's main imperative was to spread terror and despair. That was as much a goal of this operation as the field test or Zemo's own agenda, and the most certain of any of them.

The bomb would be detonated, Zemo knew, whether the ransom was paid or not.

He continued: ''On a more immediate basis, and as an incentive, we will execute one hostage every fifteen minutes, live and telecast, until such time as our terms are met.''

Two uniformed agents dragged another man into the camera's field of view. He was stoop-shouldered and beetle-browed, and tufts of white hair sprouted from his ears. A purpling bruise marked his brow, and he seemed scarcely aware of his surroundings.

''We will commence now,'' Zemo said.

''Argh,'' the balding man said.

Zemo raised his laser pistol.

The wall behind him exploded.

''Argh,'' the soft growl sounded on MACH-1's outboard speaker.

''Mr. Oglodytes!'' Jolt said, panic in her voice. Her nails dug into the bicep of Atlas, who stood beside her. ''He's going to kill Mr. Oglodytes!''

''No, he's not,'' Atlas said. ''Not if I have anything to say about it!'' He placed his hands flat against the wall.

''Atlas, don't!'' Hawkeye shouted. ''Something about this is all wrong!''

Too late. Atlas had braced himself at an angle between floor and wall, and then summoned his own super power. Deep within his irradiated tissues, exotic energies flared to life, lending strength and new mass to his body.

Atlas grew.

He grew at a controlled rate, but he grew remarkably fast. The long bones of his arms and legs grew longer, and the rest of him kept pace, bulking up and becoming even more massive. The textured soles of his boots caught on the tile flooring and held.

The wall before him did not.

Plaster board and support members gave way, and the wall erupted outward in a rain of debris.

Hawkeye cursed; Jolt all but cheered.

Still growing, Atlas rushed forward into the former dining area, his oversized body widening the breach it had created. Behind him, Moonstone and the others followed, but he scarcely noticed.

"It's the Thunderbolts," another hostage cried. "What are they doing here?"

"Whose side are they on?" came another shouted comment.

"In for a penny, in for a pound," Hawkeye said with grim resignation, nocking another arrow and following suit.

"You're not going to kill a harmless old man," Atlas thundered. "Not while I have anything to say about it." He charged the green-hooded figure before him, moving in a speedy lope made more efficient by his oversized legs. Usually, this was enough to make an enemy turn and run.

The Hydra section leader laughed

"I don't like this," Moonstone said, even as her feet left the floor and she rose within the concourse's vaulted confines.

"Of course you do not, Dr. Sofen," the Hydra overlord snapped. Apparently unshaken by the sudden commotion, he kept his pistol trained on Mr. Oglodytes's bruised forehead. "You like nothing you do not control, correct? You like to manipulate, not be manipulated."

"He—he knows you," Songbird said, as her solidified sound wings formed, and lifted her into the air. She had recognized the section leader as the one who had confronted them at the Vault. "He knew me, and he knows you!"

"I know all of you!" the Hydra section leader snarled. "I know you like a falcon knows its prey, or a teacher knows his students!"

The outlines of his green-clad form wavered and shifted.

"It—it's a trap," Atlas said, drawing up short in midstride, his sudden decisiveness fled. He had expected the Hydra commander to drop the pistol he had trained on his captive, but the masked agent seemed scarcely surprised by the team's sudden advent. His green-gloved fingers still gripped the gun firmly.

No—not green-gloved.

Yellow.

"Zemo," Atlas said in shocked dismay and recognition as the last of the cloaking illusion faded.

"Just so," snapped the founder and former leader of the Thunderbolts. His chosen attire was fully evident now, royal purple fabric trimmed with golden metal and snow-leopard fur.

"I don't know what you're doing in Hydra's ranks," Hawkeye said, "but—"

His words stopped, as cleanly and abruptly as if someone had flipped a switch.

Something was happening.

The air surrounding Helmut Zemo had begun to shimmer, like the air above a heated highway. For a brief moment, however, the walls beyond were still visible, even if distorted by the odd effect.

And then they were not.

The cloaking illusion had fallen away. As if from nowhere, eight more figures had appeared—eight golden giants, identical in face and form, glistening with barely contained energy. They towered over their master by a head or more, and wore a stylized *H* insignia on their oversized torsos.

"And as for what I am doing," Zemo continued, "for now, call it a field test and a demonstration." He laughed. "A field test for the Blitz Squad. *My* Blitz Squad."

Chapter Seven

The *Barbarossa*, deep beneath the Atlantic Ocean

The guards flanking him carried no sidearms, but they wore powered armor beneath their green and yellow Hydra uniforms. Thanks to the sensor banks in his mechanical body, the former Norbert Ebersol could "see" his escorts' hidden weapons systems, and felt a degree of approval as he assessed them—exoskeletons, base-level repulsors, microwave generators, and something that appeared to be a portable particle beam generator but probably wasn't. In all, either man commanded enough firepower to deal with almost any threat.

Not enough to deal with Techno, however, if push came to shove.

"I'm sure I can find my own way, boys," he said easily. "You can go back to what you were doing. There must be some innocent prisoners who need torturing."

The man on his left shook his head. "You are to go nowhere without a personal escort," he said.

The man on his right agreed. "The Supreme Hydra is most concerned for your safety."

The very thought that Baron Wolfgang Von Strucker cared about anyone's well-being other than his own nearly forced a laugh from Techno's artificial larynx, but he smothered it. Things had gone reasonably well thus far; he saw no need to force a confrontation, even if the outcome of that confrontation was foregone. The weaponry already in his own body was enough to deal with any immediate threat, and he could configure more systems in moments from additional, variable-use components.

More systems, and deadlier ones.

"Hard to believe anyone would be at risk onboard the *Barbarossa*," he said. He was trying hard to sound mildly sarcastic, but he knew that he could well be failing.

It was hard to tell anymore. Techno's world had become a very different place, or had seemed to, since downloading his consciousness into its current mechanical home—cleaner and more pristine, yet paradoxically invested with countless new nuances and gradations. His sensory clarity and acuity had both increased by several degrees of magnitude, providing an almost overwhelming amount of input to his still-human mind. Moreover, leaving his organic aspect behind had stripped away the biochemical fog of instinctive reaction and glandular response that overlay most human thought processes; the complex digital simulations that had taken their place were good, but not perfect.

Recently, Techno had reluctantly concluded that, no matter how much he had gained in the changeover, he had lost something, too—some aspect of his mind rooted deep in its organic origins, some minor element that did not lend itself to easy transfer or emulation. The conclusion didn't much bother him, but it was undeniable, and it had equally undeniable repercussions.

It was hard to mimic human activities when you weren't human anymore. Even his assessment of others' words was suspect, albeit to a vastly lesser degree.

Apparently he had shaped his words correctly this time. Either that, or his escorts had decided not to press the issue. Neither guard responded to his comment, so all three walked in silence until they reached Strucker's private offices. The two armed men remained behind as Techno strode through the opening. Hydra rank and file did not enter Strucker's presence unbidden.

Few sane men did.

"Welcome, Ebersol," Strucker said. Clad in full uniform as the Supreme Hydra, with the organization's distinctive snakes-and-skull emblem stretching across his chest, he cut an impressive figure. He was seated behind a desk that looked like something Frank Lloyd Wright might have designed after a bad night's sleep—all black wood, chromed steel, and heavy glass, intersecting at bizarre angles to provide plenty of work space. At the moment, however, the vast expanse of the desk's top was spotlessly empty; apparently, the Supreme Hydra had set aside all other business for this interview.

Techno wondered why.

"Events are approaching their climax," Strucker said. He gestured at an oversized video monitor set in one wall. Just now, the screen displayed a green-hooded man whom Techno knew was Zemo, disguised in a Hydra uniform.

Bet he hates wearing that getup, Techno thought. He had

come to know Zemo reasonably well in previous months—about as well as Zemo let himself be known—and had a reasonably reliable estimate of the other man's likes and dislikes.

"I thought you might wish to witness this," Strucker said. His attempt at sounding hospitable rang false even to Techno's ears. "We approach the conclusion of the exercise, after all."

"There's still more to do," Techno said. "Even if the field test plays out as expected, there are some adjustments I want to make. And it would still be nice to get my hooks on a long-term survivor of the original ionizer—Atlas, maybe. I'm concerned about longevity."

"Details, details," Strucker said dismissively. "And longevity is not an issue, when human raw material is available in unlimited quantities. When this is done, it will be time to move on to new endeavors."

"Maybe so," Techno responded, not meaning it and not really caring whether or not Strucker knew he was lying. Nor did he bother to mention that he had been monitoring the feed from Zemo with his internal circuits. He was already as current on the Fonesca situation as Strucker.

More up to date, actually, since the other baron had briefed him on his own plans, and since another corner of his mind was busily processing telemetry readings from the Blitz Squad agents.

"Good," Strucker said in what passed for an amiable tone of voice. He pressed a key on his remote control, reactivating the monitor's audio function.

". . . home of the much-vaunted nuclear particle supercollider, now belongs to Hydra," Zemo's muffled voice was saying. *"Our agents have secured the facility against any attempt to retake it. More, all within its walls are hostage to the American government's compliance with Hydra's demands.*

"Those demands are simple—the sum of ten million dollars, payable in gold bullion. Should that sum seem excessive, consider—"

Some kind of observation seemed to be expected, so Techno made it. "He's good at this," he said. "He's never been much for the limelight, but he plays well to the camera when he has to."

"We are alike in that," Strucker said.

Once again, Techno almost laughed. The world's news archives were filled near to overflowing with threats and ultimata voiced by the Supreme Hydra and beamed to every available media outlet. Wolfgang Von Strucker was anything but camera-shy.

Aloud, he said, "You may have a point."

They watched and listened in silence for a few more moments.

"Where will you go when this is done?" Strucker asked, suddenly, surprisingly direct.

"Go?" Techno asked lightly.

"Go," Strucker repeated. "Helmut tells me that your alliance with him has ended."

Techno nodded, a human habit that had proven so basic that it lived on in his new body. "Yup," he said. "At least, as a formal partnership, it has. I've gone freelance again, an independent contractor."

"Like the old days, eh?" Strucker asked, sounding positively avuncular, and perhaps even nostalgic. In years gone by, when a younger Norbert Ebersol had been known as the Fixer, he had done some work for Hydra and its various splinter organizations. During the earliest of those endeavors, Strucker had been running the show from well behind the scenes. Neither Ebersol nor the rest of the world had suspected the German's continued involvement.

In retrospect, that ignorance seemed excusable. Following World War II, Strucker has spent many years in careful hiding. The world had believed him dead, even as it came to know the fury of his greatest creation, Hydra, the terrorist cabal that he had built so carefully. Later, he had operated in a more public light, and allowed his continued existence to be known. More than once, he had faked his own death or seemed to die, and each time he had returned, deadlier than before.

Then, shockingly, he had died for real, in pitched combat with a mortal enemy, the flesh literally stripped from his bones by one of his own science staff's fiendish creations.

Only to rise yet again.

Somehow, Strucker had returned from true death, resurrected by a freak biological incident, the details of which were beyond even Techno's knowledge.

Techno wondered about that sometimes. He was quite aware that he had lost something, however inconsequential, in his transition from an organic body to a mechanical one. It stood to reason that Strucker had lost more in moving from life to death and then back to life again.

How much more? How close to human was Strucker's mind, a consciousness that now inhabited what once had been, incontrovertibly, a dead husk?

"Like the old days," he agreed.

"Tell me—do you lack for clients?" Strucker asked. He paused. "Your skills have, as ever, proven useful."

Techno didn't particularly like the way the conversation was going. Hydra's resources were considerable and he didn't particularly mind working with Strucker, at least on occasion.

Working *for* the crazed German was another matter entirely.

" 'Freelance' might have been an exaggeration," he said slowly. "I'm open to offers, but I'm picky about the ones I take. I've got some irons of my own, and some fires to put them in."

"I could accommodate that," Strucker continued. "I am not entirely opposed to initiative and—" His words broke off as he stood bolt upright and roared, "What is he *doing*?"

Techno knew what had prompted the outburst, even without glancing at the monitor. His internal receivers and processors were busily playing the same images for his mind's eye

On the screen—and in Techno's mind's eye—a wall had crumbled in the Fonesca Complex, and six costumed figures had erupted from behind it. That was bad enough, though not entirely unexpected—at least, not to Techno, who had half-expected the Thunderbolts' advent on the scene. Moreover, Zemo had chosen to reveal his true identity, pulling the cloak of invisibility from the majority of his Blitz Squad task force. None of those events qualified as good news, but Techno's best guess was that none of them were the true cause of Strucker's sudden, convulsive fury.

No, the main reason for the torrent of curses spewing from Strucker's lips had to be Zemo's words.

"A field test for the Blitz Squad," Zemo was saying. "My *Blitz Squad."*

"*His* Blitz Squad!?" Strucker roared.

To his surprise, Techno felt his optical receptors roll back in their steel sockets unbidden, obeying the prompt of deeply written personality traits.

He filed the fact of the response away for future consideration.

Avengers Mansion, New York

In the hangar space that filled much of the mansion's top floor, five turbocharged jet engines roared to life.

"Everybody strapped in?" Iron Man asked, his electronically modulated voice sounding over speakers stationed throughout the quinjet's passenger area. He was seated in the specialized craft's cockpit, steel-gloved hands on the steering yoke, more as a backup than to actually use them. The Avengers' quinjets had been designed by Tony Stark and built to his exacting specifications. Now, taking advantage of that fact, he had used a retractable cable to directly interface his armor's internal command modules with the jet-powered craft's navigation and propulsion systems. The high-speed personnel transport would effectively function as an extension of his own armor.

"Ready," came the responses from Wanda, Vision, and Wonder Man, each speaking in turn, followed by an "I'm here," from Firestar and a "Yes, sir!" that sounded postively ebullient.

That would be Justice, of course.

Tony turned to face Cap, who was settling in beside him in the copilot's seat. "What about Thor?" he asked. "Any response?"

A matter of minutes before, news of the takeover at Fonesca had reached Avengers Mansion. Literally within seconds, the alert had gone out. Fortunately, this time, most of the active team members had been available to respond.

Captain America nodded. "He'll meet us there," he said levelly. "He thinks he can make better time, solo."

"That makes sense," Iron Man said, even though he didn't fully believe it. Thor's muscle power and magic enabled him to do some pretty amazing things, but Tony had a hard time believing that they were a match for five fuel-injected, turbocharged, high-efficiency thrusters under direct mental control.

A section of roof slid back, revealing the clear blue sky above Manhattan. The roar of the quinjet's engines changed slightly as Tony revved the engines, but the craft did not rise just yet. Air traffic in the New York area was exceedingly hectic, and even the top-priority clearances that Avengers business commanded took a minute or so to process.

"I'd prefer to face this as a unit," Cap said. "Hydra has run rings around us these past few encounters, and I have to believe that's partly because we haven't been facing them as a team." He leaned forward and spoke into an intercom mike. "I want you all to follow my lead when we get there," he said. "We're facing this together, as Avengers."

Agreeing responses followed, then Iron Man said, "Uh, Cap, I think you'd better take a look at this." He pointed one steel-clad finger at the dash monitor.

Captain America blinked at what he saw. Typically, he was almost unflappable, but when he spoke, he voice carried a tone somewhere between shock and dismay.

"What in the world," he asked, "are the Thunderbolts doing in North Carolina?"

He did not seem to expect an answer, but as if in response, the quinjet's engine roar changed pitch again, and the big craft threw itself into the sky.

The Fonesca Complex, North Carolina

This could be bad, Hawkeye thought. *Very bad*.

Zemo's sudden self-revelation had been enough to give most of the Thunderbolts pause, and to make even the maddened Atlas stop dead in his tracks.

Hawkeye didn't like that. Erik Josten had some serious problems with self-esteem. He had turned on Zemo originally only under extreme circumstances, and had since shown an unnerving tendency to dither and doubt himself—precisely the kind of traits that could spell terrible trouble for people in the Thunderbolts' line of business.

Suddenly, Melissa's failure to apprehend the masked Hydra

section leader at the Vault made a lot more sense.

"Zemo!?" the ordinarily calm Moonstone said, pausing in her flight. In Hawkeye's experience, Karla Sofen wasn't surprised very often, but when she was, the effects tended to be dramatic. "What are *you* doing here?"

Yup, very bad, Hawkeye thought. They had effecively lost the advantage of surprise and ceded it to Zemo. Worse, the Thunderbolts' powers and fighting styles weren't especially well-suited to enclosed spaces. If anything blunted his teammates' edges further, the fight would be over before it started.

Atlas roared, an incoherent thunder that made him sound like an enraged beast.

"Atlas?" Hallie said, her girlish voice filled with worry.

Atlas threw himself at Zemo.

Moving with lightning speed, one of the Blitz Squad threw him back. A golden fist smashed into the giant's jaw, hard enough to make his head and entire torso snap back, and then the golden creature grasped the heavy fabric of Atlas's tunic. Without visible strain or even effort, the Blitzer lifted Atlas—at least twice his size—and threw him against the opposing wall. The felled giant smashed once more through plasterboard, bricks, and beams, and lay silent.

"Atlas!" Hallie said. This time, she shrieked the name. Even as the words left her lips, however, she was bounding, leaping, bouncing, dancing toward the same Blitzer who had felled Josten. The giant gave a growl of anger as she approached, and reached for her—but reached too slowly. Already, she was behind him, bouncing again off a wall, then driving both of her booted feet into the back of his skull.

The monster staggered, but did not fall.

No doubt about it, Hawkeye thought. *Very bad*. Their team powerhouse was down, and didn't seem to be in any rush to get up again. Aloud, he said, "Hit 'em! Hit 'em with whatever you've got!"

Now didn't seem to be the time for finesse.

"What are these things?" MACH-1's electronically amplified voice demanded. The food court area was just big enough for limited flight and even more limited maneuverability, and he was making the best use of them he could. He banked tightly, swooped, fired a trio of anesthetic gas grenades at one of the Blitz Squad members. They had no effect, except, perhaps, to irritate the creature, who unleashed a volley of lightninglike charges in MACH-1's direction. "And don't they breathe?" he continued, even as he dodged.

"We can worry about that later," Hawkeye snapped. "Just get to their boss. That's our best chance." Reflexively, he loosed his already-nocked screamer arrow at one of the titans, even though he was reasonably sure it would do no good.

He was right. The Hydra super agent snatched the arrow in midflight and broke it before the ultrasonic device in its head could activate. Hawkeye had hoped to pain the creature, or enrage it, or merely disorient it with nerve-jangling sound, but the only reward for his effort was a moment's diversion.

That would have to be enough.

He drew another arrow and shouted another command. "No more of the gas bombs," he said. "They're going to get in our way." Already, billowing clouds of vaporized tranquilizer were drifting in his direction.

"I can take care of that," Songbird said. Her solid-sound wings had sprung into being again, but not to lift her in flight. Instead, she brought them back and forward in a bellowslike motion, and blew the gas in the general direction of the hostages and guards, clustered now at the mouth of one of several corridors leading to the food court area. A moment later, armed Hydra agents dropped to the floor, unconscious.

"Good move," Hawkeye said, meaning it. MACH-1's weapons were nonlethal; even if the captives blacked out too, they were in less danger now.

Only the so-called Blitz Squad remained to be dealt with, but from the looks of them, they were plenty.

Hawkeye was a demon marksman with an bow and arrow, with a skill, speed, and accuracy that bordered on the superhuman. He augmented that innate ability with a variety of special-purpose shafts. The screamer had been one; the one he launched now was another. Customized fletches at its butt guided the projectile weapon through a looping trajectory. As it flew, the arrow trailed a slender filament behind it, a looping cord that wrapped itself around one of the Blitzers. The cord appeared too fine to have any use as a restraint, but appearances were deceiving.

Let's see you try to break an adamantium tangler, Hawkeye thought grimly.

The Blitzer tried, and for a brief moment, seemed like it would succeed. The metal cord, made of the effectively immutable synthetic metal adamantium, cut deeply into the flesh of his muscles as he strained against its tightening loops. His struggles only made things worse; the arrow's curving trajectory became a tight spiral, winding him from head to toe in the unbreakable filament. Blood flowed as the tightly drawn line bit into golden flesh, accentuated by a crackling discharge of energy.

The Blitzer gave a moan of pain and collapsed, writhing, to the floor.

One down, Hawkeye thought. *At least, for the moment.*

Aloud, he yelled, "All of you, do your best to herd them away from the civilians." Then, nocking yet another arrow, he leapt once more into the fray.

Moonstone was the first to comply, firing bursts of energy that could shatter stone from her fingertips. Here, now, all they seemed to do was splash against the enhanced beings' bodies, creating a fireworks display as two kinds of energy interfered with one another. The effect must have been painful, however, because two Blitzers turned on her, reaching in the flying woman's direction with oversized hands.

"Naughty," Moonstone said. "This isn't that kind of encounter session." She fired bursts of energy at the Blitzers' eyes. This time, they had the desired effect: the pain her blasts caused was enough to make them run.

Hawkeye drew more arrows, launched them in the path of Moonstone's targets. The weapons in his quiver had been carefully chosen to offer him the widest range of capabilities in conflicts like these—basic tools that went a long way toward levelling the odds when he faced foes more physically powerful than he. The arrows he fired now had heads containing a compressed payload of low-viscosity lubricant with properties that had been carefully engineered by Tony Stark's scientists. The arrowheads shattered, spreading a thin chemical film along the hallway's stone-tiled floor. A split-second later, the first Blitzer's left foot went out from under him. With gratifying speed, the titan fell and skidded until he crashed into the offices of a luckless engineering firm.

The second didn't follow suit, however. As if learning from his brother's mistake, the next Blitzer paused in its flight, withstanding Moonstone's onslaught as he pondered the shiny patch of flooring in his path.

Hawkeye wondered what he was thinking.

The Blitzer's hands came up, and were suddenly shrouded in energy.

"Uh, Hawk, I don't like the looks of this," Moonstone said, still trying to drive her target forward.

Energy lanced from the creature's hands, found and struck the slick that Hawkeye had laid down.

Nice idea, he thought. *But that stuff's not flammable—*

The small sea of lubricant burst into flames.

—not supposed *to be flammable,* Hawkeye amended silently.

What kinds of energies did these beings command? Hawkeye found time to wonder that, even as blue-white flames reached for the ceiling.

Where had he seen energy effects like these before?

The Blitzer laughed, turned, raised his hands again. More energy sprang into existence in the air surrounding them, then shaped itself into two lightninglike discharges. One found the roof, smashed into it, and brought rubble raining down on the multitudes even as it revealed the sky.

The other blast found Moonstone's hovering form.

There was a blinding flash as the burst of energy struck her, and then her body was tumbling through the air, somersaulting again and again as she rushed toward a wall that looked particularly unyielding. Just before impact, however, something more forgiving blocked her path.

Atlas.

Recovered from his tumble, he had increased his height to the maximum allowable. With a gentleness that was strikingly at odds with his near-berserker fury of only moments ago, he intercepted Karla Sofen, inspected her for obvious damage, and set her down.

"Are you okay?" he asked anxiously.

"Um, uh," the blonde said, a dazed tone in her voice.

"Yes. Something about the energy they shoot—"

"No time for chitchat," Hawkeye snapped, stepping closer. "We've got the keep pressing these things." He looked at Atlas. "All calm now?"

Atlas's features took on a positively sheepish cast. "Uh, yeah, boss," he said. "I don't know what came over me."

Moonstone shook her head as if to clear it of cobwebs. In response to the convulsive movement, her thick blonde mane rippled and flowed. "I've got some ideas about that," she said in a distracted tone of voice. "If—"

"Later," Hawkeye interrupted. "if you're both okay, we've got to get back to work. I think we've got them on the run."

The battle was going reasonably well actually. Outnumbered and outpowered by the Blitz Squad, the Thunderbolts certainly weren't being outfought. With a fighting style born equally of brute power and tactical cunning, they had managed to keep the Hydra agents from making best use of their own powers. The one that Hawkeye had felled still lay, writhing, on the floor, trying without success to use his own energy field to incinerate the line that held him. His partner, the one who had fallen and slid into the distance, came stumbling back, only to pause in response to an instinctive fear of flames. If they could just keep up the pace, and corner and capture—

That was when Hawkeye suddenly noticed an absence that should have been obvious. He could only assume that the noise and confusion had diverted too much of his attention for too long.

"Hey," he asked, "where the heck is Zemo?"

Five floors below, in a place of white enamel and polished steel, two men wearing severely tailored civilian attire went about their work. Far below them, in turn, in secure subbasements and heavily braced minelike shafts were the inner workings of Fonesca's geothermal tap, the source of power for its nuclear-particle supercollider.

Onboard the *Barbarossa*, Corben and Veitch had spent many long hours on simulators and mockups, practicing their assigned duties. Now, working with the genuine apparatus and live equipment, they were able to complete their tasks precisely on schedule. Even so, long minutes passed before either had completed his assignment.

"Placement complete," the first Hydra agent said calmly. He had bolted his equipment case to one primary control bank, then set the nuclear device it contained. Now, he pressed the ball of this thumb against an exposed sensor plate, then nodded in acknowledgement as an LED display clicked to life.

63:00, it read, and then *62:59*. The numbers continued presenting themselves in reverse sequence.

"Device armed," Corben continued. He turned to his partner. "Status?"

Veitch looked up from his own work. Though still clad in civilian attire, he also wore thick, heavy gloves and rubber boots. They served to insulate him against the massive energy potentials enclosed within the cabinet he had opened, one of the main power processors from the site's geothermal tap. He had spent the several previous minutes incorporating the devices within his own equipment case into the cabinet's inner workings. They were modular items, with simple, almost simplistic exteriors, and easy to work with, but he knew that their shells concealed complexities that were nearly unimaginable. He set aside the small torch he had used to secure connections, and then drew a telescoping antenna from within the cabinet's interior. At the antenna's tip was a flat metal disk, perhaps a quarter meter in diameter, and bounded by a golden filament mesh that now hung in loose folds.

"Relay in place," Veitch said crisply. He peeled off one of the heavy insulating gloves he wore, and mimicked Corben's prior action, pressing the ball of his naked thumb against a sensitized plate at the antenna's base.

In instant response, a nimbus of energy formed around the exposed length of metal and around the disk that capped it. The air in the room became charged with ozone. On one wall, a series of displays presenting power output levels from the tap suddenly went blank.

Neither Corben nor Veitch seemed to notice.

A humming noise began, and built, and built some more. The mesh that surrounded the disk seemed to take on a life of its own, first writhing like a banner in a breeze, and then conforming itself into a hemispheric shape, with the open face turned upward.

Veitch drew a communicator from his belt and pressed a key. "Hail Hydra," he said.

"Status," came his section leader's response.

"Bomb placed and armed," Veitch said. "Relay placed and activated. All systems go."

The digital clock now read *58:46.*

"Excellent," Zemo responded.

Even with the roof sundered, the food court was filled with choking smoke and final, flickering fingers of flame. Somewhat to Hawkeye's surprise, the chaos was working in the Thunderbolts' favor and not against them. Apparently, the Blitz Squad agents' enhancements did not extend to their sensory abilities; the golden titans were disoriented by the smoke and flame. Though they still fought tenaciously, Hawkeye's team still continued to herd the Blitzers away from the hostages and into a relatively empty section of the facility.

"What now, chief?" MACH-1 asked.

Hawkeye wished he had an answer.

"This can't be all of them," Atlas said, even as he drove a fist into the abdomen of one Blitzer. The force of the blow was enough to drive the Hydra agent back and away. "Zemo can't have intended to hold this place with these forces," Atlas continued. "The joint is just too big. There must be reinforcements waiting in the wings."

"Maybe," Hawkeye responded. Then, "Songbird, over here!"

From above, a ram of pink energy, solidified sound born of Songbird's enhanced larynx, smashed into two more Blitzers. They tripped and tumbled, then fell.

"Try outside," Moonstone said.

"Outside?" Hawkeye asked.

"The reinforcements. There are least five more of these things, waiting at the other entrances. I did some reconnoitering."

"Did they see you?"

"Don't think so. If they did, they didn't show it. They looked like they were waiting for orders. Still, I think that means we'll have to fight our way out of here.''

As Hawkeye considered those words, Atlas dodged yet another blow from a Blitzer, then returned the hit, with interest.

This time, the creature didn't seem to notice.

''Uh, boss,'' Atlas said, even as another fist rushed toward him. ''Boss, I think we have a problem.''

Then he went tumbling backward again.

''Something's happening,'' Jolt said. She been leading one of the Blitzers along, stinging it with bioelectric punches and then dancing out of range of its returned blows. This time, however, she didn't dance quite fast enough, and a swung fist caught her delicate chin and sent her spinning. ''They're getting faster,'' she called, scrambling to her feet and then dancing backward, more swiftly this time.

Then Hawkeye noticed something. The first of the Blitzers to fall, still tangled in its adamantium leash, was struggling to his feet. Now, an exultant expression on his perfect features, he strained again at the cable holding him.

The adamantium didn't give, but the golden flesh straining at it did.

Hawkeye fought down a faint sense of nausea as the fine cord cut into the skin, muscle and bone, slicing mercilessly into the empowered creature. It released blood and energy once more, but left no other sign of damage behind.

The thing was healing instantly, even as the metal hawser cut completely through it. Already, the first of the strands had sawed through its left bicep and, presumably, the bone beneath, then fallen away in an open loop.

The Blitzer healed so swiftly that it seemed undamaged.

''My God,'' Hawkeye said softly. ''Faster, tougher—stronger?''

Then the Blitz Squad agent laughed, and he had his answer.

Chapter Eight

Somewhere above Virginia

Seen from a distance, in images relayed from long-range cameras, nothing seemed particularly amiss at the Fonesca Complex. Above the ground, it was a fairly unexceptional exercise in modern business architecture: a tower of office space flanking a long, lower wing that was two stories tall at its highest. Part of that lower roof had collapsed now, evidently at the prompting of a blast from below, and Iron Man could well imagine the chaos that must have ensued. A lifetime before, one of Tony Stark's previous companies had maintained spaces there, so he was familiar with its basic layout, even without reference to the blueprints that federal authorities had provided.

"The background in the ultimatum broadcast looked like the food court," he said. "My guess is, that's where the hostages are. It's big enough to hold them, and small enough to be secured."

"Then that's where we're headed," Captain America responded. "The hostages have to be our first priority."

"What about the bomb?" Wonder Man asked.

"The hostages have to be our first priority," Cap repeated. He looked at Iron Man. "Any luck raising Hawkeye?" he asked.

"No," Tony said reluctantly. "They've got some kind of scrambler in place, good enough to block out our frequencies. Even their own feed has gone dead now."

Cap didn't say anything.

"I'll take a look at it when this is all over," Iron Man continued. "See if I can come up with a workaround."

"That'd be a good idea," Cap said. "It's too bad, though. If we're going to let the Thunderbolts run around loose, we should be able to coordinate with them when we have to."

"Something funny about that," Simon said, slowly. "They were already on the scene, even before the broadcast began. Does anyone have any idea how that could have happened?"

"No, and I'm not going to worry about it, either. We agreed to give Hawkeye a chance with them. We can't complain because he's managed to beat us to the scene," Cap said.

''Zemo's there, too,'' Wonder Man said. ''Don't you think that's a bit of a coincidence? He's never worked with Hydra before. The T-bolts, sure, but not Hydra.''

''We'll worry about that later, Simon,'' Captain America said, with genuine irritation in his voice. ''Any connection between Zemo and the Thunderbolts is in the past. We've agreed to trust them, and we will. That's final.''

''What about the conventional authorities?'' Wanda asked. ''What are they doing?''

''Roadblocks and cordons in the surrounding area, but we get to handle the situation itself. There are already too many loose cannons rolling around, and we don't need any civilians getting hurt,'' Cap said. He glanced at Iron Man. ''Better continue briefing us,'' he said. ''We'll be there soon.''

Iron Man pointed at the display screen in front of him and Cap and said, ''Most of the heavy-duty hardware is underground.'' A similar, larger screen in the passenger area presented the same video feed to the rest of the Avengers. ''The supercollider, the geothermal tap, the rest of it.''

''That must be where they've placed the bomb,'' Captain America said.

Iron Man nodded. ''That part of it doesn't make much sense to me,'' he said. ''Sure, they can do a lot of damage with a nuclear device—any nuclear device—but the Piedmont is relatively stable, geologically speaking; they won't get much of an earthquake effect, no matter what Zemo said.''

''What about vulcanism?'' Justice asked. ''If the engineers at the complex have already bored down far enough to tap heat from the mantle, doesn't Zemo already have the beginnings of a miniature volcano?''

Again, Iron Man nodded. The mantle, the layer of molten rock that swirled beneath the Earth's crust, was nearer the surface in the Piedmont than in most continental regions; that was one reason for putting the tap there in the first place. ''That's a good point, and I suppose a shaped charge of the right power could effect an eruption,'' he said. ''But even so, I don't know how much of an effect it would have on neighboring states. Without knowing the bomb's force, or how it's configured—''

''That's not what I meant,'' Vance Astrovik interrupted.

"From what I remember of high school geology—"

Probably more than I do, Tony thought, with grim humor. *It was so much more recent for you, after all.*

"—volcanoes kick a lot of ash and debris into the upper atmosphere. When Krakatoa blew, it was years before the last of the ash fell, and when it did, it fell all over the world."

"I don't think we're looking at that kind of eruption here, Vance," Cap said. "We need to consider—"

Justice interrupted again. He spoke urgently, and with a forcefulness that reminded Iron Man that, before joining the Avengers, Vance had successfully served as team leader for a young team of heroes known as the New Warriors. "We need to consider that, in this case, that the ash will be highly radioactive," he said. "Depending on the type of bomb, we could be looking at another Chernobyl, with much more widespread effects."

Tony felt a wave of coldness sweep through him. Setting the quinjet on autopilot for the moment, he accessed his reference schematics again and reviewed them hastily. The angle of the bore, the composition of the surrounding strata, the prevailing meteorological conditions—the specifics of the bomb comprised a missing puzzle piece and a sizable one, but even without it, the picture suddenly looked remarkably grimmer.

"Vance," Cap said, "I know you want to help, but—"

"He's right," Iron Man said. "I was too close to the problem to see it myself. Even a conventional nuclear device detonated under these circumstances would distribute highly irradiated fallout over most of the Eastern Seaboard." He paused, and turned to face his copilot directly. "We're talking about farmland, Cap, and rivers and coastal fisheries. If Zemo's bomb goes off, it could be the end of the regional food industries for centuries to come."

Cap paused, drummed red-gloved fingers on the control panel. "And it's probably safe," he said slowly, "to assume that we're not talking about a conventional warhead."

"Probably not," Iron Man said. "A 'dirty' nuke, with an enriched uranium core jacket and surrounding osmium overlays seems more likely. Something small enough to carry in a briefcase, but strong enough to pack quite a punch." He took control of the quinjet again, and sent mental commands to its roaring engines.

Moving even faster than before, the quinjet raced through the afternoon sky.

Fonesca Complex, North Carolina

"Hail Hydra!" the Blitzer roared, as the last constricting loop of adamantium cord finished sawing through his legs. Skin, muscle, and bone all healed instantly, then the bloodied cord fell to the floor, and the monster reached for Hawkeye.

"Yeah, yeah, yeah," the archer said edgily, dancing out of his adversary's path even as he drew another arrow and launched it.

It struck the golden titan on his forehead and shattered on impact. The sticky stuff it contained trickled down to find and seal the Blitzer's eyes. The monster howled in renewed anger and tore at the obscuring film.

"Learned that one from Spider-Man," Hawkeye said crisply.

"Boss, we got a problem here," Atlas called. He had grown a bit larger than was really practical in the enclosed space, apparently in order to maximize his strength.

He needed it.

Three of the Blitzers had cornered him, and were pummeling his chest and gut. Atlas was doing his best to ward off the blows and to land a few of his own, but he was losing the fight.

"They're getting stronger," the embattled Erik Josten said. "Too strong."

"Songbird," Hawkeye yelled. "Over here!"

Melissa Gold had her hands full already, figuratively speaking. She had cast a globe of solidified sound energy around the head of one Blitz Squad agent, and was clearly struggling to keep it there. "Just another second," she said. "These things are immune to gas, but they still need air. If I can just—"

"Now!" Hawkeye snapped.

Melissa nodded, released the field.

"Moonstone," Hawkeye called. "Your turn! Pour it on!"

"Really, Hawkeye, just because you're the leader doesn't make us your slaves," Karla Sofen said, but she obeyed nonetheless. Her hands came together and up, and then a double burst of energy rushed from her fingertips and caught the Blitzer who had been Songbird's target.

The twinned bolts struck squarely in his open, gasping mouth.

"Maybe your insides are more vulnerable," Moonstone said, smiling sweetly.

As if in agreement, the Blitzer gasped again, then fell.

Meanwhile, Songbird had created a new barrier, a wall of pink energy that she interposed between Atlas and his attackers. Six fists slammed into to it, once, twice, three times each.

"It's a strain, but I think I can hold it," Songbird said, wincing.

Then the Blitzers gave lie to her words. They struck again, all three in unison, and the pink wall crumbled. It broke into fragments and then into less than fragments, as the energies that composed it broke down and dispersed in a way that Hawkeye had never seen before.

Melissa cried out in pain as the feedback struck her, but, to her credit, she tried again. A second wall of force appeared, this one more massive—heavy enough to withstand four rounds of blows.

Four, but not five.

This time, Songbird's cry was not of pain, but of sheer agony.

"My turn," Atlas said. He reached with oversized hands and grasped two of the Blitzers by the scruffs of their necks. The epidermis on his hands smoldered as the creatures' energy auras flared, but only for a moment. Like a child at play, Atlas threw the pair through the roof breach and into the distance.

"They're definitely getting stronger," Songbird said, as she repeated her englobement maneuver with the third operative. This time, she wasn't interrupted, and was able to hold the sphere of energy in place long enough for it to do its work. The Blitzer clawed at it, to no effect. After a long minute, he shuddered, then fell.

"We're fighting hard, but we're not going to win unless

we fight smart,'' Hawkeye said. ''We've got to find Zemo, or whoever's ramrodding this operation.''

The rushing air of the stratosphere's lower reaches became heavier and more dense, and then gave way to the troposphere's upper boundaries. The air not only became thicker, but in effect, warmer, as its density increased enough to hold appreciable levels of heat energy.

Thor scarcely noticed.

New York City and his allies were behind him; the Fonesca Complex and his foes were ahead and below. The power of his own strong arm and godly muscles propelled him through the air at supersonic speeds. An enchantment placed on his hammer Mjolnir enabled him to use it as a mode of flight—by spinning the hammer, he could accumulate force and momentum, and use that power to pull him through the sky. The method had its drawbacks, but its merits were undeniable.

On his own, Thor could move more swiftly than all but a very few vehicles, at least within certain ranges. That was why he had chosen to fly ahead of his fellow Avengers, despite Captain America's reservations. Now, however, he was nearing his destination, and searched the world below with his keen blue eyes, looking for the Fonesca Complex.

He saw something else, instead.

He saw something golden, something glowing, something that seemed to move with increasing speed as it rushed toward him. As it came closer, more details became visible, and then he realized it wasn't a something.

It was a someone—or, rather, two someones. The figures hurling in his direction were another pair of the golden titans he had encountered in New Jersey, perhaps even the same ones.

As they came closer, they caught sight of Thor. ''Hail Hydra!'' the first roared, reaching with clawed hands as he turned in midflight and raced toward the thunder god. The giant's hands burned as they grasped him, knocking Thor from his intended trajectory and sending him tumbling across the cloudless sky.

''Unhand me, knave!'' Thor thundered.

The Blitzer's only response was to hold him more firmly.

A moment later, the creature's arms had slid around and under Thor's, grasping him in a wrestler's grip.

A moment after that, and the second Blitzer was raining blows on the thunder god's abdomen.

Watching from behind a pillar, Zemo reluctantly conceded that Strucker had a point.

There was a certain allure to chaos.

Fire and thunder filled his world now, along with shouted commands and the sounds of battle. The insufferable Avenger Hawkeye was doing a reasonably good job in his self-appointed role as leader, and the Thunderbolts, for their part, were doing their best to meet the challenge of the Blitz Squad.

It pleased Zemo to realize that their best was not quite good enough.

At first, his erstwhile associates had made surprising headway against Techno's synthetic supermen, who were vastly more powerful, at least on a physical level—Zemo still had his doubts about their artificial intelligence levels.

From the moment that Veitch had activated the relay, however, the Thunderbolts had been doomed. The relay, based on his father's prototype, sucked energy from the complex's geothermal tap and fed it to the Blitz Squad, where it was expressed as increased strength, speed, and durability.

Not intelligence, however.

Brute power was proving to be enough to turn the tide of battle, as was so often the case. Songbird's shields were shattering beneath Zehn's blows, and Füngzehn had MACH-1 on the run. Sechzehn was warding off Moonstone's blasts with relative ease and even the accursed Jolt was having difficulty keeping out of Zwölf's reach. They might last a bit longer, but the team he had founded, the team that he had created, the team that had dared to betray him—that team was certain to fall.

It was only a matter of time.

A buzzing sound drew his attention. At first, he thought it was the discharge of one of the various weapons in play, but then he recognized it as the alert from his communicator. He opened the device and raised it.

"Zemo," he said.

Techno's familiar tones came back to him. "Strucker is monitoring the situation," he said. "He's getting antsy."

"And that should concern me?" Zemo felt a wave of irritation wash over him. Techno certainly should have known better.

"Not particularly, but I thought you'd want to know that the bald man is pitching a fit."

"I assume he cannot hear this conversation," Zemo replied. There was no need to rock Strucker's boat.

At least, not at the moment.

"C'mon, Baron—you know me better than that." Techno sounded mildly offended. "I'm using my internal transceiver and accessing my vocal processors directly; these words don't even visit my larynx before you hear them. Wolfgang is ten feet to my left at the moment, and as far as he knows, I'm just watching TV."

"Good. Do you have the readings you need?"

"More or less. The relay is working at optimal efficiency and the units aren't having any trouble processing the extra energy. How are things at Ground Zero?"

"You're aware that the Thunderbolts are here?"

"We caught that before you ended the feed. Wolfie was surprised; I wasn't," Techno said. "How are they holding out against the Blitz Squad?"

"Poorly," Zemo responded, with genuine pleasure. "The odds are against them."

There was a pause, and then Techno said, "Those odds are about to change. I just picked up an alert from the Air Traffic Controller's network. There's a quinjet entering your airspace in sixty, no, thirty seconds."

"The Avengers," Zemo said, not pleased. "Very prompt."

"They made good time. You might want to make a strategic withdrawal," Techno said.

"Perhaps," Zemo said. He glanced at his watch. Nearly forty-seven minutes remained until detonation—ample time to take his leave. "Make your preparations," he said. "I will be at the rendezvous point in twenty minutes."

"What about the Squad?"

"What about them? The main purpose of this exercise is to determine how useful their new powers are in a combat scenario. I see no reason to end that scenario prematurely. Indeed, I've already diverted the perimeter forces to the main battle.''

''Uh, they're good,'' Techno said slowly, ''but they aren't *that* good. They won't survive a nuclear blast.''

''So sound the retreat at the last moment,'' Zemo said with a snarl. ''I want to assess their performance against the Avengers. Besides, they still have another duty, remember?''

''Good point,'' Techno said. ''I'll tell Strucker that you're moving on to the next phase.''

''Do that,'' Zemo said. ''Zemo out.''

He pressed a button on his belt, and the same cloak of invisibility that had hidden the Blitz Squad earlier settled on his shoulders. Hidden from any private eyes, he made his way to the nearest elevator.

It was time to go—at least, for him.

Suddenly, it seemed as if the sky had opened and it was raining super heroes.

Songbird saw them first. She had lofted herself above the main part of the fray and was using a sonic hammer to drive one Blitz Squad operative into the floor like a tent peg. Most of her mind was occupied with the task at hand, but a corner of it was reserved for tracking the other flying Thunderbolts—Moonstone and Abe—so that she could avoid trespassing on their shares of the limited airspace available. Enough of her mind was occupied that she almost didn't notice the red-white-and-blue figure dropping down from the roof breach, sliding along a line that dangled from a hovering quinjet. When she did . . .

''Captain America!'' she cried, as he raced past her.

''No time for greetings,'' the living legend announced. ''But watch your back!''

Melissa finished with her target then spun, just in time to almost avoid a pair of clutching golden hands. They burned into the solid-sound stuff of her wings, dissipating them almost instantly.

Stunned, Songbird fell.

''Allow me,'' someone said, and Melissa found herself surrounded by red-hued energy that halted her descent. This time, however, it wasn't born of her enhanced larynx, but from someone else entirely—someone she recognized.

"Justice?" she said, recognizing the young hero.

Vance Astrovik nodded. "Thought you could use a hand," he said.

"Uh, thanks for the save," Songbird said, still startled. "Now that I can concentrate, I can take over." Pink wings sprang into existence around her again, and she rose from Justice's psychokinetic embrace. "Where did you come from?"

"Just now? New York," the young Avenger said. Drawn by his sudden appearance, the Blitzer who had been reaching for Melissa reached for him instead. The nimbus of psionic energy that was his mutant birthright condensed and formed a shield.

Instantly, it shattered as the Blitzer smashed one fist into it.

"They're tough," Justice said. "Better fill me in as we go."

"They're very tough," Melissa agreed, correcting him. Usually, she wasn't one for explaining much, but she felt she owed him for the save. Hastily, as they both fended off blows and crackling energy bursts, she told him of the earlier stages of the battle. Even as she spoke, however, she had an odd sense of otherworldliness.

She still wasn't used to working with the Avengers rather than against them.

"We were making headway—good headway—when they suddenly got stronger," she concluded. "All of them, and all at once." Another Blitzer rushed in her direction; reflexively, she moved from his path and created a rippling curtain of force like a banner where she had been. It did its job and drew his attention; a moment later, the Blitzer passed through it and then slammed headfirst into what lay beyond. The force was enough to imbed him, shoulders-deep, in a brick support pillar.

"They can't be getting any smarter, though," Justice observed.

The Blitzer struggled, trying to free himself.

"I never thought I would say this," a new, electronically amplified voice announced, "but sometimes, smart isn't what's needed." Iron Man's repulsors cut an incandescent path through the air and rammed the Blitzer deeper into the barrier. His exposed arms and legs thrashed convulsively, then were still. "Sometimes, what counts is raw power."

Melissa could agree with that point of view. Too many times in her life, over too many years, she had been in positions where just a little bit more strength—physical strength, or strength of will, but not intellect—would have made all the difference. The hardest lesson that life had taught her was also the simplest: Only the strong survived.

In the air around her, more Avengers came into view. Wonder Man unleashed a volley of hammering blows at two Blitzers, driving them back. The Vision indulged in a gambit similar to Songbird's, and led a pursuing golden titan toward a solid barrier before passing through it, with gratifying effect on the Blitzer when he tried to follow. The Scarlet Witch loosed her hex at one Blitzer, who staggered and fell, then, astonishingly, dwindled into ordinary human form.

"Justice," a commanding voice called. "I could use a hand here." It was Captain America, pursued by one of the golden titans. Apparently, he had been leading it away from the still-huddled hostages.

For a brief—very brief—moment, Melissa took some pleasure in the sight, but then she remembered something.

We're on the same side now, she reminded herself.

"I'll take it," she said to Justice.

An Avenger had come to her rescue, without comment or complaint, and now it was time to return the favor.

Effortlessly, she wrapped a heavy band of solidified sound around the Blitzer's face, sealing his mouth and eyes. Blinded and choking, the enhanced human still staggered forward, moving with so much momentum that the tendril of sonic energy that stretched between him and Songbird straightened and became taut.

It didn't break, however.

"Good one," said Justice, still hovering at her side. "So they still need to breathe."

Melissa nodded. "It takes a minute or so to shut them down, but they don't seem to recover very fast. I don't understand why, but—oh!"

Below, Captain America had slammed the edge of his

shield into the exposed under-jaw of the Blitzer. Now, with a cry of pain that was muffled but not smothered by his gag, the oversized warrior toppled.

"Maybe it's—whoah!" Justice cried out in shock and surprise as another sleek, airborne form nearly smashed into him. Like a bolt of lightning, Moonstone raced wordlessly past him and strafed another Blitzer.

"The odds are better, but it's getting crowded," Melissa said, and then she peeled off in search of more targets. "We'd better get back to work," she called back at him.

As she did, over the sounds of battle, she heard a distant rumble. Reflexively, she looked back at the roof breach, and saw that the sky was still cloudless.

What now?

The oversized assailants were stronger than had been their brethren in New Jersey, but more foolish. Whereas the other pair who had attacked him had fled almost immediately, these pressed the battle, unwilling to learn the simplest of lessons.

In combat with Thor, scion of Asgard and god of thunder, the advantage of surprise was a brief one, at best.

The arms pinning his felt like hot steel, far more obdurate than flesh and blood should be, and charged with some uncanny energy. Thor had no doubt that their grip would be sufficient against almost any foe that Hydra's hellish creations were likely to encounter.

Almost.

Unmindful of the paired fists raining blows on his belly, the god of thunder flexed his muscles and strained against the ones that held him. They resisted, but only for a moment, and then, as he knew it must, the hold broke. There was a sound like snapping tree limbs, and the arms held him no longer.

"Enow!" Thor thundered. His right hand still grasped Mjolnir; he drove the enchanted mallet's head into the jaw of the Blitzer who had been pummeling him, and again, there was the sound of something breaking. The Blitzer's eyes rolled back and he fell.

Thor fell, too.

The air whistled in his ears and his cape and hair both streamed outward as he plummeted. As he fell, he renewed his grasp on the hammer's haft and swung it again, in a tight arc that displaced air and drew him upward. Rising, he saw that the first Blitzer had recovered and was coming at him again.

"Enow!" Thor repeated. "You challenge the god of thunder and the true lord of the lightning, and against me, you shall not prevail!" A golden fist smashed into him, but he seemed not to notice. Instead, he spun the hammer faster and faster, until crackling sparks accumulated at Mjolnir's uru metal head.

The Blitzer struck him again, harder.

The lightning that Thor called down struck harder still.

It came down from the cloudless sky in a long, ragged course, a rippling river of energy that splashed against the two figures who grappled in midair. Even in broad daylight, the jagged, forking energy was searing in its brilliance, enough to turn the sky white for an instant. Thor roared with delight as it struck, and laughed exultantly as its primal force bathed him.

The Blitzer, however, cried out in pain.

He cried and he fell as the lightning came down from on high to smite him. His cries echoed as he fell, until they were drowned out by the thunder that echoed, more loudly, across the North Carolina sky.

Surrounded by flame and smoke and the din of combat, Captain America dodged another flailing fist, then rolled out of the path of another Blitz Squad agent. He brought up his shield again, let it blunt the hammering blow, then ducked into a cloud of concealing smoke.

This was getting him nowhere, he realized. The conclusion was as galling as it was undeniable—a fight against the Blitz Squad was not a fight he could win, at least not in the short run. Simply put, the battle already had too many participants—the Thunderbolts and the Avengers, and Blitz Squad forces that came close to outnumbering those of the combined teams. Neither side was acting tactically, and there seemed to be no way to change that.

To put it even more simply, he had to leave this kind of battle to those who were more qualified to fight it.

The smoke surrounding him roiled, parted, and something

came in his direction. Reflexively, he raised his shield and leapt for the newcomer. Incredibly, the costumed figure evaded his lunge and lashed out at him with one booted foot. Moving quickly, he twisted, dodged, reached out with one gloved hand—then paused as he recognized the slim attractive girl who stood before him as the youngest and newest of the Thunderbolts, and the only one who had no criminal past.

"Jolt," he said, startled.

"Captain America?" she returned, clearly startled. "What are you doing—"

"No time for that," he snapped. "How well do you know this place?"

"Pretty well," she said. "We had it staked out for two days."

"Good. Then you know where the geothermal tap is," he said grimly.

Jolt nodded, obviously puzzled, and obviously eager to get back to the battle. "Five flights down," she said, pointing at a stairwell.

"Show me," Cap said urgently.

"Why?"

"Because if you know where the tap is," Cap responded, "you know where the bomb is, too."

The Fonesca Complex's former food court was nothing but a battlefield now. Colorfully costumed forms grappled with one another, and not always according to their intended allegiances. More than once, in their eagerness to reach one Blitz Squad member or another, Moonstone or MACH-1 would cross paths with Wonder Man or Iron Man, and duck or dodge at the last moment. Once, Iron Man's repulsors glanced from one of Songbird's sound constructs, shattering it and setting free the Blitzer it enclosed. In instant response, the creature surged forward, eager to exploit his inadvertent freedom, only to be felled by another burst of energy from Iron Man's gauntlets. Inch by tenaciously fought inch, the two teams of heroes drove back the empowered Hydra agents, forcing them as far as possible from the still-unconscious hostages.

"Keep the pressure on," Justice yelled, exulting. "We've got them on the run."

"Not quite on the run, but getting there," MACH-1 responded, firing another run of low-yield explosive shells at one of the Blitzers.

"The question is, what do we do next?" Moonstone asked.

As if in answer, another rolling peal of thunder sounded. Reflexively, all looked up at the roof breach, and at the majestic figure who stood there, framed against the clear sky.

"Stand back, all," Thor bellowed, spinning his hammer. "None may stand before the god of thunder."

Instantly, the combined forces of the Thunderbolts and the Avengers fell back, and, equally instantly, the Blitz Squad agents swarmed forward in a superhuman, golden tide. They moved in perfect unison, with a speed more befitting a force of nature.

They did not move fast enough.

Again, lightning lanced down from the sky. It found the gray, blurred arc that Thor's hammer described as it spun, found the orbit and bounced from it—then raced downward to the golden horde below.

Again, there was the sound of thunder, all the more deafening for being in an enclosed space.

"Yow!" someone yelled. "Can you give us some warning next time?" The words came from one of the heroes, and not their foes.

No sound came from the Blitz Squad. Not a single syllable escaped the lips of the golden forms that lay in unconscious array on the tiled floor.

"Well, that's that, I guess," Moonstone said grimly as Thor dropped to the floor. "Nice to see how easy things are, when you bring out the big guns."

"Speaking of big guns," MACH-1. "Some of ours are missing. I saw Jolt go off with Captain America, but where are Hawkeye and Atlas?"

"And where's the Vision?" Wanda demanded, genuine worry in her voice. "Where could he have gotten to?"

Two Blitz Squad agents were waiting for Zemo when he reached the donut truck at the loading dock. They waited patiently and even amiably, with no expression whatsoever on their perfect features. As he came closer, both agents came to attention and saluted. "Hail Hydra!" they said.

"Yes, yes, yes," Zemo said, testily. Less than half an hour remained before the scheduled detonation, plenty of time to escape the blast area if he moved swiftly, but not enough time to waste on formalities. "Did you secure the captive?"

The first Blitzer—Sieben—nodded, then turned and opened the rear door of vehicle. Slumped inside were two humanoid forms—Atlas, now at human size, and the Vision. Both wore metal headbands studded with electronic modules.

"The android?" Zemo demanded. "Who directed you to capture the android?"

"I did," Sieben said, speaking in a voice that Zemo found unnervingly familiar.

Techno's voice.

"Explain yourself."

"Capturing Josten wasn't hard," Techno continued through Sieben's form, "especially not with all that ruckus going on. He can be knocked out, with a bit of effort."

"That's not what I meant," Zemo snapped.

"The Vision was a bit harder, but not really that difficult," Techno continued. "Even when he's immaterial, he has some interaction with the electromagnetic spectrum. It was just a matter of generating an eddy current effect in his—"

"How are you doing this, Techno?" Zemo interrupted. "And why?"

"How? That was easy—I just built a back door in the base artificial persona before I copied it. I can take over any of these things."

"And the Vision?"

"I told you I wanted Atlas for some further research into the ionization process," Techno said. Sieben's lips pulled back in a smile. "And let's just say, I can see some uses for the Vision, too."

Zemo didn't like the situation, but he didn't have time to argue the point. Instead, he slid behind the wheel of the donut truck and started it. "They'll be secure until I reach the rendezvous point?" he asked.

"They'll remain secure until I shut down the neutralizers," Techno replied.

"How long remains until the detonation?" Zemo asked. He flipped a switch on the donut truck's dash.

"Seventeen minutes," Techno said. "Plenty of time, but none to waste."

Zemo nodded, but said nothing as the outlines of the donut truck shifted and wavered. In moments, the cartoon mascot and ornate logo had faded from view, and the vehicle presented another, more businesslike visage to the world. Still boxy and awkward looking, the apparent truck that Zemo commanded was revealed as something more distinctive and more utilitarian.

It was a Hydra multipurpose, multiple environment personnel transport, sheathed in tough armor and powered by concealed turbines. It, and the other four like it, were capable of speeds and travel modes vastly more ambitious than those of the vehicles they impersonated.

"I'll meet you at *Barbarossa*, then," Zemo said. "We will talk of this."

Techno's only response was to allow Sieben's face to go blank again.

"Volcano?" Jolt asked. "I thought we were talking about an atomic bomb."

"We're talking about both," Captain America said. "It's a long story."

They were running down a flight of stairs, taking them two and three at a time. Jolt had pointed out a bank of elevators, but Cap had vetoed the idea, only too well aware how easy it would be to become trapped in midtransit.

"Well, these stairs *are* supposed to be used in the case of emergency," Jolt continued. "The tap is on a secure level—"

Locked doors loomed. Scarcely breaking stride, Captain America executed a flying drop kick and drove one booted foot through them. Alarms bleated and fragments flew as he continued on his course.

"—but not that secure," Jolt finished.

They rounded a corner, opened a final door, and nearly tripped over two recumbent forms. Both were men, and both wore severely tailored suits, accented with tightly wound loops of nylon cord.

The cord looked familiar, and Cap actually grinned as he saw that the restraint lines terminated in feathered arrows.

A familiar voice sounded across the polished white expanse of the geothermal tap chamber.

"Hey, Cap," Hawkeye said. "Good to see you. Maybe you can help me figure out this other dingus." He pointed at the silver and gold antenna that extended from one equipment bank. "It looks like an electrical umbrella, but there's got to be more to it than that."

"What about the bomb, Hawkeye?" Captain America said urgently. He was accustomed both to his former teammate's utter aplomb and also to his sense of humor, but this was no time for joking.

"The nuke?" Hawkeye asked. He gestured at another equipment bank, where a large LED display read *23:05*. Cap watched it carefully for five seconds, then ten, before he released his bated breath.

It still read *23:05*.

"I don't see why people always leave these things until the last minute," Hawkeye said. "Especially when they're so easy to defuse."

Chapter Nine

Fonesca Complex, North Carolina

"What now?" Hawkeye asked.

He asked the question of the ten other costumed figures, men and women, who stood clustered around him. They were in the sundered remains of the Fonesca Complex's food court. The place was relatively clear now; with the Blitz Squad subdued, it had taken only minutes to snuff the last bits of fire and exhaust the residual smoke, and only a few minutes more than that to deal with the various prisoners. Iron Man had estimated that the electrical blast delivered by Thor would be enough to keep the super-powered Hydra agents unconscious for hours, certainly long enough for the conventional authorities to secure them, and there appeared to be no real injuries to the civilian hostages.

That didn't mean there wasn't plenty to do.

"Now," Simon said, "the Avengers go after your old playmate, Zemo, and we bring back the Vision."

He spoke grimly, resolutely, and perhaps even with a trace of guilt in his voice. Simon Williams and the Vision had a long and tangled history together. Years before, a recorded copy of Wonder Man's encephalographic traces had formed the basis of the Vision's artificial intelligence, making them something like brothers. Later, after Simon had returned from his apparent death, he had felt a strong attraction to Wanda—who was, at that point, married to the Vision. Now, with Simon returned from a second deathlike experience and having taken the Vision's place at the Scarlet Witch's side, there were still ties between the two. Sometimes those ties manifested themselves as dissension, and sometimes as protectiveness.

In that, at least, there was still much about them that was brotherly.

Hawkeye shook his head. "That's not how it works, Simon," he said. "I've logged more miles in this business than you have, and I've learned one thing—you don't turn your back on a teammate. Ever."

"But—"

"The Vision and I were teammates before you even met

him,'' Hawkeye continued, ''and I won't turn my back on him—or on Atlas. We're in on this.''

''All of us are,'' MACH-1 said grimly. ''We haven't come this far, made this many sacrifices, to stand aside and let someone else do our jobs.''

''They're your jobs because we let you have them,'' Simon said pointedly. ''The main reason that you people are still running around loose is because we've agreed to look the other way.'' He raised one finger, pointed it at MACH-1. ''If you want to—''

''Point it somewhere else, Avenger,'' MACH-1 said, the concern in his voice giving way to anger. ''Our teams made a deal, and *my* team wants to honor it. All I want is for you to do the same. Trust us.''

Wonder Man kept pointing. ''That's a laugh,'' he said. ''Honor among—''

''Simon,'' the Scarlet Witch said sharply. ''No more bickering. The fighting is over.'' Her red-gloved hands grasped his bicep, pulled his arm back and down. Wonder Man was strong enough to break mountains, but he wasn't strong enough to resist her. Grudgingly, he lowered his hand.

''But—''

''It's over,'' Wanda said, even more sharply this time. ''We have to worry about our missing teammates and not about who gets to be the hero.'' Her concern was obvious and immediate; it hadn't been so long ago that she and the Vision were still an item. ''The job is what matters, not who does it.''

''I think we need to look at who has the best chance of succeeding,'' Firestar said slowly. Even in her short time with the team, she had become known for her businesslike approach. ''The Avengers have clearances and formal standing here. The federal authorities called us in, and we already have jurisdiction—official jurisdiction. That means there will be questions when everything is said and done. You still have reserve status, Hawkeye; why don't you represent the Thunderbolts and help us get Atlas and the Vision back? There must be plenty of—''

Hawkeye shook his head. ''It doesn't work that way,'' he repeated. ''If I'm not going to turn my back on Atlas, I'm certainly not going to turn my back on the rest of the team.

We're in on this, whether it's with the Avengers or without you. That's final."

"I can *not* believe this," Jolt interrupted. "Zemo and Hydra have Erik—they have the Vision—and all you guys want to do is argue about who's going to do what!" She tapped one foot, providing a girlish reminder of just how young the newest Thunderbolt was. "Well, I tell you what we're going to do, we're going to do what's right."

"And we're going to do it together," Captain America's level tones interrupted the increasingly tense conversation. As he approached the costumed grouping, he moved with the effortless grace of a great athlete, and the air of one accustomed to command. He came striding up from a convenient stairwell and approached the group; a moment later, Moonstone's sleek form rose through the tiled flooring and stood beside him. The two had gone to do some reconnoitering while Hawkeye and the others conferred. Now, however, Cap was plainly concerned at the tone that the conference had taken.

The others fell silent.

Captain America clapped one hand on Hawkeye's shoulder and continued. "We made a promise to you about the Thunderbolts, Hawkeye, and we're going to keep it. You have my word on that. I hope that's good enough."

"Of course it is, Cap," Hawkeye said, somewhat abashed as he took the Avenger's other hand and shook it. "You know that."

Behind him, Simon Williams muttered something too softly to be heard—or, at least, softly enough that the others could pretend they had not heard it.

"Besides," Cap continued, ignoring him, "there's more to this than meets the eye. From all indications, this is just part of a major initiative on the part of Hydra and Zemo, much bigger than just an exercise in global blackmail. Strucker talks a lot these days about the alleged glories of global chaos; my guess is, he's moving his plans for such into high gear. Imagine how much damage he could cause—how much chaos—with an army of those creatures."

"The Blitz Squad," Hawkeye noted. "Zemo called them his Blitz Squad."

"Which proves this is one of Strucker's personal projects,"

Cap said. "Those words don't mean anything to Zemo, but they do to Strucker. He led a special operations unit during the war that used that title. He must be feeling nostalgic."

Hawkeye nodded. "A lot of Hydra splinter factions have crawled out from underneath a lot of rocks in the last few years. At first, I thought ol' Helmut must be working with one of them, but from what you say, he must have linked up with the real deal."

"That makes sense," Moonstone said. "They're very similar personality types."

"Too similar, probably," Iron Man said. "I wouldn't care to make any wagers on how long any such partnership would last."

"Which makes finding our teammates all the more urgent," Captain America said. He glanced towards the red-and-gold uniformed woman to his left, an odd expression on his face. Moonstone had been a tenacious and calculating foe of the Avengers; as an ally, she was still something of an unknown quantity, with motives that were perhaps less altruistic than others on her team. Despite that, she was undeniably competent, and had made some useful discoveries during their reconnaissance.

"We found the vehicles Zemo used to infiltrate this place," Karla Sofen said, speaking at Captain America's silent prompting. "Or some of them—a batch of trucks that are really disguised personnel transports. With a little effort, we recovered some interesting information from their navigation systems. I think we can retrace their steps, and find wherever it is that Strucker keeps his offices these days."

"Unless they left the fleet here for us to find," Wonder Man said. "It could be a trap."

Moonstone shook her head. "There's a way around that, I think." A smile that was both malicious and mischievous suddenly formed on her lips; she had a demonstrated track record at divining which buttons to push to produce a desired effect. "And I think you'll find that you need us for it to work."

"Whatever it is, we've got to get moving, and quickly," Iron Man said. "I don't want to have to explain this alliance to anyone. Looking the other way is one thing, but—"

Hawkeye grinned. ‘‘Hey, c'mon, ShellHead,’’ he said. ‘‘Since when do you worry about the company you keep?’’

***Barbarossa*, deep beneath the Atlantic Ocean**

‘‘A provisional success, then,’’ Strucker said to Zemo and Techno. His voice was so cold that icicles seemed to hang beneath each word. ‘‘And that, only if we discount our personnel losses entirely.’’

Zemo made no reply, but Techno did. ‘‘Personnel losses?’’ the mechanical man asked. He made a sound like laughter. ‘‘What personnel losses?’’

Strucker gazed at him. ‘‘Twenty loyal Hydra agents captured,’’ he said, ‘‘and ten members of the Blitz Squad.’’ Five of the enhanced agents had withdrawn from the field battle and made their way to a rendezvous point, where they had joined Zemo on his way back to Hydra's subsea fortress.

‘‘Thirty men, then,’’ Techno said. ‘‘Out of the untold thousands you command. And if there's one thing I've learned in the last year or so, Baron, it's that meat is cheap.’’

‘‘Yet you seem to have gone to some trouble to secure an excess of such an inexpensive commodity,’’ Strucker sneered. He gestured. Less than five meters distant, unmoving and unhearing, lay Atlas and the Vision. Both were securely bound to horizontal examination tables, and covered with electronic pickups and leads and other analysis equipment. Both still wore the module-studded headbands that ensured their continued unconsciousness.

Strucker glowered at Techno. Since their earlier conversation, Ebersol's demeanor had changed somewhat; he was less conciliatory, more confrontational. Strucker had seen that sort of change before, and it was usually a sign of shifting allegiance. Recruiting him to Hydra's ranks no longer seemed like such a good idea.

When this business was said and done, the former Norbert Ebersol could share Zemo's ultimate fate, the fate of all who failed Strucker, or who were foolish enough to betray him.

‘‘The relay worked,’’ Techno said. ‘‘That's what matters. We can manufacture Blitzers until the cows come home—I've already got more in process—and we can increase their base power levels to a nearly infinite extent. It's just a matter of moving energy around."

" 'Just a matter of moving energy around,' " Strucker quoted. "You are remarkably casual in your use of Hydra's resources, Ebersol. Tell me—why did no one think to retrieve the relay from the facility?"

Zemo had been silent for long minutes, listening as Strucker made one mistake after another. The first had been to mistake Techno's basically cooperative nature for weakness; the second, greater one had been to mistake Zemo's silence for compliance. Finally, wearying of the older man's self-aggrandizing management style, he spoke.

"Enough," he said. "The relay's secrets are part of my father's legacy, and are none of them Hydra's assets. The unit left behind at Fonesca was engineered to burn itself out after an hour. By now, it is nothing but junk." He paused. "Its secrets remain mine, and mine alone."

Strucker glanced in Zemo's direction now, fixed him with a steely blue gaze. "I may choose to differ with that stance," the Supreme Hydra said. He purred the words.

"Many make wrong choices," Zemo said simply. He seemed utterly at ease as he spoke, but every muscle in his body was tensed, and his hidden eyes searched Strucker's for the faintest sign of attack. He knew that his cybernetic associate was doing the same, and presumably with senses that were more varied and acute than Zemo's own. He and Techno had discussed this eventuality more than once, even quoting Strucker's own words.

"Alliances form and alliances dissolve," Strucker had said, in a cluttered, dusty bookshop, standing mere inches from that shop's deceased proprietor. *"Treaties are written to be broken."*

Was this the moment? Was this the turning point?

Strucker shrugged, and some fraction of his perpetual fury seemed to dissipate. "A matter to discuss another time," he said grudgingly. He gestured at the two unconscious forms recumbent before them. "What of the prisoners? Why have you brought the enemy to my stronghold?"

"I wanted to examine Josten," Techno said. "Just like I want to make a more extensive survey of Wonder Man.

They're the two longest-lived survivors of the ionization process, and they've both continued to mutate since their original transformation. They've gained new powers—Atlas can grow now, for example, and Wonder Man seems to have become unkillable. Their bodies might hold clues to further enhancements."

"That doesn't explain the Vision's presence here," Strucker said.

Zemo had been wondering about that, too.

"The Vision?" Techno stepped closer to the test bed that held the unconscious android. Except for coloration—red—the captive Avenger's features appeared precisely human, even peaceful, as he slumbered under the influence of Techno's equipment.

"The Vision is a machine," Techno said. "Remarkably complex, and perhaps the closest ever simulation of a living human being, but a machine nonetheless." He gave another steel grin. "I like machines. I like studying them, I like taking them apart, I like seeing what makes them tick. I want to do all that to the Vision, not necessarily in that order." He paused, and spoke to both of them when he continued. "That, gentlemen, is why he's here. I wanted him and because I could get him."

"He is an enemy," Strucker said curtly. "He must be executed."

Techno's only response was to smile more broadly.

Strucker turned his baleful gaze on Zemo. "And what of you?" he demanded. "Why have you forsaken Hydra's colors?"

"Because they are Hydra's," Zemo said testily. "They are not and never will be my own. I played your masquerade game for camouflage purposes, and because it supported morale, but no more. In this enterprise, I am your associate, not your subordinate. I will no longer allow the world to think differently."

Reluctantly, grudgingly, Strucker nodded again. "I've heard similar words from others," he said, "few of whom spoke them twice. Have a care, young Helmut, that you do not share the fate of others who spoke them."

He turned and walked away. A moment later, the steel portal to the lab space slammed shut behind him.

"Can we speak safely?" Zemo asked. "Surely he has this space monitored."

"Please," Techno said. "The first thing I did when I got here was infiltrate the alarm and surveillance systems. Right now, three decks above us, two junior grade operatives are diligently recording our conversation, both audio and visual feeds." He paused, considering. "We're talking about South America and the weather there, and how the hunting must be this time of year. Guy stuff."

Zemo nodded. "Excellent," he said. "Now, what of the Vision?"

"What of him?"

"Why did you bring him here?"

"I've answered that question once, Baron. There's no need to ask it again." Techno's artificial eyes glinted. "Both you and Wolfie have agendas of your own. Why shouldn't I?"

For a long moment, Zemo gazed at him, trying to fathom whatever secrets hid behind Techno's artificial eyes. Then: "Fair enough. See to it that he remains secure." Zemo frowned, annoyed at how much his tones sounded like Strucker's.

"Oh, I will," Techno said. "He's not going any—*uh.*"

He paused.

"Well?" Zemo demanded. "What is it?"

"I'm getting a transmission," Techno said. "It's on one of the frequencies we used as the Thunderbolts, and it's for you." He stepped closer to a wall-mounted communicator, then inserted a finger-probe in one socket on its control panel. "Here. I'll patch it through to the big screen."

Zemo nearly spat as a familiar visage filled the curved glass display.

"Hello, Baron, Norbert," Karla Sofen said, with a poisonous smile. "It's been a while."

"Would that it had been longer," Zemo snarled. "What is it you want, Meteorite?"

"It's Moonstone, remember? And what I want—what we want—is Atlas," said the woman who had once been his less-than-trusted lieutenant. "You've got him; give him back."

"You've become remarkably loyal to your fellows, all of a sudden."

Moonstone made no response, but simply smiled some more.

Zemo's mind raced as he tried to fathom the unfathomable. Sofen had always been the wild card in the Thunderbolts team. It was a given that she acted only in her own interests, but there was no telling what those interests were.

In that, he supposed, they were somewhat alike.

He looked pointedly at Techno, whose only response was an eloquent shrug.

"Don't bother trying to trace the signal, Baron," Moonstone said, noting the move. "The only way you're going find out where we are is if I let you, and the only way that's going to happen is if you give us Atlas back."

"You'll have to do better than that," Zemo said dismissively. "I've craved vengeance against the lot of you for too long to sacrifice this opportunity. Josten's sins against me, in particular, merit considerable and special attention." Atlas's ties with the Zemo dynasty were the oldest of any of the Thunderbolts, and his betrayal had been the most emphatic and most repeated. Originally a member of Heinrich Zemo's mercenary forces, Erik Josten had pledged himself to Helmut's eternal service some years later.

Pledged himself, and then reneged on that pledge. That betrayal was ameliorated only slightly by Atlas saving Zemo's life after the baron's defeat at the hands of the Avengers, Fantastic Four, and Thunderbolts.

"I can give you something you want more," Moonstone said, still smiling, but speaking now in brisk, even businesslike tones. She stepped away from her communicator so that her shapely form no longer blocked its lens. Now, the field of view showed something else—or, rather, someone else.

It showed Captain America.

Baron Zemo's oldest foe lay on the deck plates of what Zemo now realized was a Hydra personnel transport, presumably one of several left behind at Fonesca. He was wrapped in many windings of heavy rope and gagged, and his piercing blue eyes seemed to meet Zemo's as they stared out from the communicator's screen.

It looked too good to be true.

It had to be too good to be true.

"Explain yourself," Zemo snapped, but all he really wanted from Karla just now was a moment to think.

This was impossible. He had already satisfied himself that some manner of alliance existed between his former team and the accursed Avengers, and it was difficult to reconcile such an alliance with what he saw now. True, Karla Sofen was motivated by self-interest to the near-total exclusion of all else, but he couldn't see her doing this—surrendering both an ally and an alliance. To save herself, certainly, or perhaps to ransom Jolt—but not for Josten's sake.

"There's not much to explain," Moonstone said. "You've got Atlas; we want him. The reverse applies to Captain America, and I know you want him more than you want Josten."

Once, that had been true. Once Zemo's most heartfelt wish had been for vengeance against Captain America, the man who had been his father's greatest enemy. In more recent months, he had moderated his views, recognizing that it was less important to follow Heinrich's path than to extend it.

Captain America would fall, but the world might well fall first.

There was, however, another whose crimes against him cried out more emphatically for vengeance. Only a few months before, Moonstone had faced him in solo battle, and used her enhanced physical powers to hand him a humbling defeat.

It would be good to repay her for that.

Aloud, he said, "An exchange, then," and nodded.

Moonstone nodded, too. "I know the way you and Techno work. No matter what deal you've cut with Strucker, you've built an out for yourself, a back door. Let us in, meet with us, make the trade, and then you can go back to whatever game you're playing, no questions asked. We just want Erik."

That had to be a lie, too.

Zemo nodded. "And what assurances do I have that you will not act against me once more?"

"None," Moonstone said, almost cheerfully. "Except maybe strategic self-interest. As I said, I know the way you work. Whatever alliance you have going with Hydra can't be particularly stable, so you won't do anything to draw attention to yourself unnecessarily. As for us, we're not eager to take another pounding from those shock troops of yours."

"How did you capture Captain America? And why?"
Moonstone smiled.
"Answer me!" Zemo demanded.
"No more answers," Karla Sofen said. "No negotiations. I've made you an offer. Take it or leave it."
Zemo glanced again at Techno.
Ebersol shook his head, used metal lips to silently mouth the words, "It's a trap."
Zemo almost laughed. Did Techno truly think him that gullible?
"Accepted," he said. "Techno will provide you with the coordinates and recognition codes."
"I will?" Techno exclaimed. "You can't—"
"Do it," Zemo commanded, spinning on one heel and striding from the room. "I have preparations to make."

"Do you really think this will work?" Jolt asked, as the communicator's screen blanked and went dark.
Moonstone looked at her. "Of course it will," she said calmly. "For all his accomplishments, Zemo is not an especially complex man. His goals are grandiose in scale, but basic, even simple in their nature. He wants to rule the world and he wants revenge on his enemies. Offer him one or the other, and he'll eat out of your hand."
"Eat your hand, more likely."
"He's smarter than that," MACH-1 said slowly. "I know what you're saying, but he's good at scheming, too. The whole Thunderbolts scam was his idea, after all."
"And look how well it turned out," Karla said, smiling again.
"Hey, it took a while, but I think it's turned out pretty well," Jolt protested. She was still the most idealistic of the team, and had been constant in her allegiance since joining it after the death of her parents.
"Uh, that's not what she meant," Melissa said. "She meant, it didn't turn out very well for him."
"Oh."
"We'd better alert the others that the shark has risen to the bait," Moonstone said.
"What about Cap?" Jolt asked, stepping closer to the cap-

tive Avenger and kneeling to loosen his bonds.

"Leave him," Moonstone said. She looked down at Captain America, who had contended with her more than once during her criminal past. "You understand, don't you?" she asked sweetly. "Techno got a good look at you, at your bonds and gag, and he's got a photographic memory—literally. If anything's changed when he sees them again," she continued, "well, we don't want to tip our hand early, do we?"

Cap made no response.

He couldn't, really.

Chapter Ten

Somewhere beneath the Atlantic Ocean

Far below roiling, white-capped waves, long past the lingering reach of the sun's illuminating rays, fish mouths gaped even more widely than usual and the subsea creatures raced in all directions as an armored craft swept through their midst. It was an odd-looking vehicle, and scarcely seemed adapted to aquatic travel—boxy and blunt, it labored hard to push the water from its path, and harder to compensate for the rear turbulence that its angular lines created. It was driven forward by four lateral turbine engines extending from its underside on jointed mounts that shifted from one set of angles to another as the craft's pilot steered it. Each of the offset engines was about the size of a truck tire.

A short time before, that was what they had resembled.

"I can't believe this," Hallie Takahama said. "We're roaring around on the bottom of the ocean in a UPS truck." It was a toss-up which had surprised her more—the fact that the coordinates of Hydra's base were many miles from and countless fathoms below any surface landmass, or the strange nature of the craft used to span that distance.

Seated next to her in the passenger hold of the commandeered Hydra transport, Karla Sofen muted a sigh of annoyance. She liked Hallie well enough—not that she liked anyone very much—but at times, the teenaged girl's, well, *girlishness*, could become annoying. "It's not a UPS truck, Hallie. We've been over that."

"The sign on the side said FedEx," Melissa Gold interjected. She was staring pensively from a viewport set in the strange craft's hull, as if looking for something important in the darkness beyond.

Moonstone allowed herself to be annoyed, and allowed herself to show it, too. "That was a hologram," she said sharply. "Possibly Techno's work, but I wouldn't bet on it."

She had found the supposed delivery vehicle in Fonesca's loading bay. Iron Man and MACH-1 had worked together to assess its capabilities and figure out how to operate it, a procedure that seemed so easy that Moonstone had to wonder about the minimum technical competence required of a typical

Hydra agent. The most complex controls had been those of the navigation system. Operating everything else—camouflage mode, communications, weaponry, steering, and acceleration—were simple in the extreme. Inboard computers had even done the work of configuring the multienvironment vehicle for aerial and then subsea travel, once the right buttons were pushed.

The term *idiot-proof* came to mind.

"Hydra has fielded some idiosyncratic equipment over the years," she continued.

"Oh? Speaking from experience?" Melissa asked, still gazing into the suboceanic gloom.

Karla didn't answer. She didn't see much point in doing so. Melissa didn't need the information, and she didn't need anything from Melissa that would justify the courtesy. Instead, she directed her next words to MACH-1, whose armored form was tightly wedged in the driver's seat.

"Abe?" she asked. "Do you have an ETA yet?"

"Nope," came the response. "Techno downloaded a bunch of code into the navigation system. I checked it out as best I could—there doesn't seem to be anything dangerous—but he configured it so that the nav has to process it in chunks. We're on the third segment now, and there are three more to go."

"But—you have to have some idea, at least," Hallie said. Since embarking on the journey she had alternated between effusive good spirits and mild apprehension.

The girl really likes Atlas, Moonstone thought. Liked him in the purest sense of the word, and not as some kind of schoolgirl crush. Of all the team members, Jolt was probably the strongest in her desire to retrieve Josten, and certainly the most anxious.

MACH-1 had removed and set aside his domed helmet, revealing Abe Jenkins's handsome features. Now, he wriggled out from behind the control panel and stepped back into the passenger area. "Nope," he said. "We might as well be on autopilot now. Even the nav display has shut down. Ebersol may be maladjusted and pretty close to sociopathic, but he's good with machines. You've got to give him that."

Look at him, Karla thought. *His armor and weapons—the very face he wears—are all Techno's work, and he's acting like he's just realized why Techno used to be called the Fixer.*

Shortly after Zemo had brought the Thunderbolts together, one of Norbert Ebersol's first assignments had been to "fix" the faces of some members, giving them new civilian features to go with their new costumed identities. Abe had been among his subjects; Karla had not. She was quite comfortable with who she was, if not with the path her life had taken, and she had balked even at changing her code name to Meteorite.

That was one reason that she was Moonstone again.

"So we could be going into a trap," Jolt said.

Karla almost laughed. "Of course we're going into a trap," she said. "The only thing that gives us a chance of getting out of it is that Zemo hates Captain America more than he does us."

Cap, still bound and gagged, didn't make any reply. He hadn't registered any real opposition to remaining gagged as they positioned him on one seat and secured him there. Jolt had made some efforts to make him comfortable.

Moonstone hadn't.

Captain America was hardly her favorite person in the world, and among her least favorite Avengers. Their paths had crossed early in her criminal career, when she was still with her ally and mentor, Dr. Faustus, and again when she was allied with the Corporation. She didn't particularly hate the Captain—that would have been a waste of mental energy—but it didn't bother her to see him discomforted.

"Do we even know if they're following us?" Melissa asked. She spoke more softly now, apparently more at ease with Abe seated beside her, but her large, expressive eyes were still fixed on the darkness outside. "We don't know what we're in for. I'd feel better if I knew my back was covered."

"It is, Melissa," Abe said. He draped one armored arm around her shoulders and drew her close. "I'm not going anywhere."

"Yet," Melissa said even more softly.

Moonstone considered the exchange and mentally filed it for future reference. Melissa had shown some fascinating psychological tendencies of late, and this might explain some of them. Fairly obviously, she was severely stressed by the fact that Jenkins intended to face the music for his past crimes.

The ramifications of that promised to be interesting, and worth observation.

"She meant, covered by the Avengers," Jolt said.

MACH-1 nodded. "Iron Man took care of that," he said. "Phased-frequency, scrambled-protocol transponder as a backup to the nav coordinates." Now, he looked out at the darkness, as if trying to see what fascinated Melissa so. "They're out there," he said. "You can count on that."

"How do you think Hawkeye's doing?" Jolt asked. The archer had remained with the other team, so that his presence with the Thunderbolts would not reveal their ruse earlier than necessary.

"I'm sure he's enjoying the Avengers' hospitality just as much as their leader is enjoying ours," Moonstone said dryly. She wasn't surprised when no one laughed at her witticism.

They rarely did.

The *Barbarossa*

Techno unplugged his fingertips from the first databank and stepped to the second. He inserted the articulated connectors into another set of ports, then recommenced the data download. Immediately, data began to flow from the computer to and into his fingertips, then along the oxygen-exhausted superconductor linkages that ran along his arms and led to the modular, microembossed silicate hard drives hidden in his chest. He had installed the small-size, high-capacity storage units there against precisely this moment—the moment when the simmering tensions between the two barons reached a flashpoint.

That was what this was about, of course. Zemo's motive for inviting the Thunderbolts onboard wasn't as clear-cut as even he seemed to think. He wasn't doing it to capture Captain America or even to avenge himself on the others. He was doing it at least partly to spite Strucker. Techno could see that, even if Helmut himself could not.

Sometimes, there were advantages to being an observer of the human condition, rather than a full participant in it.

The hard drive in the console clicked to a halt, and the one in his chest flashed a signal to his mind's eye, telling him that the job was done. The first databank had held all that he had been able to glean from Heinrich Zemo's notebooks and prototypes; the second had held the field-test telemetry and diagnostics data from the Blitzers, along with their artificial personality configuration parameters. With this data stored safely away, he would be able to re-create what he had done here this day, in safer circumstances of his own choosing. He hoped that the facilities would be as good, but he had to doubt it.

This lab space had been the biggest advantage of his three-way alliance with the two German barons. Equipment, staff, data processing capabilities, and test subjects—all had been available in effectively limitless quantities. His own assets were considerable, but Hydra's went far beyond them.

And, of course, they had something else, too.

Techno withdrew his finger-probes and ambled over to the two testing stations that held Atlas and the Vision. Automated probes had already recovered most of the data he wanted from his former teammate, but the android was another matter entirely. The Avenger demanded his personal attention, and time that he had been unable to spare.

Time that was running out.

He thought about that for a moment, considering the opportunity and regretting the need to pass it by.

Need?

With a slight grin, Techno retracted the data probes and extended another set of different, sharper ones. His downloads were complete, and he could leave at a moment's notice, which meant that he could spare a second or two. He placed his hand on the Vision's face, and grinned more widely as the whirling drill bit at the tip of his index finger bit into the android's red synthetic flesh. Curlicues of red plastic fell as it bored deeper. In moments, the initial probe had found a primary nerve conduit, and a moment after that, Techno had connected with and was scanning the impulses it carried.

Won't hurt to take a peek, he thought.

The Vision twitched.

• • •

Somewhere else beneath the Atlantic Ocean

"Hey, ShellHead," Hawkeye said. "Answer a question for me?"

Iron Man didn't look up from the submarine controls as he responded. "Go ahead."

"If the Avengers are really the best-equipped super hero team in the world, how come Hydra's the outfit with the flying submarines?"

It had taken the better part of an hour to return to New York, board the Avengers' submarine, and launch it from its berth beneath the mansion. Ten minutes later, the sleek, futuristic craft had emerged from a hidden underwater tunnel and into the East River, and thence into the Atlantic Ocean. It had been a quick process, but not quick enough for Hawkeye, who was champing at the bit to return to the field of battle.

"Different needs, different priorities, Hawk," Iron Man said. "The quinjet is a high-speed, quick-response tactical vehicle, optimized for atmospheric travel—it's even capable of low-orbit hops. Hydra made a different tradeoff—sacrificing speed for flexible use. Besides, the quinjets are capable of being used underwater, but they're less reliable the deeper you go. And the sub has more room to ferry all fourteen of us back when this is over."

He was seated at the submarine's controls, carefully monitoring a computer-generated, three-dimensional representation of the surrounding sea bottom. Just now, the Avengers' submarine was moving swiftly through a ragged maze of underwater mountains. It stayed close to the hidden peaks to minimize the chance of detection, but never strayed far from the course coordinates provided by the captured Hydra vessel.

Hawkeye asked, "Any idea on our ETA?"

"None at all," Iron Man said. "I can't even tell where they're heading—it's been a zigzag course that covers a lot of territory. I'd guess that someone thinks the T-Bolts might be followed."

"Sounds like a pretty smart someone," Simon said. He had been the least enthusiastic of the Avengers regarding this gambit, and didn't mind saying so. "He probably wouldn't let his team leader be used as a bargaining chip, especially not to ransom someone like Josten.''

''And the Vision, our own good comrade,'' Thor noted. ''E'en so, the wheel has turned, and Josten is our comrade at arms now, and merits our concern.''

''Hmph,'' was Wonder Man's only response.

Atlas was not and never would be the Avengers' favorite member of the Thunderbolts. In his earlier criminal career, as Goliath, he had been among the Masters of Evil task force that had invaded and nearly destroyed Avengers Mansion. That was bad enough; what was worse was that he had helped beat one Avenger, Hercules, nearly to death. Not even Moonstone, then Zemo's second in command, had gone that far, and not even she had earned such a long-held grudge from the team.

''He had mental problems in those days,'' Hawkeye said softly. The words sounded weak, even in his own ears.

''He's always had mental problems,'' Wonder Man said doggedly. He knew Josten from his own days working for Heinrich Zemo, and had gone up against Goliath plenty of times since, both with the Avengers and on his own. ''If we were going after only him—''

''We aren't,'' Hawkeye said. ''And the past is past. Cap's willing to trust Erik, even risk his life for him—if you can't do the same, could you at least zip it?''

Simon's eyes sparked, literally. ''Who died and made you boss, Hawkeye?'' he asked angrily.

''I'm going to ignore the first part of that,'' Hawkeye said, in a voice from which all humor had suddenly fled. ''And, as to who made me boss—well, I've paid my dues leading the Avengers. It wasn't so long ago that I was running the West Coast branch, remember? Cap's busy with my team. I figure, right now, I'm the best qualified to take his place, even if just for a while.''

''Are you sure you haven't lost your edge, running a bunch of jailbirds?'' Wonder Man asked, derisively. He had been a member of the West Coast team that Hawkeye spoke of.

''You're out of line, Simon,'' Iron Man interjected. ''If the Thunderbolts haven't finished paying their dues, they haven't missed any installments yet, either.''

"But, Cap is—"

"And, if Cap is putting himself at risk for a member of their team, MACH-1 and the others are doing the same for one of ours. Or have you forgotten that this isn't just about Atlas, but about the Vision, too?"

There was a long pause.

"That doesn't mean Hawkeye's running the show," Wonder Man said slowly.

"Maybe it does. Not in terms of strict protocol, but he's got the experience and the savvy," Iron Man continued. "And he's the only one of us who knows how both teams work. I'm comfortable following his lead."

"As am I," Thor said, in level, confident tones. "Clint Barton is a doughty warrior and a skilled leader. I would serve gladly at his side."

Simon blinked, then shrugged, then settled back in his padded seat, but he didn't say anything.

Neither did anyone else.

Hawkeye, however, smiled.

"My God," MACH-1 said softly. He had returned to the controls for a status check.

"Something on the scanners?" Moonstone asked.

"You might say that," the former Beetle replied. "Take a look."

"I don't see anything," Melissa said, still peering into the ebon depths.

"Take a look here," MACH-1 repeated. "This shows an infrared image."

The Thunderbolts clustered around, and stared in awe at the image the screen presented.

" 'My God' is right."

"I never dreamed—"

"What—what is it?"

Abe Jenkins pointed at a string of characters that had suddenly flared to life in one corner of the screen. They presented a single word.

Barbarossa.

• • •

"We have visual contact," Iron Man announced. "Long range, upshifted from infrared and down from microwave emission. I'm putting it on the big screen."

"My God," Hawkeye said softly.

The others made similar noises as they stared with something approaching genuine shock at the image presented to them. Bit by bit, the image resolved itself. Vague outlines became less vague, and then distinct; as the image definition increased a halo of annotating callouts came to life, green-fringed frames with arrow indicators. Swiftly, the frames filled with data that provided details about various aspects of the displayed image.

"The computer's still processing," Iron Man said softly. "It's got enough to give us the big picture, but not all of the details yet."

"The big picture is bad enough," Wanda said. "I never imagined—"

"How could anyone imagine?" Firestar asked. "What—what is it?"

"I've heard rumors about something like this," Iron Man said, "But I never credited them. I knew that Hydra had some amazing facilities, but had a hard time believing that they could do anything on this scale."

"What is it?" Firestar repeated, sounding even more serious than usual.

"It's the *Barbarossa*," Iron Man said grimly.

It was an armored fortress, mounted on mammoth tractor treads and carving a path along the sea's bottom. Larger by far than an American aircraft carrier, the *Barbarossa* moved implacably through the eternal night. Its treads gouged huge trenches in the sea's floor and clouded the surrounding water, but not enough to mask the behemoth's contours completely.

It had a squat, domed shape, and an outer skin studded with weapons launchers and communications relays, but the thing's sheer scale made them hard to see—even the largest embellishments faded into insignificance against the sheer size of the gigantic craft. Only the treads that drove it, that raised it slightly from the seabed, were large enough to make impressions of their own; easily the size of a railroad train locomotive, even they were dwarfed by the massive structure that rode them.

"Cold fusion power," Iron Man said tightly, reading the analyzer displays. "Magnetohydrodynamic engines. Heavily armed. Force field reinforcement of the hull. That makes sense—on this scale, at this depth, metal alone wouldn't be enough to maintain a pressurized environment."

Hawkeye, rarely at loss for words, stared at the screen in silence. For a long moment, the others did the same.

Then, Thor said, "Such an abomination cannot stand. We cannot allow it. An evil such as Hydra needs to have a heart, and this is surely it."

"I agree absolutely," Iron Man said. "This must be Strucker's nerve center. Rescuing Josten and the Vision may have brought us here, but we're going to do more than that. This might be our chance to put an end to Hydra and Strucker, once and for all."

"Barbarossa," Justice said. "He was a twelfth-century German king; headed the Holy Roman Empire. The legend is that he didn't die but merely sleeps, and will return when his people need him."

"The legend is wrong, then," Hawkeye said. There was no humor in his voice. "After we're done here, *Barbarossa* won't be seen again."

The docking bay that Techno had selected for the meeting was on *Barbarossa*'s lowest level, ordinarily reserved for utility runs. As Techno had explained things, it was a low-traffic bay and only rarely staffed; typically, it was sealed electronically by computer interlocks whenever it wasn't in use.

Computer interlocks meant little to Techno of course, except perhaps for a moment's diversion. It had taken him less than a minute to override the locks and the operating software, and a bit more than that to provide artificially generated feeds to the various surveillance systems.

Whatever business Zemo conducted here in Hydra's very heart, would be unseen by any other.

He stood in that bay now, watching the deck plates before him separate as the heavy steel slabs comprising the airlock's inner seal moved apart. The Blitz Squad agents standing at his side tensed as the scent of seawater filled the air. A moment later, it faded as hidden pumps came to life and drained the last of the water that had filled the lock. Then other, more powerful motors throbbed as they lifted the lock's remaining contents into the bay area.

It looked like a FedEx truck once more.

Zemo thumbed a switch on the control panel before him and the transport's hull split along a longitudinal seal, then peeled back. Splitting open like an oyster, the utility vehicle opened to reveal its contents.

''Hello, Zemo,'' Moonstone said.

The Blitzers accompanying him moved forward one step, then two; he gestured for them to halt.

Moonstone scarcely seemed to notice the aborted advance. She remained where she stood, poised at the front of her group, taking the point. Not for the first time, Zemo felt grudging respect for Karla Sofen's leadership qualities and, yes, even her courage. Sometimes, it was difficult to discern the specifics of what motivated the woman—certainly not loyalty—but her diligence in acting on those motivations was to her credit. It was almost a shame that she had to die.

Almost.

He didn't bother to acknowledge her greeting, other than by saying, ''If any of you move, however slightly, in a way that displeases me, you will die immediately.''

He looked at them, hating them, fighting down the impulse to roar curses and invective, to strike out at them with the weapons he wore. There would be time for that later. For now, it was enough to look at the tableau the transport had revealed, and to feel the hate well up within him.

He saw Moonstone, Songbird, and MACH-1—three failures whom he had taken in and given new identities. He had given them new lives and new reasons for living, only to have them turn against him.

He saw Jolt, the impudent and imprudent child on whose part he had led the Thunderbolts against a crazed geneticist and his legion of monsters. She had repaid him by insinuating herself into his creation, his Thunderbolts, and encouraging the others when they embarked on the path of betrayal.

He saw the helpless and bound Captain America, the man

who had put an end to his father's dreams. Once, Zemo had allowed his hatred for the Avenger to shape his life; now, the accursed hero was merely another on a long list of those who had earned his vengeance.

"Where's Atlas?" Moonstone demanded, in a tone of voice inappropriate to one of her station. "We had a deal."

"Nonsense. There is no 'we.' I have you, and you have whatever I choose to allow." He stepped closer.

"Big words. Too bad you need a pair of oversized associates to back them up."

Zemo shook his head. "Your ploys are transparent to me, Dr. Sofen. You will not goad me into imprudent acts." He paced slowly around the standing quartet, pausing and assessing them one by one, watching for any move against him. The final stop on his circuit was the recumbent Captain America, whose restraints seemed quite solid and adequate to the task.

"Hello, *Herr Kaptainn*," he hissed. "We meet again."

The American's eyes met his gaze. They were blue eyes, no less blue than the mask that surrounded them. For a long moment, Zemo gazed into those eyes, looking for fear and thinking he found it.

Perhaps Moonstone's offer was legitimate, after all, he thought.

No matter.

He stepped away from the motley quintet again.

"Where is Atlas?" Moonstone asked.

"You will see him again, and soon," he said. "In hell."

Then, impossibly, Captain America leapt at him.

The Hydra cadet was a slight and slender fellow, scarcely as tall as Strucker's shoulder and plainly terrified at being in his master's presence. "Hail Hydra!" he cried, in a voice that quavered with fear and the feuding hormones of late adolescence.

Strucker set aside the pen he held and looked up from his work. He did not bother to return the salute, but merely demanded, "Who authorized your entry into my office?"

"Lieutenant Hopkins, sir," the youth said, still at attention, still trembling.

"When we are done here, you are to inform Hopkins that

he will be executed at the stroke of ship's midnight,'' Strucker said crisply. ''That will teach him to send another in his place.'' He had long since wearied of the ambitious young bravoes who enlisted in this service, and then allowed a little thing like concern for their personal safety to stand between him and what he needed to know. He continued, ''And what is Hopkins's title?''

''Director, Management Information Systems, sir.''

''His duties are yours, now. Report.''

''We have detected unauthorized access to archival files, sir. Someone has downloaded the primary laboratory backups and purged the memory, despite the safeguards.''

Strucker knew who that someone had to be, and at whose behest he had most likely acted.

He spat and stood. With scarcely a glance at the still-trembling cadet, he strode to a cabinet in an office corner, opened it, and withdrew one of his specialized Satan Claws. Red energy flashed as he exchanged it for the more conventional prosthesis he had been wearing.

''Betrayal,'' he said angrily. ''Always, betrayal. Always, my allies think they can move against me before I strike at them.''

The cadet had relaxed some fractional increment. ''Shall I alert the security forces, sir?'' he asked.

Strucker shook his head. ''See to Hopkins,'' he snapped. ''I'll tend to the prodigal son.''

The ropes binding Captain America broke and fell away. He felt no soreness, no stiffness from his long confinement as he drew his legs under him and then leapt.

''But—!'' the ordinarily unflappable Moonstone gasped, obviously surprised. For his part, Zemo barked something in German, short, angry words that Captain America had heard before. He ignored them both.

''MACH-1,'' he snapped in midleap. ''Now!''

Gravity pulled him down again, even as he reached for Zemo with open hands. He had gambled that surprise would make Baron Zemo pause for a fateful instant before reaching for his weapon or issuing orders of his own.

His tactics were partly successful, at least.

Cap's right hand clamped down on Zemo's left wrist, immobilizing the German's hand before he could secure the pistol that hung at his belt.

The two Blitzers had moved, too. One reached for Cap, while the other moved for the Thunderbolts. Moonstone fired an energy blast at his eyes as she dodged his embrace, and Songbird created a ribbon of solidified sound in his path at ankle level. He tripped and tumbled, and as he did, MACH-1 raised one armored hand and pressed it against the back of the creature's skull.

There was a searing flash of light as electrical capacitors discharged, and then the Blitzer collapsed.

"That's one," Abe Jenkins said. Working with Iron Man, he had been able to patch together an electrical weapon, sufficient to re-create, at least to some degree, the searing energies unleashed by Thor.

"How long until it recycles?" Cap demanded. Zemo struggled in his grasp, trying hard to avoid Cap's second hand and managing.

"Neunzehn!" Zemo shouted. "Kill him!"

Neunzehn tried. He moved forward with remarkable speed for someone his size, but not as quickly as Captain America, who relaxed his grip, then released it, then tumbled from the path of the golden giant. When the pair of energy-charged fists found home, they found it on the deck plates, striking hard enough to send chips of steel flying.

"He's getting away," Jolt cried, pointing at Zemo. She leapt then, moving so swiftly that she seemed to bounce as she struck wall, then floor, then the rolling muscles of the Blitzer's shoulders, ricocheting each time in a zigzag trajectory that carried her toward Zemo.

Toward, but not to; even as she launched herself for him, the baron ducked through a suddenly open hatch, a hatch that slammed shut instantly behind him. Hallie's feet slammed into structural steel and she rebounded one last time, back into the docking bay.

Cap, for his part was still scrambling, trying to evade the pounding fists of Neunzehn, who was still lashing out at him. "Songbird," he said grimly. "I could use some help here."

A split-second later, and a bubble of pink energy formed

around the Blitzer's head. Moments after that, he collapsed.

Moonstone raced for the hatch, reaching for the control keypad with one hand even as she extended the other through the metal's gleaming surface. "I'll go after him," she said. "You follow—"

"No," Cap commanded. He brought one hand down on Karla Sofen's shoulder, where she was still material, and pulled her back. "You're not going anywhere until I say so."

He knew that Moonstone could slip his grip even more easily than Zemo had, but, for whatever reason, she didn't.

"Unhand me," she snapped, turning to confront him. "Now!"

Cap released her, then spoke in level, grim tones. "Listen to me, all of you," he said. "You see how big this place is. Even with reinforcements on the way, we're in for the fight of our lives. Our job is to clear the way for the Avengers and try to find the hostages. We have to face what's ahead as a team, if we want even the faintest hope of getting out of here alive."

None of the Thunderbolts spoke for a moment, and then, more calmly, Moonstone said, "I take it that you're in charge?"

Cap nodded. "You're a good leader, Moonstone, but a better deputy. Think about that the next time you decide to play games about leaving an ally tied up."

"As I said, Techno has a photographic memory," she said.

"Uh huh." Cap allowed his skepticism to show in his voice. "I'm sure that was your only reason."

"And—and you got loose," Melissa interrupted. "How did you do that?"

Now, Captain America smiled. "Tricks of the trade, Songbird," he said. "I'll tell you when this is all over." He gazed upon each team member in turn and said, "We're in this together, team. I've trusted you. I think you can trust me."

"I'll say," MACH-1 commented. He almost sounded cheerful. "I never thought I'd be led into battle by Captain America!"

Chapter Eleven

Somewhere

The sky was bleeding—not merely the color of blood, but actually bleeding. Great gouts of red stuff oozed from the bruised-looking dome above Techno, dripped down, and splashed against the irregular terrain surrounding him. As the streamers of clotting gore fell, they passed between his eyes and the purplish sun that hung low in the bleeding sky, passed before it but did not block the bilious rays that lent light to his new world.

There were no shadows here.

"What the heck?" Techno said. He was so surprised that he actually voiced the words, only to be even more surprised at how they sounded in his own ears. Instead of his more typical, hollow and electronic-sounding tones, he had spoken with the reedy, nasal voice of Norbert Ebersol.

The voice that had once come from the lips of his human body.

Techno tore his gaze from the diseased-looking sky and examined himself instead. He saw his body in its most recent configuration—red and black armor plate, external connectors, oversized forearms and hands—and felt a sense of relief at seeing something, anything familiar. That much, at least, was right. The next step, logically, was to run an internal diagnostics check. That was a matter of a simple mental exercise, a systems command to—

Nothing. There was no response, no report to the network of recorded engrams that made up his consciousness, not even the appropriate hint of feedback as the diagnostics subroutine engaged.

Something was terribly wrong—wrong with the world and wrong with him.

Desperately, he thought back, trying to remember his last actions, trying to determine what had brought him to this strange situation. He remembered lowering his hand to the Vision, extending a probe, accessing the android's nervous system.

He remembered seeing the Vision twitch, and a brief, transitional instant of disorientation.

That was it. Something had happened to him then. If only he could access his system logs.

A yellow fist smashed into his face, driving away all considerations except pain.

Pain? Not damage, not malfunction alerts, but genuine pain?

"Techno!" the Vision said, hitting him again. The android's voice sounded different than it usually did, and it took Techno a moment to recognize its new quality—a very real, very human anger. "Surrender, and we can end this," the Vision commanded.

Then his gloved fist rushed forward again, striking Techno's jaw for a third time.

This time, the explosion of pain prompted something else—not wonderment, but rage.

"Don't think so," Techno snapped, still speaking with Norbert Ebersol's voice. He sent the mental signal that should have brought a plasma cannon to life, and was only slightly surprised when it failed to work. For some reason, his internal weapons systems refused to engage—another mystery—but that was okay. His body's primary functions were still fully operational.

Physically weak during his organic life, he had constructed this frame to be very strong, indeed.

He brought both hands forward, clamped them around the Vision's neck, and began to squeeze. Acting more on reflex than anything else, he half-expected the android to turn immaterial and ooze from his steel grip—but to his surprise, the Vision did neither. Instead, he made a choking sound and clawed with gloved fingers at Techno's oversized hands.

Even more surprisingly, Techno felt him do it. Felt him the way a human would feel him, and not simply as a series of impulses relayed from his external sensors.

What was going on?

The *Barbarossa*

Zemo hated running.

More precisely, he hated to flee. Far better to meet your foe on the battlefield, to stand before whatever he could throw against you, to meet the challenge and defeat it, then prevail. Running was a concession of defeat, no matter what euphemisms were used to describe it, no matter how tactfully it was expressed. One mark of a good military mind, however, was to recognize when the better option is unavailable, and only a fool fought on when defeat was inevitable, and when flight could bring ultimate victory.

Zemo did not regard himself as a fool.

Somehow, MACH-1 had felled Zwanzig, and the *verdammt* Captain America had evaded the grasp of Neunzehn. That meant he had only one ally against five super heroes, most of whom had more-than-human powers.

Those weren't odds that Zemo cared to face.

He raced along the *Barbarossa*'s winding corridors, shouldering aside the occasional Hydra operative he encountered, with little concern for their startled exclamations or tentative salutes. He ran with a long, loping stride that devoured the distance, but which scarcely placed any strain on his excellent physique. He ran in an erratic route, that took him from the main corridors and into side passages and then back again, working hard to lose Captain America and the others—were they pursuing him—and yet at the same time, working hard to reach his new goal.

Techno had failed to respond to Zemo's hurried alert, so he had settled instead for using his communicator to deploy the available Blitzers. At least ten of the enhanced agents should be on hand, given that Ebersol had manufactured a new batch during the preceding hours. Zemo had issued the coded commands that activated them all, and set them to maximum available power. The Blitzers had been programmed not just to obey their leaders, but to recognize specific enemies—the Avengers and the Thunderbolts among them—and act on that recognition. Zemo could take some consolation from that fact, and from the fact that his father's relay system had been recreated in the *Barbarossa*'s generator room, but he could not count on either factor being enough to turn the tide of battle.

Muscle and force won wars, but only when yoked to skilled command.

There was another angle to consider. The Thunderbolts had comported themselves remarkably well at Fonesca. Now, with experience, and with the aid of Captain America, they would doubtless do better.

And who could know what allies might follow?

No, he could not rely on his own forces, at least not here and now. There was another option, however. If he could reach Strucker swiftly enough and slay him, he might still salvage this unfortunate situation. As the Supreme Hydra, Strucker had access to weapons and defenses that Zemo did not.

If he could could commandeer those resources and make them his own . . .

Zemo ran faster.

Time was running out.

"MACH-1," Cap called, "to your left!" His words were barely audible over the wail of sirens that had begun moments after he and his team had emerged from the docking bay.

Abe Jenkins raised his left arm and fired another round of anesthetic shells. They struck three green-suited figures who had just emerged from a side passageway, then spewed thick, clinging vapors. A second later, the trio of Hydra agents fell.

"Got 'em, Cap," MACH-1 said.

Cap scarcely noticed. He had taken the point, as was his wont, and had already lunged beyond the corridor intersection. He moved with remarkable speed, half-leaping, half-running, sometimes crouching, sometimes standing erect, always working to present the least possible target to his enemies. He had to trust that the others, close behind him, followed suit; he was too busy to verify.

Ahead of him, four more Hydra agents abruptly emerged from behind a sliding steel door, moving in teams of two. Each team held a rocket-launching device that looked similar to a bazooka. They worked much the same way too, as their operators now demonstrated. Jet-powered, explosive shells came rushing at Captain America, moving in a vector precisely opposed to his line of attack. Without breaking stride, he raised his shield, braced the muscles of his back and arms, then grunted as the missiles slammed home and detonated.

As they erupted, they made a deafening thunder and a blinding flash, both amplified by the corridor's tight confines. Bits of shrapnel flew, found the hall's steel walls, bounced, and flew some more, but Cap ignored all the various effects and continued in his headlong charge, raising his shield higher and leaning into the protection it offered. The special properties of his shield had absorbed most of the blast effects, and he was confident that the others could protect themselves from the remainder.

The Hydra agents fired again.

This time, Cap felt something different, even as the shells slammed into him. This time, he felt the impact of small feet as someone small and light, actually ran up his body and launched herself into the air from his shoulders.

"Jolt," he snapped angrily. "No loner tactics."

"Correction, Cap," Hallie Takahama called back to him. She was bouncing from floor to wall to ceiling now, moving with increasing speed as she gathered momentum. With each rebound, the bioelectricity her body generated sparked and flashed. "We're a team, and we work as a team!"

Jolt's last bounce was bringing her down on top of the Hydra quartet. She swung clenched fists, caught two of the men on the back of their heads. Again, organic electricity flashed, and the men fell, dropping their weapons. Again, Hallie bounced, and this time her trajectory brought her back down behind Cap. A split-second later, and a flash of heat and light from Moonstone's fingertips felled the other two goons.

"Good work, Jolt, Moonstone," Cap said, in what he had to admit were grudging tones. He hadn't expected the Thunderbolts to work so well together, let alone work so well with him. Despite that, in the minutes since boarding *Barbarossa*, the five had functioned as a well-oiled team, showing precisely the appropriate measures of consideration and initiative, all the while following his lead. "MACH-1," he said. "I need a situation report."

"Another thirty, thirty-five meters," Jenkins responded. "Left at the next branching, then ahead, I think. Resonance imaging is a little fuzzy." Before the Avengers and the Thunderbolts had parted ways, Iron Man had jerry-rigged one of MACH-1's internal scanners to read the distinctive energy fingerprint of the relay system that had powered the Blitz Squad. No one had been surprised to find that the relay was active here on the *Barbarossa* now, and no one had argued when Cap decided that their first priority was to disable it, and reduce the threat that the super-powered agents offered.

"Good," Captain America said. "If we can just make it before we run into one of those things—"

Then they did.

Turning, Cap slammed headlong into one of the golden giants as he charged down the corridor that MACH-1 had indicated. Sparks flew like lightning as his shield tried to absorb the energy of impact—tried, and failed.

"Hail Hydra!" the gleaming titan roared, smashing its fist into the ringed star of Cap's shield. More sparks flew and the Avenger grunted in pain as the hammering strike knocked him off his feet, to sprawl on the steel flooring.

"Cut off a limb and two more shall take its place!" the Blitzer thundered. He reached down, grasped Cap with glowing hands that made the blue chainmail mesh of his uniform smolder and smoke. He raised the living legend above his head and threw him at Songbird.

"Nice to see they can learn," Moonstone said as the two costumed figures fell in a tangled heap. "They know Songbird's a threat." Still racing along at about two meters above the floor, she hurled past the titan and then curved around again. "MACH-1, see to them. Jolt, follow my lead."

"Gotcha," Jolt called. She repeated her leap-and-bounce maneuver, but was careful not to come too close to the monster's flailing reach. Instead, she carefully kept just beyond his grasp, bounding and rebounding, tempting him and tantalizing him.

"Okay, now," Moonstone called.

Jolt raised her hands, brought them together. Another bioelectrical discharge flashed and found the Blitzer's eyes. It roared in pain, and as his mouth opened to release the roar, Moonstone fired twin bursts of energy down his gullet.

"They can learn," she repeated, as the monster fell. "Good thing that we can, too."

"I'll second that," Captain America returned, and he scrambled to his feet again. He shrugged off MACH-1's supporting hand, then leapt once more into the lead. "Good work," he said again. "Now, let's see some more."

Looming ahead were four more Blitzers.

"This is too convenient," Moonstone said. "They aren't just trying to capture us, they're trying to protect something."

Cap nodded. "The generator room," he said. "They must have been stationed to guard it."

Then more ionic lightning flashed, and there was no time for talking.

Only for fighting.

Techno struck the Vision again, and felt a grim sense of satisfaction as he seemed to hear artificial bones break under the impact. The Vision fell and tumbled, then rebounded as if from a rubbery gymnasium mat and threw himself at Techno once more.

"Give it up, android," Techno snarled. "I'm the stronger man." His oversized arms lashed out yet another time. His steel knuckles dug deep gouges in the roiling surface on which they stood. This time, the stuff behaved less like rubber and more like stone, shattering into chips—but the chips writhed and pulsed as they flew, and then splashed like water when they struck him.

What kind of place was this?

"I would argue the point," the Vision said. He still spoke in human tones rather than his usual monotone, but he sounded calmer now—though that calmness was not reflected in his actions. Abruptly, a cluster of ragged projections sprouted from the heaving surface at his feet; the Vision broke one loose easily, then swung it.

Techno cried out as the bludgeon came down on his head, unleashing a Niagara of pain that swept through him. He heard a roaring sound in his ears and saw blacks spots form in his field of view. Uncounsiousness reached out, tried to claim him, but he forced it back.

The Vision hit him again.

This isn't possible, he thought as the second wave of agony swept through him. Years before, in his human body, he had done some research for Hydra into just how much pain the human physique could withstand before shutting down completely. If what he felt now didn't meet that threshold, it surely came close—and Norbert Ebersol would never have placed himself at the high end of the pain tolerance scale.

What he was feeling now should have been more than he could bear.

He held onto the thought as the Vision hit him a third time, then inverted the club he held and drove its narrow end—sharp now, Techno noted—into his chest. Sparks flashed as plate steel broke, and then the mechanisms behind it shattered. The pain—the damage—wasn't what made Techno gasp in shock, however.

No; what did that was the river of blood that gushed from his sundered chest, red, viscous stuff as warm and clinging as what dripped from the sky.

"I'm bleeding," he said.

"Apparently," the Vision replied, moving in for the final attack.

"*I can't bleed!*" Techno snarled. As he spoke the words, a realization of their full meaning swept through him. "I can't bleed," he repeated. "I'm not organic anymore. I can't feel pain and I can't bleed."

The Vision punched him again.

"This—this isn't reality," Techno said. The pounding in his ears faded and his vision cleared. The broken remains of his chest twisted and convulsed, then spat out the spear that had stabbed through them. Even as the chunk of stonelike stuff fell down and away, Techno's thorax smoothed itself and healed.

"It's real enough," the Vision said through gritted teeth. He punched Techno again, hard enough to make his ears ring some more. "I'm real and you're real, and whether this place is real or not doesn't matter."

"But," Techno said, confusion setting in again, "this can't be happening."

The Vision's next blow said that it was, however.

"Hit 'em high and hit 'em low," Hawkeye called, as he released his taut bow string and launched a special arrow up and away. Even as the magnetic head caught and held, he clasped the line the arrow trailed. When it retracted, it took him with it, drawing him at an impressive speed and at a sharp angle toward the corridor's ceiling. Along the way, he swung his booted feet forward, hard, at precisely the right moment to ensure that they pounded the jaws of two onrushing Hydra agents.

He grinned as they fell. This was the Avengers' third skirmish with Hydra forces under his tempoarary leadership, and the experience was still novel enough to enjoy.

The others felt differently. Right now, the broad corridor they occupied was crawling with Hydra agents, both normal humans and Blitzers. The expressions on the faces of the Avengers as they plowed through their opponents ranged from wearied to worried.

"Impressive, Hawk," Iron Man acknowledged. "Too bad the big guns don't go down as easily." A Blitz Squad agent was racing in his direction, and electrical bolts were crackling back and forth between his extended arms. Iron Man ducked forward, into the creature's embrace, then brought the dome of his helmet up hard against the Blitzer's out-thrust jaw. Sparks flew, but the Blitzer did not fall. Instead, he grabbed Iron Man in an impromptu hug and drew him closer.

More sparks flew.

"Iron Man," Thor cried, "stand fast! Aid comes!"

The Blitzer contending with the thunder god disagreed. He pounded on Thor's barrel chest, then wrapped golden fingers around the haft of the hammer that the immortal of Asgard bore.

Thor smiled and released the hammer. A force more powerful than gravity pulled the hammer down, smashing it to the deck plates, and crushing all in its path.

Specifically, the Blitzer's left foot.

The super-powered agent gave a wail of pain that was genuine, then tried to dislodge his trapped toes. The strength of his leg muscles was not enough, so he stooped to add the power of his arms to his effort—to no avail. Immutable and immovable, the hammer remained where it was.

So did the Blitzer's foot, and so did the Blitzer.

"None may hold Mjolnir, lest he be worthy," Thor said, kneeling and grasping the enchanted weapon again. "And, though there be those other than Thor who may make that claim, you are not among their number." He lifted the hammer, fast and hard, and let its head smash into the Blitzer's, moving with enough force to shatter granite.

This time, the creature had no time to express its pain, but only time to fall.

Thor spun, ready to come to the aid of his comrade, only to pause in astonishment as Iron Man's opponent fell, too. "What blow did you strike?" he demanded. "You were sore pressed by your foeman."

"No blow at all," Iron Man said grimly, "but it's not a trick I can repeat for a while. These things run on ionic energy, and that's a kind of electricity. All I had to do was open my own transducer system and drain off most of its life force. I'm fully charged now, and maybe a little bit more than that."

"Life force?" Firestar asked. She was using her microwave powers to herd more Hydra operatives through an open doorway. A moment later, the doorway slammed shut, and Justice used his psychokinetic powers to seal it, twisting and crumpling the metal into a fused mass. "We—we aren't trying to *kill* those things, are we?" she asked.

"I hope not," Iron Man replied. He spoke with renewed vigor, and seemed to fairly sparkle with the colossal amount of energy he had absorbed. "I said 'most,' after all." He raised one hand, fired a repulsor beam. The coherent pulse of phased neutrons found another Blitzer and punched a hole completely through his chest. The hole healed almost immediately, and the Blitzer, his attention drawn, came loping toward his attacker.

"Uh, uh," Wonder Man said, "play nice." He swung a fist in a short, sharp arc intersected by the Blitzer's jaw. The golden creature tumbled back and slammed into a steel wall, hard enough to punch through it.

"Besides," Iron Man said grimly, "I'm not even sure these things can be killed, not while they're at this power level."

"They don't seem to be as strong as they were in North Carolina, though," Hawkeye said, as he dropped from the ceiling and rabbit-punched another of Hydra's seemingly limitless array of green-garbed foot soldiers.

"Good call," Iron Man said. "According to my analyzers, they aren't. There might be a reason for that. Maybe the power's not available, or maybe someone's concerned about this boat's structural integrity.''

''Hate to punch a hole through an outer hull,'' Simon said, punching a hole through an inner one instead, as he felled another Blitzer.

''I just hope Cap and the others can do their jobs,'' Iron Man said.

''Have a little faith, ShellHead,'' Hawkeye called. He was already bounding down another corridor. ''They'll do their part of the job; we have to do ours.''

Then there was another rush of small-arms fire, and the battle was on again.

''Generator room, dead ahead,'' MACH-1 said tightly, pointing at an open doorway flanked by armed, uniformed sentries. As he spoke, the two men raised and fired laser pistols. The crimson energy discharge found his armor and splashed against it, then he fired a few rounds of rubber bullets at the pair.

''Sorry, boys,'' he said softly. ''We're in a rush.''

''No time for small talk,'' Cap said. He leapt ahead, bouncing and tumbling into the gleaming white spaces of the generator room. ''Jolt, you and MACH-1 come with me. Moonstone, Songbird, bring up the rear and secure us.''

''Easier said than done,'' Moonstone said grimly. She was firing burst after burst of energy at a quartet of Blitzers who were hot on their trail.

''He doesn't want us to say it, he wants us to do it,'' Songbird said, even more grimly. ''Scared of a little tag team all of a sudden?''

''Don't be ridiculous,'' Moonstone snapped, scarcely noticing Jolt leap and bounce past her. ''I'm just being realistic.''

''Realistic doesn't win matches,'' Melissa snarled. Sometimes she got like this; sometimes in the rage of battle, her persona as a professional wrestler surged again to the fore.

Sometimes, it served her well.

Songbird raised her hands and sang. A sheath of pink energy encased them and then extended itself. By the time it reached the lead Blitzer, it had taken the form of a bulldozer blade. It caught him and his fellows, and sent them sliding back.

"That's it, that's it, keep them disoriented," Moonstone said encouragingly.

"I know what to do," Songbird said, her voice a snarl again.

Her words echoed throughout the corridor. Inside the generator room, MACH-1 heard them and felt cold worry well up within him. "I wish I did," he said.

"What?" Cap asked, startled. "But Iron Man briefed you—"

Abe Jenkins shook his head. "He gave me his best guess about what I'd likely find and what to do about it," he said. "And it was probably a pretty good guess." He gestured at the control panel, at the various LED displays and meters. "The reality, though—these readings are bad."

"How—how bad?" Jolt asked.

"Very."

Zemo's pistol was in his right hand as he raised his now-ungloved left to the sensor plate outside the door to Strucker's offices. Techno's infiltration of *Barbarossa*'s systems had extended even to the locking systems, so the sensor recognized his hand as Strucker's and the door slid open.

Something flew towards him, something that glinted silver in the indirect lighting. It flew in a high, spiraling arc, moving swiftly enough to make a ringing sound as it cut through the air. Reflexively, Zemo dropped his pistol and caught it.

It was a sword—a heavy, angled blade, with a slight curve to it, suggestive of a scimitar. The weapon's balance was excellent, and Zemo was surprised to realize how comfortable its hilt felt in his hand.

"That steel has been in my family since the twelfth century," Baron Wolfgang Von Strucker said. He stood poised in the room's center. He held another, similar weapon clutched in the red steel prosthesis that ended his right arm. "Your father and I had a match or two with these very blades. It's better steel than you deserve, either to fight with or to fall before."

Zemo looked at him levelly, felt fury and disgust well up

within him. After long weeks of working together, the endeavor was finally ending, ending as he knew it would, ending as even Strucker had said it would.

" 'Allies become enemies, foes become friends, and the cycle begins anew,' " Zemo quoted, sneering. "I have no time for your nostalgic games, old man." He stooped to retrieve his laser pistol.

Red lightning lanced from the tip of Strucker's blade, found the sidearm and reduced it to slag.

"You have time for nothing else," the Supreme Hydra hissed. "Now, to use the words of ignorant gutter folk—*en garde*!"

He lunged.

Chapter Twelve

The *Barbarossa*

The Avengers continued toward the center of the subsea fortress, fighting and smashing and hammering their way along, even as they met wave after wave of armed resistance. Again and again, squads of heavily armed Hydra agents, summoned by shrieking alarms, erupted from behind sliding doors or secret panels; again and again, they fell before the Avengers' combined might.

Hawkeye launched yet another arrow, this one headed with a smoke bomb, and waded into the roiling clouds it created, striking at the assailants they hid.

Iron Man, meanwhile, had extended the powered wheels that were hidden in his boots and skated into the midst of another cluster of Hydra foot soldiers. Metal weapons flew from gloved hands, drawn by magnetic fields that his own gauntlets generated, and then there were grinding noises as he crushed them into useless shrapnel. The suddenly disarmed Hydra agents manifested the better part of valor and retreated.

"This is like taking apart a hornet's nest," Wonder Man said. "The further we go, the more progress we make, the less fun we have."

"We aren't in this for fun, Simon," Hawkeye said. "We find the prisoners, then we find Strucker and Zemo. After that, you can find other ways to amuse yourself."

In the long minutes since making their entrance, the Avengers had arrived at a fairly simple strategy—keep together, present a united front, and keep moving. They moved through the corridors in a tight cluster, with the team's real powerhouses—Thor, Iron Man, and Wonder Man—working the outer perimeter and dealing with Blitzers when they showed up. In the center of the group, Hawkeye, the Scarlet Witch, Firestar, and Justice focused primarily on the Hydra rank-and-file operatives.

The formation was plastic, of course, as were the assigned duties. Sometimes a Blitzer made it past Thor or Iron Man and had to be dealt with by Justice or Firestar. Sometimes, the proverbial hordes of Hydra were sufficient to overrun the group completely, and Iron Man or Wonder Man was forced to deal with them. Justice and Firestar especially, thanks to their flying powers, shuttled back and forth between the perimeter and the center. Through it all, however, the formation remained relatively stable and undeniably effective. They were making admirable progress as they stormed the hidden fortress, and Hydra agents and Blitzers alike were falling before them in respectable numbers. Hawkeye was beginning to allow himself to think that it was only a matter of time now before they claimed their triumph. Unfortunately, to Hawkeye, time seemed to be in short supply.

"ShellHead," he called out. "How much further? I'd need a quiver the size of a house to keep up this pace much longer."

"Fifty meters west," Iron Man said. Now that they were actually inside the armored citadel, his telemetry equipment was sufficient to detect the energy signature of the Vision's unique artificial metabolism. "Looks like Atlas is in close proximity too, but it's hard to tell. There are too may ionic energy sources in the neighborhood."

"Yeah, I'd buy that," Hawkeye muttered as golden hands reached for him.

Wanda loosed another hex in his general direction. It found the Blitzer and did something to the thing's artificial biochemistry. With a guttural moan, the golden titan fell back, his hair abruptly white and his flesh hanging in folds.

"Just keep moving, Hawkeye," Wanda snapped, stepping over her assailant. "You're not the only one wearing down, and we still need to find the Vision."

"We need to do more than that," Iron Man said, his voice suddenly even more grim. "I'm getting a message from MACH-1. We're running out of time." He paused. "There's a problem in the generator room."

"So?" Hawkeye asked. "Does that mean the lights are going to go out?"

"Worse than that. If my theory about this place is right, things are about to get worse." He paused. "A lot worse."

Techno fell, tumbled, and rolled backward until he lay beneath one of the red streamers that dripped down from the sky. He felt it splash against his metal skin, find his eyes, and sting them, then fill his mouth with a taste like rotting flesh.

None of that should have happened. His cybernetic body had many senses that his organic one had lacked, but the reverse was also true. In mechanical form, he had no tactile sense, no sensory pain receptors (or simulators) in his eyes, and no taste buds whatsoever.

He couldn't be feeling what he felt now, but he was.

That meant it wasn't happening.

The knowledge broke over him like dawn on a battlefield, banishing darkness and doubt, and leaving behind certainty and triumph.

This isn't happening.

He wasn't in his body, but in a mindscape—what his erstwhile partner, the telepath Mentallo, had called the astral plane. It was a phantom world created from shared memories, perceptions, and impression when his mind and the Vision's had collided. He remembered now, boring into the Vision's skull to access his cranial mechanisms, and he remembered seeing the captive android twitch.

The Avenger must have awakened then, or tried to.

Techno gathered his feet beneath him and threw himself at the Vision again. This time, certainty lent new vigor to his blows. He pounded and hammered at the synthezoid, driving him back toward a chasm that had suddenly opened in the roiling terrain. The Vision grunted and tried to strike back, but Techno was faster.

A thought drifted through Techno's disembodied consciousness, a memory of words he had spoken to Strucker: "*The Vision is a machine,*" he had said. "*Remarkably complex, and perhaps the closest ever simulation of a living human being, but a machine nonetheless.*"

The day had not yet dawned when Norbert Ebersol couldn't get the better of a machine.

Yet the Vision declined to fall. Even when Techno pushed him into the chasm, he hovered above it instead, ignoring whatever passed for gravity here.

"You cannot defeat me," the Vision said calmly. "I will not fall before you."

Techno begged to differ. Rage roared through him as he leapt again at his opponent, hoping to trap him in a steel embrace. Instead, his body passed completely through the Vision's, and he fell.

Then the world twisted again, heaved and convulsed, and he was somewhere else entirely.

The sound made by the two pieces of centuries-old steel as they smashed into one another was almost a thing of beauty. Like the striking of church bells, the sound rang out and filled the entirety of Strucker's quarters, before echoing back to Zemo's ears.

Strucker's blade came lancing toward him now, stabbing through a hole in the silvery lattice that Zemo's dancing steel wove through the air between the two men. Zemo moved his wrist a bit and his forearm a bit more, and then his sword blocked Strucker's and knocked its point aside.

"Skillful," Strucker said. "Your prowess in this, at least, is no sham."

In his months as Citizen V, leader of the Thunderbolts, Zemo had made the sword—any sword—his weapon, and seen more action with a blade than most saw in a lifetime. He had faced his enemies with nothing more than a length of edged steel, and he had always come out the victor. He didn't mention that now, however.

"Part of my heritage," he said calmly. He kept his words to a minimum. Talking at all during such a match was risky; it expended breath and vitality better devoted to battle. Zemo was all too aware, however, that this battle was being fought on more than one front, and that Strucker was striving to obtain a psychological edge.

Zemo would not let him do that.

He slashed again. This time, the tip of his blade found Strucker's left bicep and pinked it. Redness oozed forth, staining the Supreme Hydra's uniform.

"First blood," Strucker acknowledged. "Not the last, but the first." He brought his sword forward, fast and hard, and muttered a curse as Zemo danced out of its way.

"We shall see," Zemo returned, moving back and to his left, but remaining careful not to move too far. Their duel had taken them over most of the room's area, and brought him perilously close to the paneled walls more than once. If he was to win this conflict, he needed room to maneuver. Allowing himself to be cornered would be tantamount to suicide.

"I honor you with this, you know," Strucker said easily. "Or, rather, I honor your father. I could slay you as easily as I destroyed your pistol, and as easily as I have put an end to your dreams of betrayal." He slashed again. "Already, my forces are securing the base and putting rout to yours. They tell me that you even admitted your precious Thunderbolts to the facility. Did you truly think that you could commit such transgressions and live to tell of them?"

How could the man talk so much, and still keep the breath to fight? Zemo had to wonder about that, but he suspected he knew the answer—even as his own aging had been retarded by one of his father's inventions, Strucker's vitality had been greatly enhanced by the biological incident that had returned him from the dead.

He wondered if Strucker even needed to breathe at all.

Slash, stab, parry, then slash some more—the two swords smashed into one another again and again, moving with a rhythm and grace that seemed self-contained. Zemo could almost believe that the weapons themselves were the warriors, that the two blades battled one another, and that he and Strucker were only along for the ride.

Stucker's blade found Zemo's left shoulder, stabbed, then withdrew as Zemo drove it back with a series of slashing feints.

"You are ambidextrous, *ja*?" Strucker asked, mocking. "I am told that you are equally skilled with either hand. Well, not here, not now, *nicht wahr*?"

"I don't need two hands to bring you down," Zemo said. His breath was coming a bit more raggedly now, so he forced himself to speak slowly as he continued. "And at least I have two, *nicht wahr*?" He repeated the interrogative in a mocking imitation of Strucker's tones.

Strucker laughed. "What another foe robbed me of, my own scientists replaced. My good right hand for the Satan Claw. It was a fair exchange."

Despite his assurance, however, something in his voice told Zemo that the older man had taken more offense at the barb than he chose to admit.

"As you say," Zemo responded. His wounded shoulder throbbed and ached now, and his heart pounded. Swordfighting was excellent aerobic exercise, and he was beginning to feel the strain.

Beginning.

"You could have been my right hand, Helmut," Strucker continued. "There was no need to let it come to this. You would always have had a place in Hydra."

"Perhaps," Zemo said. "I suspect that place would have had a locking door, however."

Again, Strucker laughed, and again, he lunged.

"Yeah, that's what I thought," MACH-1 said into his communicator. "I just wish I were wrong." He paused, listening to Iron Man's words, then responded. "I'll tell the others. MACH-1 out."

"What is it? What's wrong?" Captain America asked.

MACH-1 looked up from his work. He had removed his masking helmet and his handsome features were pale and drawn in the generator room's light. "We've got problems," he repeated. He was holding the last of three components he had stripped away from a main equipment console. This one was an umbrellalike antenna, copper surrounding a bulging disc. A moment ago, that mesh had been arrayed in a graceful curve, but now, de-energized, it hung in loose folds.

"Can't you power down the Blitz Squad?" Songbird asked urgently. She and Moonstone had fought off the last of the guards and secured the chamber; now the four Thunderbolts and Captain America stood close together as Abe spoke.

"I've done that," he said edgily. "Iron Man says their power levels dropped the moment I cut the first wire. But I think we're too late." He gestured again at the systems status display, at the numbers and values shown there. "This place runs on fusion power," he said. "And the generators are destabilizing, fast—probably as a side effect of all the power this other gadget was sucking out of them." Abe shook his head again. "It's never a good idea to retrofit key functions without backups. That's probably why they ran their field tests at Fonesca."

"What are you saying? What does this mean?" Moonstone asked. "Is this place going to explode?"

"No, no, nothing like that," MACH-1 said. "Fusion generators pretty much can't." He paused. "They can shut down, though, and when that happens, I have a hunch we're dead."

"Dead?" Jolt asked. "But the Blitzers—"

"The Blitzers aren't an issue anymore," MACH-1 said. "But when these generators shut down, the force fields buttressing this joint's hull will collapse." He looked at Cap. "We've got to evacuate," he said.

"Can't you do anything?" Moonstone asked. "There must be some way—"

Abe shook his head, then snapped his helmet back in place. "No once can do anything; the process has gone too far." He repeated, "We've got to evacuate this place.

"What—what about Atlas?" Jolt asked.

MACH-1 didn't have an answer to her question.

Zemo's blade was becoming heavier in his hand, but he could not let Strucker see that. Instead of relenting, he redoubled his efforts, slashing and stabbing in a series of strokes that seemed wide and sloppy, but were, in fact, quite precise. Each time Strucker's blade stabbed toward him, his blade was there to block it. Each time there was an opening, no matter how slight, in Strucker's guard, Zemo's blade raced for it. Once, twice, three times, the curved steel's razored tip found its target; bright flowers of blood suddenly adorned Strucker's chest, shoulder, and jaw.

It was Strucker who gave ground now, backing away slowly but surely. The older man was hard pressed in the most specific sense of the term: driven back by his enemy until he was less than a meter from one wall.

"Perhaps as a whole man you could have defeated me," Zemo said. "Not as the old, maimed thing you are now."

His blade stabbed out again, racing for Strucker's eye. At the last moment, the Supreme Hydra twisted and dodged, but still Zemo managed to strike his monocle. The glass lens did not shatter, but dislodged and spun away into the distance.

"Look at you," Zemo said, trying hard not to gasp and

succeeding. "Maimed, half blind—it will be a mercy when you die once more."

Strucker roared then, an inarticulate cry of outrage and pain and raw fury. The metal contours of his Satan Claw twisted, convulsed, and were suddenly shrouded in a halo of red energy. "No mercy for you, ungrateful cur!" he thundered, finally shaping his rage into words. "Only death, swift and eternal!"

The crackling redness flowed from his artificial hand and into the blade it held, bathing the steel in a rippling, crimson haze. He lunged, with no finese or skill, but only brute force, the glittering length of his energy-charged blade stabbing at Zemo.

Or, rather, at the place where Zemo had been.

Zemo was the smaller man. Younger and nimbler, he ducked beneath Strucker's attack and inside his guard. As he ducked, he made his own attack, jabbing his blade at the skull emblem on Strucker's chest.

Unlike Strucker's weapon, Zemo's found its mark. It stabbed into the skull's left eye, punched through the fabric and cut into the flesh and bone beneath.

Strucker gasped, choked.

Zemo rammed the blade home, unmindful of the one his foe still held or the blood that gushed from the wound he had created. Strucker's sword was just steel now, dead and without charge; the only redness evident was that of his life's blood. Zemo knew that the older man's plasma still held the deadly contagion of the Death Spore Virus, but he gave that no mind; Techno had immunized him to such trash.

Strucker gasped again, staggered backward. Zemo moved him, still pressing the attack. As Strucker fell back, his tall, muscular form slammed against one wall's oak panelling—slid along it, then stopped, as Zemo's blade pinned him there, nailing him to the dark wood like a butterfly specimen's pin.

Strucker's lungs rattled and his lips twisted, but no sounds came. His fingers relaxed and his weapon fell.

"And now," Zemo said, "I believe I shall take my leave of this place."

Strucker's lips twisted again. He spat a milky blob of mucous, a sticky globule that found Zemo's tunic and clung there.

Zemo ignored the final gesture of contempt. Instead, he gazed for a moment at Strucker's hate-filled features. They had gone from pale to paler now, and the electric blue of the older man's eyes was becoming clouded. As they continued to dim, Zemo felt an odd sensation well up within him—the grudging realization that an era was passing.

Stucker gasped and wheezed. His eyes closed and his breathing slowed.

Confident now that it would not be seen, but not really knowing why he did so, Zemo raised his arm in a final, silent salute—and then lowered it.

He had work to do.

The world twisted, convulsed, then remade itself. Where there had been a bleeding sky and heaving landscape, the Vision now found himself surrounded by gleaming whiteness and complex lab equipment. Without pausing to consider the situation, he reached up and tore Techno's steel hand from his brow.

Then he drove his own synthetic fist into the mechanical man's face.

Still stunned, still confused, Techno didn't even try to avoid the blow, struck by an android who had increased his physical density to its absolute maximum. The mechanical man went flying back, staggering and stumbling. Even as he tried to right himself, the Vision punched him again. This time, the impact drove him back into a bank of machinery—specifically, a carousel-shaped device with six transparent modules arrayed around a central console. Plastic shattered and steel bent, and then long, arcing electrical sparks flew.

The Vision paid them little mind. Moving swiftly, he peeled loose the various restraints that held Atlas to the other lab table and set about reviving the Thunderbolt.

"Huh—wha—what happened?" Erik Josten asked when consciouness had returned.

"We're in some manner of Hydra facility," the Vision said crisply, once again speaking in his trademark monotone. "If you're able, I think it's time we took our leave of this place."

Atlas looked around and caught sight his former teammate, still sprawled in the center of the shattered mechanism.

"Uh, what did you do to Techno?" he asked.

"I merely showed him who was the better man," the Vision replied.

"But, uh—but Techno's not really a man at all, not anymore."

"Precisely."

"Things just got a lot worse," Iron Man said.

"I'd have to disagree with that," Wonder Man said. He lashed out at another Blitz Squad agent, and grinned in savage satisfaction as the ionic superman fell. "The fight's going out of the big guys, and the green pajama boys are running out of steam, too."

In the last several minutes, the tide of battle had finally ebbed. Of the Blitzers, only one or two remained, and most of the Hydra agents had given up the fight.

"That's not what I mean," Iron Man said. He upped the gain on his external speakers, so that all could hear him. "There's a problem in the generator rooms. We're looking at a complete system shutdown in a matter of minutes."

"So?" Hawkeye asked. "You must have a flashlight or two in that outfit."

"It's more than a blackout, Hawkeye," Iron Man said. "The hulls of this place are reinforced with force fields. When the power goes, so will they."

"And when they go?"

"When they go, we go too," Iron Man concluded. "We've got to evacuate, and soon."

"But what about the Vision?" Wanda asked anxiously.

"And Atlas," Hawkeye reminded her.

"And Atlas," she said.

"We'll find them first, of course," Hawkeye said. "But we've got to hurry."

Two steel doors slid open, revealing two costumed figures framed in their opening—Atlas and the Vision, stepping out from the chamber that had been, minutes ago, the Avengers' goal.

"Hurry?" the android Avenger asked coolly.

Chapter Thirteen

In the distance, there was a sound like thunder.

It was a low, bass rumble, so low that it was felt as much as heard, as it resonated through the countless tons of steel that comprised *Barbarossa.* Like thunder, it came in rolling waves, building in power and then fading into faint echoes before beginning anew.

And begin anew, it did.

"You were right," Iron Man said to MACH-1. "I had hoped you weren't, but you were. The structural members are starting to shift already."

The other armored man nodded, but said nothing.

The Avengers now stood with the Thunderbolts in *Barbarossa*'s generator room, where fusion reactors processed hydrogen into helium, and released the excess mass as energy. With Atlas and the Vision at their side, it had taken the Avengers only minutes to fight their way there, following the prompt of MACH-1's communicator, and even less time to confer hastily and compare notes. Now, cables connected Iron Man's armor to the generators' operating systems, as the armored Avenger ran one test sequence after another on the failing devices.

They all told the same tale.

Iron Man pointed at the dismantled relay system that lay in scattered components on the floor. "There's the real problem," he said. "I can only assume that someone should have been monitoring that, making adjustments to it when necessary."

"The one at Fonesca had a dedicated operator," Hawkeye said. "Until I—uh—undedicated him and disconnected the gadget."

"I'm surprised that Techno wasn't in personal attendance. This is his kind of toy, after all," Moonstone said. "Maybe we could find him now, make him—"

"He was otherwise engaged," the Vision said. "And I doubt he is available even now. I could verify that, however. There is also the matter of our hosts, Zemo and Strucker, and the need to apprehend them." His outlines wavered, became less distinct.

"Hold it," Captan America said. "You aren't going anywhere. We didn't come this far to lose you again."

"Nor to lose everything, if it can be avoided," the Vision responded. "See to your own safety; I will rejoin you." He turned slightly to face Wanda, an unreadable expression on his face.

"Vision," she said. "I—"

Too late. He was gone, drifting down through the steel of the deck plates as if they were not there.

Hawkeye turned to Moonstone. "You can do the walk-through-walls bit, too. Wanna give him a hand?"

Before Karla Sofen could reply, Captain America spoke instead. "No," he said. "We're not splitting up again. We're leaving this place together." He turned to Iron Man and asked, "How long do we have?"

"Not long. The generators' power feed has already destabilized, and the force fields are showing the strain."

"How long?" Cap repeated.

"I don't know, exactly. The generators will shut down completely in less than an hour. I don't imagine the hull will last long after that. We've got a whole ocean sitting on top of us, after all."

"Any way to reverse the process?"

"I can't do anything, and I'd be very surprised if even Techno can."

"Or would," MACH-1 said.

"Or would," Iron Man agreed. "We've got to get out of here." He glanced in Thor's direction, and his voice took on a bleak quality as he hearkened back to the immortal's earlier words. "It looks like we put an end to this place, after all, even if not in quite the way I had in mind."

The thunder god's only reply was a puzzled expression.

"The generators destabilized because of the power the Blitzers were draining from them. The Blitzers needed power because we were fighting them."

Thor nodded. "Hydra's own foolhardiness has brought them down," he said. "And Strucker's own ego has writ the end to his tale."

"That's another point," Wonder Man chimed in. "We can't come this far, fight this hard, without capturing the bad guys. If we leave without them, they win."

"If we don't leave now, we die, from what Iron Man says,"

Cap said. "I'd imagine the same applies to Strucker and Zemo."

"And to everyone else on board," MACH-1 said. He looked urgently at Cap. "There must be hundreds of people on board—maybe thousands—not the best people in the world, sure, but people. We can't just leave them here to—"

"There's no time to save them all, Abe," Songbird said gently. "We've got to—"

"MACH-1 is right," Iron Man said. He stepped to a wall intercom unit, extended a screwdriver from one fingertip and removed the device's cover. "We can't save them, but maybe they can save themselves."

Reboot.

The world came back to Techno in bits and pieces. Even before his consciousness returned, there were internal status reports—*system integrity, eighty percent; operating system; seventy-eight percent; self-repair at ninety percent.* Next the environmental sensors kicked in, giving him back sight and sound and a half-dozen other information gathering systems, followed by gyrostabilizers and balance mechanisms. Finally, the major motor systems came online and he stood. The entire process took perhaps eleven minutes—about four more than it should have.

The damage had been more extensive that he would have believed possible. The Vision's dense fist, the mammoth discharge of ionic energy . . .

"Oh, my," he said softly, as he rose from the cluttered pile of wreckage in which he had lain. "This is going to take some explaining."

Or would it?

His audio receptors were receiving distress alarms and calls to combat. A quick scan with his in-built radio transceiver revealed more of the same. Moving quickly, the mechanical man stepped to a nearby computer console and plugged in, then accessed *Barbarossa*'s computer network.

This was very bad.

Something was wrong with the fusion generators; some excessive drain had thrown them into a state of imbalance. He wondered at the cause, but decided that determining it could wait.

The issue of survival could not.

His best projection showed less than an hour until the reinforced hulls failed, at least, unless the situation changed. Still working from the remote node, he opened the generator systems' configuration subroutine and began making adjustments. It would only take a moment to divert power from the main engines and use it to shore up the fields. That would immobilize the craft, of course, but might save it, as well. Once that was done, he could recalibrate the generators themselves to—

The laboratory door opened, startling him. Zemo stumbled in, clutching one bicep. The purple fabric of his sleeve was stained a darker color, and the stain was growing.

"Baron," Techno said, still engaged with the computer. "You're wounded."

"It is nothing," Zemo said. His words came in ragged gasps and he seemed on the verge of collapse, but not so much from his wound as from sheer physical exhaustion. "What means all this commotion? Give me a status report, now."

Techno spoke quickly and concisely, telling him about the generators and their status.

"And what happened here?" Zemo demanded, indicating the sundered bank of machinery. "Where are our prisoners? Where are Atlas and the Vision?"

This time, there was a pause before Techno answered.

"Escaped," he finally said. "The Vision got loose, took me out, and freed Josten."

Zemo cursed softly, but at great length. Finally, he said, "It was to be expected, I suppose. All else has gone poorly."

Techno wasn't sure what to say to that.

Zemo looked at him balefully. "I assume Strucker has some manner of private escape vessel? His kind always does." He paused. "I know that I would."

A quick review of a hidden inventory file provided an answer. "A private sub," Techno said, nodding, "moored to a central launch corridor. It's not far, but I assume that Strucker will race you for it."

"Strucker is dead," Zemo said simply, and with a mixture of emotions in his voice that Techno found curious. "And from what you tell me, we will be, too, unless we take our leave of this place.''

''Uh, I may be able to pull a save, but—''

''Leave it.''

''I can delay—''

''Leave it!'' Zemo snapped. ''*Barbarossa*'s time is done. Let it serve as a tomb for our erstwhile ally and, if fortune favors us, for our enemies, as well.'' He paused again, gasping, and more redness spilled from the wound on his shoulder. ''Look to the future for triumph, Techno, not to the past.''

''Okay, fine,'' Techno said. As he spoke, he disengaged from the generator operating systems and then broke his physical connection to the computer, withdrawing his fingers from the input jacks. Events would take their own course now, but that wasn't his concern.

''Now let us be gone,'' Zemo said. ''I weary of this place.''

A moment later, and both had exited the lab space through another pair of sliding doors.

A moment after that, the Vision's green-hued form drifted through one wall, looked around, and then exited through another only a moment later.

Nothing worth noting had met his impassive gaze.

''Attention! Attention!'' Iron Man's voice rang out from a thousand intercom speakers throughout the *Barborosa*. He spoke quickly and clearly, in the very voice of command. ''A hull rupture is imminent! Abandon ship now. This is not a drill! I repeat—a hull breach is imminent. You must abandon ship now!''

He had made a few hasty changes to the intercom system, annexing it tempoarily to his own suit's communications suite, so he was reasonably confident that his announcement would be heard in all quarters. Despite that, he repeated the call several times, prefering to err on the side of excess.

He didn't bother to identify himself. Hydra agents were, by and large, a subservient lot, and tended to obey orders, provided that those orders were delivered properly. Telling them that their words came from Iron Man—or from any of the assembled heroes—wouldn't have done much to encourage cooperation. Better to command now and present credentials later.

The Vision drifted silently through a world that, at the moment, had no claim on him. Walls, floors, air, bulkheads, human beings, hatches—all were the same to him, and none offered him any resistance. With the ease of long practice, he steered by adjusting his tangibility by fractional increments, so that one air current or another could change his path, or to permit himself to feel gravity's pull. He moved through *Barbarossa*'s various levels, pausing only long enough to measure and assess, and then he moved on.

He saw many things.

He saw metal plates bend and buckle, split and tear—then, finally, collapse completely, allowing the cold darkness without to rush within. In instant response, emergency hatches slammed shut and hidden pumps labored, so that the collapse, though widespread, was slowed.

Slowed, but not stopped.

He saw men and women in Hydra uniforms, fleeing desperately through crowded corridors that were knee-deep in frigid water. He saw them throw themselves into emergency escape pods, five and six at a time, and activate launch sequences, and then he saw those same pods throw themselves into the inhospitable sea. Would the evacuees survive their sudden assent? Would they escape or be apprehended?

The Vision could not know.

He paused many times in his zigzag course, but he stopped completely only once. That was on an upper deck, in a large, abandoned chamber decorated to resemble a hunting lodge's interior—obviously the private preserve of a high-ranking Hydra official, presumably Strucker. Certainly, it made a striking contrast to the utilitarian spaces that preceded and followed it in the Vision's course. The floor was inches-deep in rich carpet and the steel walls were masked with dark oak slabs, decorated with mounted trophies.

One wall bore something else.

Making himself solid again, the Vision stepped closer to inspect what he saw. It was a ragged gouge dug deep in the old wood, overlaid with a splash of red wetness that could only have been blood. More blood stained the carpeted floor there, and nearby lay a curved steel blade, obviously the tool that had cut the wood. Still more blood sheathed the razor-edged weapon.

He saw no sign of a body, however.

The Vision considered the tableau a moment, thinking. Then more, distant rumbling roused him from his reveries. Another moment's thought, another effortless mental exercise, and, immaterial once more, he sank through the floor and continued his search for Techno, Zemo, and Strucker.

He had to wonder, however, if any of the three were to be found.

Barbarossa took a long time to die.

The subsea citadel died in fits and starts, as one section after another collapsed. After the first few convulsions, however, the process assumed an eerie kind of momentum, and a sense of inevitability set in. Steel bent and tore as the hidden energies sustaining it failed, and then the air trapped inside erupted in clouds of murky bubbles. As each section collapsed, it weakened the next, so that the muffled sounds of rending steel soon become almost continuous, and the bubbling chaos came almost as steadily.

"How long can this last?" Jolt asked.

"A while yet," Iron Man responded. "It's a big place, and it was built well."

"Not well enough," Hawkeye commented.

The Thunderbolts had joined the Avengers on their submarine that hovered a safe distance from the crumbling fortress. Nearly an hour had passed since they had launched themselves from the lower-deck docking bay. They had spent that hour watching *Barbarossa* die by increments, pausing only to place a few calls to the authorities, alerting them to what was happening.

When the escape pods reached the surface, their occupants would find a welcome committee waiting for them.

"I think this is it," Cap said, staring at the screen, a look of grim fascination on his face.

"But—but the Vision," Wanda said. "He's still in there—"

"No." The single word filled the air as a familiar form dropped into the submarine's passenger area, moving as though the hull were not there. "I am not." When he had entered the fuselage completely, his outlines wavered again and then he was solid once more. He showed no sign of having been exposed to crushing tons of deep sea pressure, or even of having been underwater at all; he had passed as easily through the waters as he had though all other material media.

"Neither are those I sought, however," he continued. "I believe they have made good their escape."

"What?" Atlas said, stunned. He had been very vocal in his desire to repay his captors for their hospitality. "That's not possible! Even if they're in one of the pods, they'll be caught!"

Captain America raised his hand for silence, then pointed at the monitor screen.

It had gone white, and the world had turned to thunder

"I thought you said fusion reactors couldn't explode," Hawkeye said sourly, as the submarine shook and rocked in the ensuing shockwave.

"Technically, it didn't explode," Iron Man explained. "It had already shut down completely, for that matter. But the generators and the engines were still superheated. When the water hit them—"

His words trailed off into silence.

All that the screen showed now was churning chaos; water and air and light and steel debris had all combined into a single boiling cloud that marked the end of *Barbarossa.*

"I suppose it's too much to hope that Zemo, at least, was in there," Hawkeye said as the chaos showed its first signs of subsiding.

"He's tough," MACH-1 responded. "He's gotten out of worse. I wouldn't believe him dead until I saw him buried."

"Maybe not even then," Wonder Man said. "Those things have a way of reversing themselves."

"Hold it," Moonstone said. She raised one hand for silence. "I'm getting something on my radio." She shot a questioning glance at MACH-1.

Jenkins nodded. "On the old T-bolts frequency," he said.

"I can patch it to external." One of several speakers on his armor's exterior crackled and came to life.

"Impressive, isn't it, Thunderbolts?" Zemo's familiar voice sounded in the submarine's tight confines. "If you can hear this, you're seeing a man's dreams die. They die hard, eh?" He paused, and his labored breathing was barely audible. "Not as hard as the man, but die they do."

Hawkeye mimed words to Iron Man, shaping each one with exaggerated movements of his lips, but making no sound. *Can you trace?* he asked.

"If you can hear these words—when your ends come, they will come at my hand," Zemo continued. "And each day that joyous event is delayed merely serves to make my inevitable triumph all the sweeter."

"Too much interference, too much debris blocking my probes," Iron Man said softly.

"Bold words," MACH-1 said suddenly, angrily. "Especially from someone running with his tail between his legs."

"Ah, Beetle," Zemo said. "So you are alive and can hear me. And if you live, the others doubtless do, as well. A pity, but that will one day be corrected."

"Try it, Zemo!" MACH-1 yelled into his microphone. "Try it and we'll—"

The connection broke.

"Too much interference," Iron Man repeated. "He was close, but I can't pinpoint him."

"He wouldn't have bothered contacting us if he thought there was any way he could be captured," Jolt said. "That means he's not in any of the pods."

"So he's alive, at least. That means Techno probably is, too," Moonstone said. She didn't sound happy. "That leaves Strucker."

"Does it?" the Vision asked.

Epilogue

Avengers Mansion, New York

This time, Doug Deeley came calling without Jasper Sitwell's company. Perhaps to make up for that, he met with both Captain America and Iron Man. He nodded amiably as one Avenger showed him to a chair and the other handed him the files that he had left behind on his other visit.

"Thanks, Doug," Cap said. "The information was useful."

"Thank you, Cap," the SAFE agent replied. "From what we understand, the Avengers dealt Hydra one heck of a blow. That makes everyone's job a bit easier." He slid the folders into his briefcase and locked it.

"How much easier?" Iron Man asked.

The handsome African-American man shrugged. "Not as easy as we'd like, I have to admit. Hydra's a big outfit, and there are a lot of splinter outfits using the name, like the one that Skrull was secretly running," he said, referring to a recent difficulty that the Avengers—particularly Cap—had had. "They'll still be thorns in our side for some time to come."

"Strucker said something about that once," Iron Man said. "A botched quote, to the effect that the object of chaos is chaos. It wouldn't surprise me to learn that he engineered some of those splinter groups himself, just to see what kind of fruit they bore."

"Any word on Strucker?" Cap asked, in a serious tone of voice. "From what the Vision said—"

"He hasn't turned up yet," Deeley responded, "but that doesn't mean anything. He's died more times than anyone this side of Dr. Doom, and he keeps popping up again, alive if not well."

"Zemo seemed to think he had killed him," Iron Man said.

"Well, I'll ask him when and if we track him down, but you'll pardon me if I don't take his word for it," Deeley responded. "There are only a few loose ends that need tying up, and then I'll be out of your hair for a while."

"Shoot," Iron Man said.

"I've got some folks who would like an interview with Ms. Maximoff. Six Blitz Squad agents remained behind at Fonesca, and she might be able to help us with them."

"How so?" Cap asked.

"Word is, she managed to revert one to human form. If she could do it again, they'd be a lot easier to keep behind bars."

"I'll let her know," Cap replied. "She's in the Adirondacks with Simon this week."

Deeley nodded. He wasn't a man who took notes, but more than once, he had demonstrated an excellent memory. Neither Avenger doubted that Cap's response would be reported and recorded accurately.

"How about Hawkeye?" the SAFE agent asked. "Is he around?"

"He's on a leave of absence," Iron Man said quickly. "Mind telling us what it's about?"

"Oh, Colonel Morgan wanted to ask him a few followups about the events out at the Vault. One of our men stationed there had a silly—" Deeley paused. "Well, let him know we were asking, would you?"

Cap nodded and stood. "I will," he said. "But if you'll excuse us—?"

"Of course. Guess you folks are always busier than you'd like to be, right?"

"Something like that."

Deeley nodded again, smiled, and shook both men's hands. "Always a pleasure, then," he said, then turned and walked towards the door that would take him outside. Just before he reached it, he paused and turned again. "One last thing," he said.

Cap and Iron Man waited expectantly.

"Cap, you spoke to Colonel Morgan from onboard the Avengers sub, immediately after the explosion."

Cap nodded. "I wanted him to know what was going on," he said easily.

"And he appreciated it. He wanted me to ask you something, though—was there a reason you had turned off the video feed on your communicator?"

"It wasn't on?"

"No pictures at our end," Deeley said. "I've watched the tape."

''If anyone turned off the feed, it wasn't Cap,'' Iron Man said carefully.

''Probably an accident, then,'' Deeley lightly. ''After all, if it were turned off deliberately, that would mean that someone didn't want us to see who all was on that sub, right?''

Thunderbolts HQ, Colorado

''You did good, guys,'' Hawkeye said. ''We did good.''

The Thunderbolts were seated around a table in the dining area of the lodge they had rented, and that did double duty these days as a command center. Just now, it being used for its original function—half-empty cartons of Chinese food sat on the table's worn surface, and most of the team members were lifting forkfuls of the savory stuff to their mouths.

''We couldn't have done it without the Avengers,'' Jolt pointed out. She had already stowed away more kung pao chicken than her trim form should have been able to hold, but she was reaching for more even as she spoke.

Hawkeye nodded. He said, ''But—''

He paused, long enough that MACH-1 realized that someone else was supposed to finish the sentence. He complied. ''But they couldn't have done it without us,'' he said slowly.

Hawkeye nodded again.

''Think we'll get any good press out of this?'' Atlas asked.

''Probably not. That's not the point, though. You do the work, and the recognition follows. You guys have made a lot of bad first impressions, but people forget about stuff like that, given enough time.'' Hawkeye grinned. ''Once upon a time,'' he said, ''there were warrants out for my arrest too, remember. Now I'm the idol of millions.''

''You hadn't earned those warrants,'' MACH-1 said in a low, soft voice.

Hawkeye looked at him. ''Actually,'' he said mildly, ''I had. But that's not the point, Abe. What's done is done; you can't undo the past, but you might be able to make up for it. Most of you guys made a lot of mistakes, and worse than mistakes, but that's the past. What you did at the Vault, at Fonesca, on *Barbarossa*—those are the present.''

This time, Abe didn't say anything.

Hawkeye continued. "When most of us were trying to figure out the fastest way off that boat, you were the one who pointed out that we had to evacuate the place, too."

"Someone else would have thought of the same thing," MACH-1 said slowly. He toyed with an egg roll. "I just spoke up first."

"My point exactly," Hawkeye said. He grinned. "You've got some miles to go," he said, "and some dues to pay, but you'll be a hero yet."

"He already is, actually," Melissa said. "If you ask me, I mean."

Castle Zemo, South America

"You're certain?" Zemo demanded.

Techno nodded—or, rather, his image did. There was no telling if the mechanical man actually stood before a camera in his headquarters or if he were simply beaming a computer-generated image of himself to the transceiver.

Zemo supposed it didn't make any difference, either way.

"Fried," Techno repeated. "That was a heck of a jolt—uh, shock—I took when the ionic transformer blew. I managed to reboot, but my supplementary data modules didn't make the trip back."

"And why is that?"

Techno shrugged. "Cheap Hydra goods?" he asked. "I was using off-the-shelf processors from Strucker's stores. That may have been a mistake."

"May have?"

"Okay, okay—it *was* a mistake. Anyway, they were wiped. I lost all my downloads."

"Unfortunate," Zemo said.

"Tragic, actually," Techno responded. "With time, I can recover a lot of it, but most of the telemetry's gone for good, and about a third of the core schematics. Without your father's notes and his prototypes, the project will take a long time to re-create."

"So this has all been for naught," Zemo said.

"You nailed Strucker," Techno reminded him. "That should count for something. No two ways about it, that guy was trouble."

Zemo made no reply.

"Ah, Baron," the former Norbert Ebersol said slowly. "If we're done, I have some tests I need to run and some things I need to check. I set some projects of my own aside to support you in this, and I really need to get back to them."

"Of course, Techno," Zemo said easily. "But first—none of these projects would involve ionic transformation, would they? You wouldn't be seeking to mislead me?"

"Of course not," Techno said. He sounded genuinely indignant. "That's your franchise." A smile twisted his metal lips. "Besides, I solved the problems associated with that stuff. I'm looking for new challenges."

"A good view to take," Zemo responded, then broke the connection.

He slumped back in his padded chair, trying to take some solace from Techno's words. The affair had been a debacle, but not an unmitigated one—he had given the Thunderbolts some trouble, and taken a new measure of their current capabilities. He had eliminated one rival, while providing an object lesson to others. And, if he had not claimed the future that he knew was his, at least he had regained a portion of his past.

Of his legacy.

Zemo opened the drawer to his left and lifted out the small, leatherbound volume that Strucker had handed him in a small used bookstore in Virginia. He opened it to the page where his marker waited, and, after adjusting a nearby lamp, he began to read. Coded words in a familiar handwriting met his gaze. Slowly, a smile formed on what was left of his lips.

For now, at least, the future could wait.

A shining beacon of hope to his friends, a shadowy figure of terror to his foes, **PIERCE ASKEGREN** has drunk deep of life's rich cup, and spat its dregs in destiny's dark eyes! Esthete, scholar, philosopher, jerk—others have called Pierce all these things and more, yet no single word can come close to encompassing his complex majesty. Some three other writers are blessed enough to call him "collaborator"—Danny Fingeroth and Eric Fein on the epic Doom's Day trilogy of Spider-Man team-up novels, and John Garcia, on the story "Better Looting Through Modern Chemistry" in *Untold Tales of Spider-Man.* Loyal readers know him as the author of *Fantastic Four: Countdown to Chaos* and as a contributor to the anthologies *The Ultimate Silver Surfer*, *The Ultimate Super-Villains*, *The Ultimate Hulk*, and the forthcoming *Untold Tales of the X-Men.* Comics fans with extremely long memories for obscure anthology stories know that he wrote for Warren Publishing's *Creepy* and *Vampirella.* These days, the laughing daredevil of literature dwells in a bucolic land named Virginia, works as a technical writer, and continues to create stories featuring other people's characters. What's next on the big man's plate? Well, even as this is written, he's busily developing a science fiction trilogy, and there are plans afoot for him to take his derivative genius into new venues.

MARK BAGLEY was the winner of Marvel's "Try-Out Book" competition, which led to doing large amounts of work for Marvel. He was the original penciller on the popular *New Warriors* comic book, and had a distinguished run on *The Amazing Spider-Man*, including that title's thirtieth anniversary issue and landmark 400th issue. He cocreated the Thunderbolts with Kurt Busiek in 1996 and continues to pencil the book to this day. He lives in Georgia.

JEFF ALBRECHT has worked as a commercial illustrator inside and outside the comic book field for over ten years. He has extensive credits as an inker for the major comic book publishers, and occasionally serves as penciller. In addition to comic book art, he spends a large part of his time creating licensing artwork for Warner Brothers, the Walt Disney Company, DC Comics, and others. His other book illustration work can be seen in *Spider-Man: The Octopus Agenda*, *Fantastic Four: Countdown to Chaos*, and the *Untold Tales of Spider-Man* anthology. He lives with his wife, Dorothy, and son, Lucas, in Missouri.

CHRONOLOGY TO THE MARVEL NOVELS AND ANTHOLOGIES

What follows is a guide to the order in which the Marvel novels and short stories published by Byron Preiss Multimedia Company and Berkley Boulevard Books take place in relation to each other. Please note that this is not a hard and fast chronology, but a guideline that is subject to change at authorial or editorial whim. This list covers all the novels and anthologies published from October 1994–May 1999.

The short stories are each given an abbreviation to indicate which anthology the story appeared in. USM=*The Ultimate Spider-Man*, USS=*The Ultimate Silver Surfer*, USV=*The Ultimate Super-Villains*, UXM=*The Ultimate X-Men*, UTS=*Untold Tales of Spider-Man*, and UH=*The Ultimate Hulk*.

If you have any questions or comments regarding this chronology, please write us.

Snail mail: Keith R.A. DeCandido
Marvel Novels Editor
Byron Preiss Multimedia Company, Inc.
24 West 25th Street
New York, NY 10010-2710
E-mail: KRAD@IX.NETCOM.COM.

—Keith R.A. DeCandido, Editor

X-Men & Spider-Man: Time's Arrow Book 1: **The Past [portions]**
by Tom DeFalco & Jason Henderson

Parts of this novel take place in prehistoric times, the sixth century, 1867, and 1944.

"The Silver Surfer" [flashback]
by Tom DeFalco & Stan Lee [USS]

The Silver Surfer's origin. The early parts of this flashback start several decades, possibly several centuries, ago, and continue to a point just prior to "To See Heaven in a Wild Flower."

"In the Line of Banner"
by Danny Fingeroth [UH]

This takes place over several years, ending approximately nine months before the birth of Robert Bruce Banner.

X-Men: Codename Wolverine ["then" portions]
by Christopher Golden

The "then" portions of this novel take place while Team X was still in operation, while the Black Widow was still a Soviet spy, and while Banshee was still with Interpol.

"Spider-Man"
by Stan Lee & Peter David [USM]

A retelling of Spider-Man's origin.

"Transformations"
by Will Murray [UH]
"Side by Side with the Astonishing Ant-Man!"
by Will Murray [UTS]
"Assault on Avengers Mansion"
by Richard C. White & Steven A. Roman [UH]
"Suits"
by Tom De Haven & Dean Wesley Smith [USM]
"After the First Death . . ."
by Tom DeFalco [UTS]
"Celebrity"
by Christopher Golden & José R. Nieto [UTS]
"Pitfall"
by Pierce Askegren [UH]
"Better Looting Through Modern Chemistry"
by John Garcia & Pierce Askegren [UTS]

These stories take place very early in the careers of Spider-Man and the Hulk.

"To the Victor"
by Richard Lee Byers [USV]

Most of this story takes place in an alternate timeline, but the jumping-off point is here.

"To See Heaven in a Wild Flower"
by Ann Tonsor Zeddies [USS]
"Point of View"
by Len Wein [USS]

These stories take place shortly after the end of the flashback portion of "The Silver Surfer."

"Identity Crisis"
by Michael Jan Friedman [UTS]
"The Liar"
by Ann Nocenti [UTS]
"The Doctor's Dilemma"
by Danny Fingeroth [UTS]
"Moving Day"
by John S. Drew [UTS]
"Out of the Darkness"
by Glenn Greenberg [UH]
"Deadly Force"
by Richard Lee Byers [UTS]
"Truck Stop"
by Jo Duffy [UH]
"Hiding"
by Nancy Holder & Christopher Golden [UH]
"Improper Procedure"
by Keith R.A. DeCandido [USS]
"Poison in the Soul"
by Glenn Greenberg [UTS]
"Here There Be Dragons"
by Sholly Fisch [UH]
"The Ballad of Fancy Dan"
by Ken Grobe & Steven A. Roman [UTS]
"Do You Dream in Silver?"
by James Dawson [USS]
"A Quiet, Normal Life"
by Thomas Deja [UH]
"Livewires"
by Steve Lyons [UTS]
"Arms and the Man"
by Keith R.A. DeCandido [UTS]
"Incident on a Skyscraper"
by Dave Smeds [USS]
"A Green Snake in Paradise"
by Steve Lyons [UH]

These all take place at various and sundry points in the careers of Spider-Man, the Silver Surfer, and the Hulk: after their origins, but before Spider-Man got married, the Silver Surfer ended his exile on Earth, and the reemergence of the gray Hulk.

"Cool"
by Lawrence Watt-Evans [USM]
"Blindspot"
by Ann Nocenti [USM]
"Tinker, Tailor, Soldier, Courier"
by Robert L. Washington III [USM]
"Thunder on the Mountain"
by Richard Lee Byers [USM]
"The Stalking of John Doe"
by Adam-Troy Castro [UTS]
"On the Beach"
by John J. Ordover [USS]

These all take place just prior to Peter Parker's marriage to Mary Jane Watson and the Silver Surfer's release from imprisonment on Earth.

Daredevil: Predator's Smile
by Christopher Golden
"Disturb Not Her Dream"
by Steve Rasnic Tem [USS]
"My Enemy, My Savior"
by Eric Fein [UTS]
"Kraven the Hunter Is Dead, Alas"
by Craig Shaw Gardner [USM]
"The Broken Land"
by Pierce Askegren [USS]
"Radically Both"
by Christopher Golden [USM]
"Godhood's End"
by Sharman DiVono [USS]
"Scoop!"
by David Michelinie [USM]
"The Beast with Nine Bands"
by James A. Wolf [UH]
"Sambatyon"
by David M. Honigsberg [USS]
"Cold Blood"
by Greg Cox [USM]
"The Tarnished Soul"
by Katherine Lawrence [USS]
"Leveling Las Vegas"
by Stan Timmons [UH]
"If Wishes Were Horses"
by Tony Isabella & Bob Ingersoll [USV]

"The Silver Surfer" [framing sequence]
by Tom DeFalco & Stan Lee [USS]
"The Samson Journals"
by Ken Grobe [UH]

These all take place after Peter Parker's marriage to Mary Jane Watson, after the Silver Surfer attained freedom from imprisonment on Earth, and before the Hulk's personalities were merged.

"The Deviant Ones"
by Glenn Greenberg [USV]
"An Evening in the Bronx with Venom"
by John Gregory Betancourt & Keith R.A. DeCandido [USM]

These two stories take place one after the other, and a few months prior to The Venom Factor.

The Incredible Hulk: What Savage Beast
by Peter David

This novel takes place over a one-year period, starting here and ending just prior to Rampage.

"On the Air"
by Glenn Hauman [UXM]
"Connect the Dots"
by Adam-Troy Castro [USV]
"Summer Breeze"
by Jenn Saint-John & Tammy Lynne Dunn [UXM]
"Out of Place"
by Dave Smeds [UXM]

These stories all take place prior to the Mutant Empire *trilogy.*

X-Men: Mutant Empire Book 1: **Siege**
by Christopher Golden
X-Men: Mutant Empire Book 2: **Sanctuary**
by Christopher Golden
X-Men: Mutant Empire Book 3: **Salvation**
by Christopher Golden

These three novels take place within a three-day period.

Fantastic Four: To Free Atlantis
by Nancy A. Collins
"The Love of Death or the Death of Love"
by Craig Shaw Gardner [USS]
"Firetrap"
by Michael Jan Friedman [USV]

"What's Yer Poison?"
by Christopher Golden & José R. Nieto [USS]
"Sins of the Flesh"
by Steve Lyons [USV]
"Doom^2"
by Joey Cavalieri [USV]
"Child's Play"
by Robert L. Washington III [USV]
"A Game of the Apocalypse"
by Dan Persons [USS]
"All Creatures Great and Skrull"
by Greg Cox [USV]
"Ripples"
by José R. Nieto [USV]
"Who Do You Want Me to Be?"
by Ann Nocenti [USV]
"One for the Road"
by James Dawson [USV]

These are more or less simultaneous, with "Doom^2" taking place after To Free Atlantis, *"Child's Play" taking place shortly after "What's Yer Poison?" and "A Game of the Apocalypse" taking place shortly after "The Love of Death or the Death of Love."*

"Five Minutes"
by Peter David [USM]

This takes place on Peter Parker and Mary Jane Watson-Parker's first anniversary.

Spider-Man: The Venom Factor
by Diane Duane
Spider-Man: The Lizard Sanction
by Diane Duane
Spider-Man: The Octopus Agenda
by Diane Duane

These three novels take place within a six-week period.

"The Night I Almost Saved Silver Sable"
by Tom DeFalco [USV]
"Traps"
by Ken Grobe [USV]

These stories take place one right after the other.

Iron Man: The Armor Trap
by Greg Cox

Iron Man: Operation A.I.M.
by Greg Cox
"Private Exhibition"
by Pierce Askegren [USV]
Fantastic Four: Redemption of the Silver Surfer
by Michael Jan Friedman
Spider-Man & The Incredible Hulk: Rampage (Doom's Day Book 1)
by Danny Fingeroth & Eric Fein
Spider-Man & Iron Man: Sabotage (Doom's Day Book 2)
by Pierce Askegren & Danny Fingeroth
Spider-Man & Fantastic Four: Wreckage (Doom's Day Book 3)
by Eric Fein & Pierce Askegren

Operation A.I.M. *takes place about two weeks after* The Armor Trap. *The "Doom's Day" trilogy takes place within a three-month period. The events of* Operation A.I.M., *"Private Exhibition,"* Redemption of the Silver Surfer, *and* Rampage *happen more or less simultaneously.* Wreckage *is only a few months after* The Octopus Agenda.

"It's a Wonderful Life"
by eluki bes shahar [UXM]
"Gift of the Silver Fox"
by Ashley McConnell [UXM]
"Stillborn in the Mist"
by Dean Wesley Smith [UXM]
"Order from Chaos"
by Evan Skolnick [UXM]

These stories take place simultaneously.

"X-Presso"
by Ken Grobe [UXM]
"Life is But a Dream"
by Stan Timmons [UXM]
"Four Angry Mutants"
by Andy Lane & Rebecca Levene [UXM]
"Hostages"
by J. Steven York [UXM]

These stories take place one right after the other.

Spider-Man: Carnage in New York
by David Michelinie & Dean Wesley Smith
Spider-Man: Goblin's Revenge
by Dean Wesley Smith

These novels take place one right after the other.

X-Men: Smoke and Mirrors
by eluki bes shahar
This novel takes place three-and-a-half months after "It's a Wonderful Life."

Generation X
by Scott Lobdell & Elliot S! Maggin
X-Men: The Jewels of Cyttorak
by Dean Wesley Smith
X-Men: Empire's End
by Diane Duane
X-Men: Law of the Jungle
by Dave Smeds
X-Men: Prisoner X
by Ann Nocenti
These novels take place one right after the other.

The Incredible Hulk: Abominations
by Jason Henderson
Fantastic Four: Countdown to Chaos
by Pierce Askegren
"Playing It SAFE"
by Keith R.A. DeCandido [UH]
These take place one right after the other, with Abominations *taking place a couple of weeks after* Wreckage.

"Mayhem Party"
by Robert Sheckley [USV]
This story takes place after Goblin's Revenge.

X-Men & Spider-Man: Time's Arrow Book 1: **The Past**
by Tom DeFalco & Jason Henderson
X-Men & Spider-Man: Time's Arrow Book 2: **The Present**
by Tom DeFalco & Adam-Troy Castro
X-Men & Spider-Man: Time's Arrow Book 3: **The Future**
by Tom DeFalco & eluki bes shahar
These novels take place within a twenty-four-hour period in the present, though it also involves travelling to four points in the past, to an alternate present, and to five different alternate futures.

X-Men: Soul Killer
by Richard Lee Byers
Spider-Man: Valley of the Lizard
by John Vornholt

Spider-Man: Venom's Wrath
by Keith R.A. DeCandido & José R. Nieto
Spider-Man: Wanted Dead or Alive
by Craig Shaw Gardner
"Sidekick"
by Dennis Brabham [UH]
Captain America: Liberty's Torch
by Tony Isabella & Bob Ingersoll

These take place one right after the other, with Soul Killer *taking place right after the* Time's Arrow *trilogy,* Venom's Wrath *taking place a month after* Valley of the Lizard, *and* Wanted Dead or Alive *a couple of months after* Venom's Wrath.

Spider-Man: The Gathering of the Sinister Six
by Adam-Troy Castro
Generation X: Crossroads
by J. Steven York
X-Men: Codename Wolverine ["now" portions]
by Christopher Golden

These novels take place one right after the other, with the "now" portions of Codename Wolverine *taking place less than a week after* Crossroads.

The Avengers & the Thunderbolts
by Pierce Askegren
Spider-Man: Goblin Moon
by Kurt Busiek & Nathan Archer
Nick Fury, Agent of S.H.I.E.L.D.: Empyre
by Ray W. Murill

These novels take place one right after the other, and several months after "Playing It SAFE."

X-Men & Spider-Man: Time's Arrow Book 3: **The Future [portions]**
by Tom DeFalco & eluki bes shahar

Parts of this novel take place in five different alternate futures in 2020, 2035, 2099, 3000, and the fortieth century.

"The Last Titan"
by Peter David [UH]

This takes place in a possible future.

FREE COMICS!!
GET A FREE 3-MONTH SUBSCRIPTION TO ANY ONE OF THE FOLLOWING COMIC BOOK TITLES:*